CASTING STONES

Jeff Gafford

Chaparral Publishing Company
Chandler, Arizona

ISBN 978-0692681138

The Publisher wishes to thank the following for their contributions to this edition:

Howard Moses, Editing
Jennifer Oneal Gunn, Interior Layout & Design
Marian Oprea, Cover Design

To my wife, Pam. Your love and encouragement have made my life better than I could ever have imagined—far better than I deserve.

Chapter One

The light from the full moon reflected brightly off the deck of the vessel as it sat at anchor near a small cove two kilometers east of Jacmel, Haiti. It made the eight men dressed in black very nervous. As clear as the sky was tonight, they could be spotted for miles around. At least it was an upscale yacht, no more than two years old, with the lower decks gutted to accommodate an extra-large hold, with easy access that would make loading quick. The vessel had about twice the speed of the last three boats, all of which met with disaster at the hands of the U.S. Coast Guard.

With practiced speed the men pushed, shoved and dragged their cargo, double-time, across the white sand of the beach, over the rocks and into the fishing boats which then ferried them to the side of the vessel. Then they climbed up the ladder, waited for the hatch to open, then quickly and efficiently threw the merchandise into the hold. Silently, they made their way back to the rock outcropping and watched to make sure the cargo hatch closed tightly and locked. The second the muffled, metal-on-metal click of the locks was heard, they dispersed so silently that anyone watching might have thought they had been an illusion.

Five miles away, at the once-beautiful Hotel Sur Mer, Police Captain Francois Boudreaux had just hung up the phone. Reno Chatelaine, his civilian liaison officer from the UN Mission in Haiti, who had been working closely with him for the last two years, stood on the balcony looking out on the ocean.

"Well, Reno," the captain said in their native Kreyol, "it appears that the first shipment to our new customers has gone off without a problem."

Chatelaine nodded but didn't speak.

"Is there a problem, my friend?" Boudreaux asked with an edge in his voice.

"I just have a bad feeling about this," Reno shrugged. "I wasn't in favor of this deal…"

"But we *have* a deal," Boudreaux snapped. "And *you* have outlived your usefulness."

These last words were said with an ominous grin that sent a chill down Reno's spine. What he had feared for the last two years had happened; his cover was blown. He always knew the risk was great. His sister had married into a well-known, upper class family and he had only been gone from the country for eight years before returning and working his way into the inner circle of this organization.

"You did well for us, Reno," the older man said. "But now that my pipeline is in place, you are no longer of any use to me."

"I don't understand," he replied.

"Of course you do," the captain smiled and said patronizingly. "We have been using you to send false information to MINUSTAH." He added, smiling even more broadly, "You were specially selected by my business partner for this assignment. He said you were such an earnest, naïve little soldier that you would accept anything I gave you and pass it on." Realization showed clearly on Reno's face and Boudreaux laughed at the sight. He was pointing a pistol at him now; it looked to be a Colt .45 automatic. "Ah, poor *'ti Frere*," he said, contemptuously emphasizing the nickname given him by his father's closest friend. "All these years you thought your father loved you. And now you know the truth." He stepped closer and said, "How could you truly believe that he could have ever loved the child of a whore?"

Reno Chatelaine's blood went cold as the words struck home. The fact that his mother had been a Carrefour prostitute when she became pregnant with Reno and his twin sister, Mireille, was true. But the man who fathered them took her as his mistress and moved her to an apartment in Delmas. If this thug knew that, then he knew about...

"I've already sent Michel to your *whore* sister's home in Thiotte. He's probably having a wonderful time with her right now," Boudreaux's voice broke through his thoughts with a dark menace. "Or, maybe he's already finished with her and is starting on your sweet little niece."

The stricken look on Reno's face pleased Captain Boudreaux, a sadistic man who derived great pleasure from seeing the fear in his victims' faces. He began to laugh, and laugh hard. He was trying to catch his breath when Reno took advantage of that millisecond of distraction. With adrenaline-charged speed, he clamped his hand over the top of the gun and slipped his little finger between the hammer and the firing pin. With his other fist he punched the captain with all of his strength once, twice, three times in the throat as his would-be killer stood frozen in place, stunned by the sudden, brutal attack. The captain lifted his free hand to stop the oncoming blows, but it was now too late; his throat was crushed. Chatelaine wrenched the gun from Boudreaux's hand and watched him fall to the floor, clawing vainly at his windpipe. Then he quickly stepped behind the wall leading to the room's entryway and took out the folding knife from his back pocket. He watched as the dying man's thrashing about became weaker. In just another moment, Francois Boudreaux would go from gloating victor to dead man.

"Was that what you had planned for me, *'Capitaine'?"* Reno whispered as he worked to catch his breath and calm his nerves. "You're lucky. If I had time, I would have done it much more slowly." He knew that St. Martin, Boudreaux's bodyguard, would be wondering what the noise was all about.

"Capitaine?" As if Reno's thought had made it so, St. Martin knocked on the door then began to open it. *"Capitaine?"* he said again as he stepped warily into the room, past the nook where Reno was hiding.

St. Martin froze only for a moment when he saw the body of his commander on the floor. But a moment was all Chatelaine needed to deliver a hammer-fist strike at the junction of the man's neck and shoulder then slap a hand over his mouth, pull his head back and drive the knife into his throat, twisting the blade to open the wound and then forcefully slicing a deep gash across his neck, severing the jugular vein and carotid artery. Then Reno took him quietly down to the floor and watched the thug in his last moments of life. The man's eyes bulged and darted about, his face a mask of terror as he laid there watching his own blood spray everywhere, too weak to try to stop it, waiting in torment until death made it stop.

Reno closed the door, went to the bathroom, removed his bloody clothes and showered off as quickly as possible.

He went to the closet where he pulled down one of Boudreaux's tailored tropical-print shirts and put it on, noting that it was just barely too large for a perfect fit. The dead man's pants were even more loose-fitting, requiring Reno put an additional hole in his belt then cinch it tight to hold them up. Then he searched both bodies for items he could use in his escape. From Boudreaux, he took military ID, five thousand U.S. dollars in cash and pulled a Ruger SP101 .357 magnum snub-nosed revolver from a holster on the dead man's ankle. From the guard he took a hundred dollars U.S., twelve dollars Haitian, a double-edged boot knife, a Beretta 9mm pistol and the Uzi submachine gun St. Martin had in his hand when he entered the room. He checked himself in the mirror then went to the door and opened it. The hallway was clear. The rest of the security detail that the captain always had with him was asleep in their room a few doors down.

Closing the door quietly behind him, he walked casually to the staircase and headed downstairs and out to the parking lot where he took the time to slash two of the tires on every car to slow his pursuers down—and he knew he was going to be pursued when the next guard went to relieve St. Martin in a few hours and discovered the bodies. He located Boudreaux's dark-blue Land Rover, climbed into it and drove slowly out of the lot. He was a mile down the twisting, pothole-riddled road before he pushed the gas pedal to the floor and drove as fast as he could. His heart was pounding, his breathing hard and ragged as he fought to control the sobs that escaped; his vision was blurred from tears in his eyes. He knew the odds of his family still being alive were virtually nonexistent, but he had to go to Thiotte and see for himself.

Chapter Two

The sound of my own screaming pulled me out of yet another nightmare. My heart felt as if it would pound itself out of my chest. And I felt wet and clammy as I tried to catch my breath. Then I heard the voice of my wife, complaining that I had awakened her—again—with my stupid bad dreams.

"*God*, Jimmy!" she growled. "You can go into the office anytime you want 'cuz you own it. But I have to be at school early in the morning." She looked over at the alarm clock on the nightstand. "Dammit!" she said. "I have to be up in an hour and now I won't be able to fall asleep. Might as well just get up now."

"I'm sorry," I said. "It isn't like I want to have nightmares, you know."

"Yeah, well if you keep having them, then you should see a psychiatrist about it. Maybe they can give you some medicine that will help you sleep through the night."

"Yeah, I guess you're right."

"I know I'm right. And until you do, will you please just go back to sleeping in the guest room?" the request was said more as a command. "I need my sleep if I'm going to function at work during the day."

"All right," I sighed. "I'll sleep in the other room from now on."

"Don't get all pouty about it," she said. "We both sleep better alone. You said it yourself." She added, "And it sure isn't like there's anything but sleep happening in this house, anyway."

"I'm sorry I'm not the man I used to be," I replied.

"Not that you were much in the first place," she jabbed again.

"Thank you. How sweet of you say so."

"What?" she shrugged. She was getting her rhythm now. "You can't tell me that's a surprise to you. You mean to say that you actually thought all my moaning and screaming was real?" She laughed at my naiveté. "That was just me trying to psych myself into an orgasm. It hardly ever worked, but it was all I had."

"Why is everything about our relationship centered on sex?" I asked, trying to ignore the pain of that last barb.

"It isn't centered on sex! That's the problem! Sex is a thing of the past and we never really had anything else in common."

"That isn't true," I insisted. "We believe the same things. We're members of the same church, we love children…"

"You *know* I can't have children!" she said indignantly. "How dare you bring that up? Just how heartless can you be?!" Her eyes began to fill with tears. She covered her face and headed toward the bathroom.

All I could do was stare, dumbfounded. I had no idea how to talk to her when she was like this. She found offense in the oddest of things yet had no compunction about cutting me to ribbons with her words. When were things going to change for the better? Would they ever?

I picked up my pillow and headed to the guest room. I'd learned all too well that it was no use trying to patch things up with Tara. I had to wait for her to want that. Her moods were far too erratic lately. She'd changed so much that I was sure that she either was going through a horrible early menopause or she had some kind of mental disorder that had never been detected before. Whatever it was, I had to try to help. I had to be patient even though my inner voice was begging me to pack up and leave. My vows were "'til death" and as hard as it was, I needed to trust that things would work out.

As I lay down on the double bed in the guest room, staring at the ceiling and waiting to drop off to sleep I wondered why, after all these years, I was being tormented again by the memories of something that had happened twenty years earlier.

Chapter Three

I couldn't believe my eyes. I was sitting at the counter of the café just before going to my office for another tedious day of work, when I looked up and saw in the reflection on the coffee maker, someone that looked remarkably like Jason Hadley, the man who got me involved with the Haitian Missionary Fellowship years ago. I turned around to get a good look and, sure enough, it was him. He had gained about thirty pounds and lost half of his hair since I last saw him, but it was Jason. I watched him sit on the stool two seats to my left and ask for coffee.

"Yes, sir," Chad replied with his usual polite smile. "Bold or regular?"

"Um…Bold, I guess," he answered, smiling back. "I like mine strong." The boy nodded and turned toward the coffee dispenser.

"I'm jealous," I said. "They won't give me bold coffee. 'It's bad for your delicate stomach,' they tell me." I watched him try to recall where he knew me from.

"Jimmy Stone?" Hadley said when it dawned on him. "Hey! Great to see you again!" He laughed and shook my hand vigorously. He must have been in his late sixties yet his grip was as strong as ever. "What are the odds of me seeing you here after all this time?"

"Pretty good, actually, since I moved here about ten years ago," I smiled. "The really long odds are on the chances of you coming here from Port-au-Prince. What brings you all the way out here? It's been...what? Twenty years or so?"

"Well, for one thing, I retired from the Fellowship about twelve years ago," Jason said. "After we lost our second volunteer to kidnappers I just couldn't do it anymore."

"Oh, my!" was all I could say. Jason loved the Fellowship and the group of missions and churches it helped start and support. But kidnappings were common in Haiti, just as it was in many other less-developed countries, as gangs used it as a means of making a quick buck. These armed thugs had no respect for human life and often killed or maimed their victims even after they'd been paid off.

"Yes, it was terrible. The worst of it for me was seeing their families." A brief silence passed before he shrugged and said, "So anyway, for the past several years I've been working part-time as a freelance consultant to non-profit organizations—mostly missions and charity work in developing countries. It takes me to a lot of new places and I meet people of all walks of life."

"So, are you just passing through or headed somewhere in the area?"

"Oh, I'm retiring right here," he smiled. "I've owned a lot over on the south ridge, overlooking the Graham Ranch, for about nine years now."

"Really?!" I said in surprise. "I have *got* to get over to the store and buy a lottery ticket today."

"Yeah," he laughed. "It sure looks like million-to-one-odds, but I guess we were meant to be neighbors."

"Well, you sure couldn't have picked a more different place from the Caribbean than this," I said. "The warm season only lasts about four months here."

"I grew up in a little town on the Upper Peninsula of Michigan," Jason smiled. "If you want to know cold, go there."

"But what made you choose Summertown of all places?" I pressed. "There are so many other towns…"

"Actually, it was just blind luck," he laughed. "I was looking for a quiet place with four seasons and lots of trees, kind of a getaway spot. The more I looked, the more places I came up with that filled the bill. So, finally I just printed out a list of the top ten, closed my eyes and pointed."

"So we were a blind choice?"

"God guides everything in our lives, Jimmy. As long as we let Him lead, there are never any truly 'blind' choices. He always has a plan. And meeting you today just confirms that I made the right choice!" he said patting me on the back.

"Well, we'll be glad to have you," I said. "It's a nice town with lots of friendly people. I'm sure you'll like it. Oh, and there's a Presbyterian Church a couple of blocks over that has a terrific pastor."

"Great," he smiled. "But hey, you look pretty healthy," he squeezed my shoulder. "What's with this talk of having a delicate stomach? If I remember correctly, you'd eat the greasiest, spiciest *grillot* you could find and never have any problems. Did it finally catch up to you?"

"No," I laughed. "I just got hurt last year and ended up spending some time in the hospital."

"You got shot, you mean," Earnest said from his booth behind me. He was a wiry little man with a full head of snow-white hair, age-spotted sagging skin and a slight tremor to his voice. "You got real lucky, Jimmy. I told you what happened to a buddy of mine after he got the same kind of wound at Inchon."

"Yeah, I remember Ernest," I said. Earnest was a veteran of the Korean War, and proud of it. Everyone knew not to bring up anything having to do with Asia, especially North Korea or China.

"He got shot protecting my brother," Chad put in. "The doctor said that if he hadn't slowed the bleeding with his t-shirt, Jhoon would have bled to death before anybody could get to him."

Every time I heard him say something like that I almost cringed. I shook my head and tried to dismiss it.

"I didn't do anything that anybody else in this town wouldn't have done in the same circumstances," I said emphatically. "Ernest here would have done the same, and he would have had the sense to stay down and wait for help. If I'd done that, I would be in better shape than I am now."

"Now, Jimmy," Ernest scolded. "Hindsight isn't the way to look on something like that. You just have to remember that you did your best and the Lord will judge the rest."

"Amen," agreed Jason. "That took some real guts, brother." He added, "I can see you're not comfortable hearing it, so I won't belabor the point. But you really did a heroic thing."

I grinned at that, but I didn't reply. Chad filled my coffee mug then turned it so that Jason could see the picture of the Rock of Gibraltar with the caption 'The Stone of

Summertown' printed on it. Now it was getting embarrassing.

"My dad got this made for him," he said.

"That's great," Hadley smiled. Detecting my discomfort he changed the subject. "My name's Jason, by the way. Jimmy and I are friends from a long time ago."

"Chad," the boy introduced himself. "Chad Shirazi. Pleased to meet you."

"Shirazi. Is that Iranian?"

"Wow, you're good," Chad replied. "No one every guesses it right. My first name's actually Amjad, named after my grandfather."

"I see. I would have guessed you might be Japanese, or maybe Korean," Jason remarked.

"Korean," Chad replied, a note of tension in his voice. Growing up a military brat, living in all parts of the world, he had learned to be wary of people who asked questions about his heritage. "Why do you ask?"

"No offense intended," Jason said. "I was just curious."

Chad relaxed. "I'm sorry," he said. "I get a little defensive sometimes."

"I understand."

"My mom is from Korea," Chad explained. "She married my dad when he was stationed there in the Air Force."

"She's from *South* Korea, son," Ernest cut in. "Don't forget that, now. I wouldn't have nothing to do with her if she was from the north, and you know why."

"Yes, sir," Chad replied.

"I watched too many of my friends die at the hands of them butchers," the old man told Jason. "Them and the Chinese. I'll never feel anything but hate for 'em. South Korea, on the other hand, they've always been our ally, even when the rest of the world up and turned their backs on us."

"You were at Inchon, you said?" Jason asked.

"3rd Battalion, 5th Marines," Ernest nodded proudly.

"3rd, Vietnam, '68," Jason reached out. "Semper Fi."

"Semper Fi," Ernest nodded and shook the proffered hand. "It's nice to see new folks move into the area."

"What's happening with the mission?" I asked before Ernest could get started on one of his war stories. "Is Pastor Jacques still there?"

"No," Jason replied. "He just couldn't stay there after his wife died. Just as well," he added. "His cover was blown, so he couldn't help the State Department anymore. And if he stayed around much longer, they'd have killed him, too."

"He was an informant?" I asked in shock.

"You didn't know that? I thought everybody knew that by the time you started going down there."

"No one ever told me," I said. "All I ever saw him do was pray and help children. That's not what my father did and he worked for the CIA in Europe way back when."

"Wow! Really?" Hadley replied, surprised.

"I don't remember him very well," I said. "I was seven when my mother divorced him and took me to the States to grow up."

"You weren't born in the U.S.?"

"No."

When a few seconds passed and I didn't elaborate he asked, "You never saw him again?"

"Nope. I wouldn't recognize him if he walked up to me on the street."

"That's too bad."

"Not really," I replied. "My mom was a good parent and I grew up without *too* many neuroses. But what about Pastor Jacques? What's he doing now?"

"He lives in Miami now and runs a children's ministry we helped him set up. It was the least we could do for him after what he'd lost. "He lowered his voice and looked to make sure no one was listening before adding, "I heard what you did, and I want you to know that...well...I probably would have done the same thing in your situation."

I nodded slightly and looked away. I didn't want to talk about that night. I had spent much of the last nineteen years trying to forget it, which was no easy task. I wasn't able to talk to anyone about it for fear those State Department goons would find out, so I just walked around with it; a dark cloud over my head that I had to consciously push away every morning just to be able to think clearly. As time went by I eventually put it behind me. But lately, the memories were coming back to me in my dreams, along with the guilt, the shame, and regret.

Chapter Four

Corinda Stone was one happy lady. She had been through a great deal over the last two years and was only now able to enjoy her life again. First Nerville left her, although that turned out to be a blessing in disguise because it woke her up to how lazy she had become. Two months later her Jessica was married; what was supposed to be the most wonderful night of her life turned into a living nightmare when she allowed a young man from the wedding party to seduce her. Of all nights for Nerville to come back. Poor Nerville. He found her with this other man and went crazy, but he just wasn't strong enough. In a matter of moments both men were dead; Nerville at the hands of her young lover, and her lover from the knife wounds she inflicted on him trying to defend Nerville.

If not for Ray, she would have gone to prison. Ray Brandt, Marshal of Summertown, watched over her and helped her find a good attorney. He even gave her Gaucho, a trained German shepherd to protect her. And now he was her man. She loved cooking for him. She wanted to make sure that when he left from her house, it was with a full stomach.

Little did she realize that Ray was not too happy with his expanding waistline. He had always been careful not to get too soft around the middle, making sure to exercise regularly, the same way he did when he was a deputy sheriff in Phoenix. He knew that everyone's safety, especially his own, could depend at some point on his endurance and strength. But ever since he started dating Corinda, she'd been feeding him...and *feeding him*. And the food was so good that at first, he didn't hesitate to eat...in large quantities. But after a few weeks, he noticed that he wasn't able to just work the extra calories off like he did when he was younger. His gut was starting to show now and it didn't make him happy. And when Gary, his deputy, teasingly asked him, "When's the baby due?" he knew something had to be done.

Here he sat at Corinda's table, about to be fed more starchy food, swimming in that red sauce he loved so much. The problem was, he had just finished the left-overs she brought him from last night, just a few hours before and for whatever reason, it didn't quite agree with him. He was still a little queasy and the very smell of the greasy enchiladas was making him nauseous. The last thing he wanted to do was throw up, but that was exactly what he was on the verge of doing. It was all he could to hold it down.

"Mira, querido," she said, smiling broadly, carrying the serving dish full of red enchiladas and oversized burros over to the table. "I made something special for you."

"Whatever you make is special, honey," he said. The bile began to travel up his throat, but he fought it down as she laid the plate in front of him. He forced a smile and looked up at her. *For God's sake hold it, Brandt.* But he couldn't. He jumped up from his chair and ran to the bathroom with his hand clamped tight over his mouth and the moment he got the toilet, he threw up everything he'd eaten earlier.

After washing his face and stealing a few swallows of mouthwash he found in the cabinet he walked back into the dining room to find Corinda gone. Following the sound her loud crying, he found her sprawled across her bed, her face buried in the pillow. He sat next to her on the edge of the bed and stroked her back, but she shrugged his hand away.

"Don't touch me!" she wailed, her face still in the pillow.

Holy crap, she can scream, he thought. He took his hand off of her back and just sat with her until her wailing subsided. When she seemed to calm down, he spoke very quietly so as not to cause her to start all over again.

"Corinda?" No response. "Corinda, dear."

She pulled herself up from the bed and sat up but didn't look at him.

"Now, sweet—"

"Don't call me sweetheart." She snapped.

"OK," Ray sighed. "I'm sorry I did that."

"You threw up at my food!"

"I didn't mean to," he said, in as earnest a voice as he could. "I was just so full from everything else you fed me…"

"So you don't like anything I make for you!" she shouted accusingly. "When I ask you, you always say 'It's delicious, sweetheart.' But now I know you're lying to me. Why? Are you waiting to get me in bed? Is that it? Then you'll just throw me away and joke with your hot-pants deputy how long you had to eat my cooking until I let you have me?"

"Where the hell did that come from?!" He demanded indignantly. "I have *never* even hinted that I…"

"No, you don't!" she cut him off. "What's wrong with me, hah? I dress like this for you, I cook all of this for you and the most I get at the end of the night is, 'Goodnight, sugar. I better go or people will talk.'" She said this mimicking his deep voice, and the face she made when she did it made Ray cover his mouth to conceal his smile.

"What? You think this is funny?" she demanded. "Oh, you think this is so hilarious. I dress up for you, I cook for you, and you throw it up in *my toilet* then laugh at me when you *know* you broke my heart!" She began crying again, this time wrapping her arms around her legs and bringing them up to her chest, closing herself off from him.

Oh, God, he said to himself. *I've done it this time.* He tugged at her arms until she finally allowed him to open them, then he wrapped his own arms around her and whispered softly, "It isn't like that at all, Babydoll, and you know it. You just fed me too much, that's all. I've eaten so much lately that the idea of eating again—no matter how much I love your food—caused it all to come back up. I'm sorry, but that's all there is to it. You've been feeding me so much that I even had to go buy a bigger uniform."

"You never said anything," she mumbled, now sounding like a little girl.

"Because I love you, and I saw that it was making you happy," he replied.

"What?"

"I said you were so happy cooking for me, I…"

"You love me?"

Only then did it occur to Ray that this was the first time he'd actually said those words. He certainly did love Corinda. He never wanted anything so much as to make her happy. But he never came out and said "I love you" to her. *Brandt, you can really be an idiot sometimes.*

"Yes, sweetheart," he said, sitting back and brushing the hair away from her face so he could look into her eyes. "I love you. More than anything in this world…God help me."

"Why do you say it like that?"

"Because if you keep feeding me the way you have, I'm going to pop!"

"Then I won't! Just say something from now on! *Ay, Dios!*"

"OK," Ray said seriously, after thinking about it a moment. "I'll say something right now." He got down from the bed, putting one knee on the floor, then took her hands and looked into her eyes. "Corinda, I love you. Will you marry me?"

For the first time in who knew how long, Corinda was speechless. Her mouth dropped open, her hands went to her chest and she gasped so loud that Ray thought she was having an anxiety attack. Then she let out a squeal that caused Gaucho to bolt into the room and pounce on Ray, knocking him over.

There, lying on his back on the floor of the bedroom, with a big, snarling German shepherd standing on his chest, Ray heard the love of his life say, "Yes".

***

I had been in the office only a few minutes when my caffeine cravings took control. I usually waited an hour or so, but today I felt like spending a little extra time with friends. So I headed down to the Little Creek Café for their famous pancakes and bacon breakfast and a cup of coffee.

"So, what'll it be, Uncle Jimmy?" Chad Shirazi asked me as I sat down at the counter. Chad's eldest brother married my daughter, Jessica last year, which made me his uncle. I still got a kick out of hearing him say it.

"The usual, Chad," I replied. I was beginning to get used to the lightly brewed coffee they served me, but I still missed the strong stuff.

"What did the doctor say on your last visit?"

"That I have to watch what I eat from now on, that I should stay away from beer, no spicy foods and no more than one cup of light coffee per day. At least he said I can start running again. Remember to stay in shape, Chad; when you get to be my age, it's hard to lose weight once you've gained it."

"My dad tells me that all the time," he chuckled. "Usually when he's eating a big piece of pie or something."

"You bad-mouthin' your old man?" came the voice of the café's proprietor from the back room.

"Jeez, he has good ears," Chad said, sheepishly.

I covered a laugh as best I could. "Parents have eyes in the backs of their heads and bionic hearing, didn't you know that?"

"I forget sometimes," he grinned.

"OK, son. I'll take the counter," Ken told Chad as he entered from the back room. "How about you go ahead and stock us up on dinnerware?"

"Yessir."

I thought it was kind of odd to be stocking up a counter that didn't need stocking until I heard familiar footsteps at the front door and turned to see Gina Albright, the school principal push her way into the restaurant. She was about five-five, late twenties, blonde, blue-eyed and a kind of outdoorsy-pretty that didn't need makeup. And, more pertinent to the current moment, she had become quite the distraction for Chad.

At this moment, however, I was sure Gina was feeling anything but pretty. She was eight months pregnant last June when she suddenly, tragically miscarried, leaving a deep emotional scar that was still healing. She was slowly beginning to get back to her confident, assertive self, but her usually athletic figure was still hiding under a baby bump that seemed so cute when she was pregnant, but was now a painful reminder of what she had lost. No one had seen her around much outside of the school; the café was about the only place she would go, and then only during the quieter hours. She was my closest friend and it pained me to see her going through this.

"Good afternoon, Principal Albright," Ken greeted her in the sing-song way her students would say in class. It made her wince.

"Please," she said. "I'm off the clock. Give me a big cup of coffee and a little, tiny slice of apple pie."

"Little tiny?" Ken repeated. "I don't give out tiny pieces."

"Well then, I'll share it with Jimmy. I am now officially on a diet. It's time to start working this fat ass off."

"Language, Gina," Ken chided her. He was a devout Christian who did not abide any kind of foul or off-color language in his restaurant. Unless, of course he was the one using it.

"Oops, sorry, *Dad*," she said sarcastically. "I will now begin to work on losing weight."

"Don't go losing too much," I said. "You look very pretty just as you are."

"Said the guy to the fat chick," she grimaced.

"I did not say you were fat," I protested.

33

"You didn't say it, but you meant it," she insisted. "'Oh, you have such a pretty face.'"

"Now that's not fair…"

"Sure it is," she cut me off. "You used to steal glances at my a–butt when we went running. Now, it's eyes forward. About the only thing you steal glances at now are my boobs."

"Wh–what?!" I stammered. "I never—"

"Yes you do," she cut me off again. "And so do you," she pointed at Ken, who simply shrugged.

"I can look," he said. "But I touch only the one who belongs to me."

"Well, at least you guys notice me," she said. "Whenever I go to the grocery store in Flag, I feel invisible. All the tiny little college girls get the attention. I'm sick of it. I'm getting hornier by the day."

"Gina, for Pete's sake, will you stop talking like that?" Ken said.

"I can't help it," she said. "I haven't done it in a year and I'm going nuts."

Ken just closed his eyes and shook his head.

"Anyway," she went on, "I'm going to drop this flab and get my body back."

"Well, that may not be completely possible," I said. "Some things just don't go back to the way they were."

"Read my lips," she said, facing me eye to eye. "I am getting rid of this fat body and getting my thin one back." She paused a moment then cupped a breast in each hand and added, "I might keep these, though. They're eye-catchers."

Just then, Chad came walking through the kitchen doors with an armful of clean plates. He caught one look at Gina squeezing her assets and the dishes came crashing to the floor. I thought Ken was going to cry.

"Son, go back in the kitchen. I'll take care of that."

"But..." Chad was pointing at the mess he'd made, but his eyes were still glued to Gina's chest.

"Don't worry about it," his father said trying valiantly not to yell at him. "Now put your eyes back in your head, close your mouth and go back in the kitchen, please."

"Y-Yessir." Chad turned and stumbled through the doors as requested.

"Thank you, Gina," Ken said. "His hormones are out of control as it is. Now he won't be good for anything the rest of the day."

"I'm sorry," she replied meekly.

"What's gotten into you?" Ken asked, sincerely concerned. "You've never acted like this before. What's wrong?"

"I don't know," she sighed. "All I know is I feel like jumping the nearest man I come across. And don't think either one of you are safe, by the way."

If only, I thought. Then I drove it from my mind. I was married and had no business being attracted to anyone, especially my best friend. She needed my support, not my lust. And as bad as things with Tara were, I wasn't about to commit adultery.

"Now, Gina," I said, "it will come in good time. Don't go trying to rush things, or you'll end up with some guy who doesn't deserve to tie your shoes. Be patient."

"I'm sick of being patient," she said. "I'm horny *now!*"

The sound of silverware hitting the floor advised us that Chad had been listening in. He stuck his head out the kitchen door and said sheepishly, "Everything's OK. I'll clean it up." Then he ducked back into the kitchen.

"Nice, Gina," Ken said with narrowed eyes. "Very nice."

"What?" she shrugged. "How is it my fault your son eavesdrops?"

"Let's change the subject," I suggested.

"Let's," Ken seconded. "How is the hiring going at school? Any good candidates?" After we lost three teachers last year, we had to get emergency help from the town's general fund to pay substitutes. One of the spots was filled now, but there were still two more teachers needed.

"Oh, yeah," Gina nodded. "I sent three files over to Pedro. I'm sure he'll get the board to approve them; we don't have any choice."

"They any good?" I asked. I sat on the school board along with two other residents.

"One's from Albuquerque. She plans to retire in four years and wants to live in a small town where she'll settle in for good. I think she'll be a good one. She has a Special Ed certificate."

"Sounds good," I nodded. "The others?"

"Both fresh out of NAU, just got their Elementary certifications. One's a kind of pudgy guy with chipmunk cheeks and a goofy laugh. Teaches English. Kinda cute in a cartoony kind of way."

"Where's he from?"

"Flagstaff. A Mormon boy. Smiles a lot, cracks dumb jokes. Perfect elementary school teacher."

"He sounds pretty good, too," I said.

"Yeah," she nodded. "I might do him."

Ken's jaw dropped open. He tried to speak but the words wouldn't come out.

"G-Gina!" I sputtered.

"What!" she snapped. "Beggars can't be choosers," she replied. "The way I look, I have to get it where I can."

"Not with a future employee," I said. "When you sent that file over to Pedro Mendoza you shot your chances of anything but a professional relationship with that young man, unless you want to risk a sexual harassment lawsuit."

"Oh, crap. That's right," she said as it dawned on her. "Oh, well," she sighed. "I guess I'll have to wait until I look human again." Her voice broke with the last few words. Suddenly the veneer of good humor that she'd been hiding behind gave way and she covered her face in her hands and cried, taking in gasps of air only to bawl them out again. Ken reached across the counter and patted her shoulder as I put my arm around her and tried to console her.

"I'll be OK," she said, straightening up and drying her face with a napkin. The mask of business-like invulnerability that she wore at school was up. "Thanks. I just have to let it out a little sometimes. I'll be fine. I'm getting better...aren't I?"

Without waiting for a reply, she got up from her stool and turned to go. I got up and followed her out, waving to Ken as we went. I wasn't about to let the conversation end there. I knew Gina too well.

"So, what's happening, Sissy?" I asked once we were across the parking lot.

"Nothing, Jimmy," she shrugged.

"C'mon now, tell me what it is."

"I'm lonely, I guess," she said tentatively.

"You guess?"

"Well, I don't know. I never really minded being alone before. It's weird…"

I waited for her to finish the thought that seemed stuck between her brain and her tongue, but she didn't say any more. So, I just walked with her past my office, down to the west entrance to the residential district and strolled two laps around the neighborhood until she'd had enough.

"OK, I am lonely," she said as if it were something to be ashamed of. "I'm finally getting over losing the baby—or at least getting past it, but there's still this huge hole in my life. It took me months to get used to the idea of raising a kid and just when I started to get excited about it, she was taken away from me." She didn't cry this time. She spoke as if this were someone else's story, not hers. Knowing Gina as I did, I could tell that she was keeping a safe distance from her feelings whenever she could. I guess they kind of got away from her in the café.

"I know, Sis," I said. "I was there. I wish I could have done something more than just sit there and pray. I felt so powerless."

"Don't, Jimmy," she said patting my cheek. "Let's talk about something else before we both start bawling."

It had been a beautiful June day when she called me and asked for a ride to her doctor's office in Flagstaff. That raised a red flag in my mind, since Gina preferred to drive herself to her appointments, even though driving pregnant was not a comfortable task. When she told me that she was cramping badly, was running a fever and wanted to puke, I insisted on taking her to the ER immediately.

The moment we arrived, someone put her on a gurney and wheeled her in to the Labor and Delivery department, but it was too late. The doctor told her that the baby had died in the womb and that they needed to induce labor to prevent her from having severe complications. I was waiting in the lobby when a nurse called me back to the examination room. As I entered, Gina reached out to me like a little girl needing her daddy. She buried her face in my shoulder and held me tight, as if she was holding on for dear life. I sat on the edge of the gurney with my arms around her, rocking her, trying to soothe her anguish. But, of course, I couldn't. She was a young mother who had just been told her baby died before she could even hold it in her arms.

With all of the grief and depression she'd gone through since then, this was the first time she admitted to being lonely. I took it as a good sign, since that probably meant she was willing to do something about it. The trick now was to keep her from seeking the wrong company. Namely, the man who got her pregnant in the first place, Deputy Marshal Gary Callan. He wasn't *bad* company, just the wrong kind for Gina.

Gary was a great guy, who was very well liked among the residents of Summertown. Young, powerfully built and boyishly handsome, he was also very shy around women. He and Gina dated very briefly then suddenly broke up, but not before Gina found out that she was carrying Gary's child. Although he was ready to help financially with the care of the child, I always felt that Gary got the sweet end of that deal; he didn't have to help raise a baby he didn't want, and he didn't have to deal with the pain and depression that a mother experiences after losing a child.

"I think I'll go for a run before I have to stand in for Tara," she said. "This fat won't disappear on its own."

"For Tara?" I asked. My wife never mentioned she needed to do anything during school hours.

"Yeah," Gina replied. "She never told you about her doctor appointment?"

"What doctor's appointment?"

"I don't know," she shrugged. "We don't talk anymore, remember? She just said she needed to leave early today for a doctor's appointment." She gave me a probing look. "She never told you about having to go to the doctor?"

"She doesn't talk to me, either."

Tara had become increasingly distant and cold to me in the past few months. Even though I'd healed enough to take care of myself, I wasn't able to be as physical as before when we made love and she was not very understanding about that. It was as if, just because I couldn't satisfy her in the bedroom she had no time for me in any other part of our life together. As much as she had told me she loved me, no matter what, the reality was that she didn't. She didn't talk about work, or anything else anymore. We just lived in the same house, shared the bills and slept on opposite sides of the same bed.

"Not even about medical issues?" Gina asked. "Who would she talk about this stuff with, if not you?"

"I don't know that she talks to anybody," I said. "Min asked me last week what's up with Tara; apparently, they don't spend any time together anymore, either. I don't know, Gina. Things were rocky before I got shot. Maybe this marriage was meant to disintegrate and we've just been delaying the inevitable."

"I'm sorry, Jimmy," Gina said sympathetically.

"It's fine," I replied. And I meant it. I was finally at the point of accepting the inevitability of divorce.

"You sure?"

"Absolutely."

"Good."

"You didn't want me to take her back in the first place," I said. "I wish I'd listened. It would have saved time and heartache."

"No, I don't think so," she replied. "You would have just moped around, wondering if you could have done something different. Now you know there's nothing you could have done to save your marriage, because it wasn't your fault things went to hell in the first place."

"Well, I wouldn't go *that* far…"

"I would," she insisted. "In fact, I'm expecting Tara to just take off sometime soon, without notice and leave me stuck with another open position. She's changed somehow. I don't know why, but she has. Or, maybe she was always this way and she's just been pretending to be squared away; only now she's gotten tired of the masquerade."

"You're suggesting I married a sociopath?" I asked skeptically.

"Maybe not a *sociopath*, but someone with serious personality issues."

"Well…"

"Look," she said as we arrived at the front of her house. "Let's talk about this later; maybe after school?"

"Sure," I shrugged. "If you think talking about it will make any difference."

"Probably not," she allowed. "But it would be nice to hang out for a while. I like hanging out with you; you make me feel better."

"Ditto," I said, giving her a quick hug.

I watched to make sure she made it up the steps and into her place safely, then headed down the walk toward my office. I was so glad I had Gina to talk to. As close as Ken and I were, I couldn't talk about my marital problems with him. Not that he wouldn't be supportive; Ken was the kind of man who would give anything to see his friends and family happy. I had told myself I didn't want to burden him with my problems; that he wouldn't be able to understand. But the real reason was that I was jealous. I wanted the kind of marriage he and Min had. They argued but never for too long; they showed affection to each other, even after twenty-some years; their love was the kind that made everyone around them feel at home, while my marriages had been the exact opposite. The first one I endured for over twenty years because of my daughter, Jessie. My second started out beautifully. I really believed that Tara was my soul-mate—the one that was meant for me, for life. Then, two years into it, she started to change.

It wasn't obvious at first. If it had been, I would have seen it. No, it was subtle things that changed, that I didn't pay attention to until her mood swings—which I had attributed to being part of a difficult PMS cycle, became more dramatic and her sexual inhibitions began to diminish. In fact, by the time it occurred to me that she was going through more than just her "time of the month", she had already begun to openly flirt with men she never would have spoken to before; used language I never thought she knew and, when she was really agitated, she spoke in disjointed, sometimes nonsensical phrases. When I was bed-ridden, she had become a doting, dutiful wife, waiting on me hand and foot, although there were times when she became really irritated, over-all she took very good care of me. But as I began to heal and become more and more capable of taking care of myself, she started drawing into herself. She began berating me for my appearance, even though she knew I couldn't exercise the way I had before I was shot. She complained that I didn't "perform" as well as I used to—one time, she said she wished she hadn't saddled herself with a broken-down tub of lard that couldn't do anything unless I took a nap first. After a few months she didn't even show any interest. We were roommates, not husband and wife.

I stopped myself from getting any more stressed over my home life and decided to let it all go for the moment and just free my mind, like my physical therapist taught me. I looked up and saw that it was a beautiful, early fall day; the air was crisp and damp from a light rain that had fallen just before dawn. Fluffy white clouds floated above the tree tops in the distance and I mentally tossed all of the worries of the day, one by one, onto them and watched them float away. By the time I got to the door of my little storefront I was feeling a little better.

Chapter Five

Reno Chatelaine drove as fast as he could along Route 203, going east along the southern coast then veering up into the mountainous country. He couldn't go any faster than 55 kph, even when the road was straight and clear, which was rare. The terrain was simply too rough and the road too poorly maintained to be able to go any faster for any distance. He passed UN checkpoints with ease because of Boudreaux's Police Nationale ID, which he only needed to flash at the soldiers quickly; they didn't even take the time to look closely at the picture since the car had government license plates. It took only two hours of hard driving to get to the home of Mireille and her husband Robert Narrette. When he arrived at the gate he found it standing open and the gardien, Hubert, on the ground to his left, his pistol-gripped shotgun lying next to him. The man who swore he would protect the Narrette family with his life had kept his promise. Reno struggled to keep his mind on the task of clearing the house of armed intruders and not the carnage that probably awaited him inside. He scanned the yard for strange vehicles and saw a late model, mother-of-pearl colored Landcruiser parked blocking Mireille's and Robert's matching Pajeros. He ran to the kitchen door at the back of the house and kicked it open, holding his weapon close to his body and aimed forward.

The Narrette home was a big, Spanish-style palace with eight bedrooms, each with its own bathroom. A large, open mezzanine was located toward the front where Mireille loved to entertain guests and the top floor was a maze of bedrooms and sitting areas. There were so many places to hide that it was going to be a death-defying act just to clear it all.

After taking a quick look through the door, he stepped into the house and walked swift down the hall from the kitchen to the dining room where he almost tripped on the bloody body of Dieu Donne, the Narrettes' yard boy. He was only fourteen years old but he worked hard and sent his weekly pay to his family in Cite Soleil. He was a good boy, and now he was dead, hacked to pieces by some machete-wielding bastard who obviously enjoyed killing. With his heart racing Reno continued into the living room, checked Robert's office where there looked to have been some sort of struggle; three chairs and a table were overturned, a trail of blood ran from Robert's big leather desk chair into the hallway and up the steps to the mezzanine where the body of the housekeeper lay across the big oak coffee table, stripped of her uniform, mutilated, her face a terrible mess of drying blood that oozed from multiple wounds to her mouth, nose and eyes. On the floor next to her lay one of the invaders. He was face-down in a pool of dark, sticky blood. There was no weapon near the body, so someone may have picked it up. He moved slowly and silently up the stairs to the right that led to the second floor landing as the hair on the back of his neck bristled and his hands trembled uncontrollably.

When he was four steps from the top he could see two bodies, tangled together across the back of the sofa in the center of the parlor. He scanned the room while ascending the last few steps and saw the door to his niece, Soraya's room open and the large body of a man lying face-down in front of it. The back of the dead man's shirt had several small red stains from bullet holes. He had been shot from behind, by someone outside the room.

Taking a closer look at the two bodies on the sofa his heart broke. The twisted knot of arms and legs that lay draped across the back of the couch like a pile of laundry told of the final struggle of Robert Narrette as he tried to protect his family. Robert's left hand was still gripping the neck of his enemy whose face was twisted and blue, his tongue distended and his eyes bulged. Judging by the pistol with its slide locked open in the hand of the invader and the blood—so much blood—that had drained from Robert's body, Reno's brother-in-law made it his dying act to take as many of them with him as he was able. *You did well, frère,* Reno thought as tears welled up in his eyes. *Two of them...*Then he saw the bullet hole in the back of Robert's head, and his sadness became a deep sense of dread; somebody else was here. He pushed open the door of Soraya's room and found the very thing that he feared.

The bodies of both his sister and her beautiful daughter lay across the bed in grotesque positions, horribly mutilated; their precious blood splattered around the room. Reno gazed on the scene, unable to look away, unable to scream, unable to weep. He was numb...so very numb that as the invader who had been hiding in the closet jumped out and shot him twice, he hardly felt the bullets strike him. Out of reflex born of intensive training, he shot back, unaware of where his bullet landed. He sensed himself sinking to the ground, still unable to feel the pain as his body struck the floor. Everything that he lived for until now had been taken from him. He now had only one reason to live and he would not allow himself to die until he had accomplished it. As he lay on the floor, he swore that if he survived he would find and kill Michel and whoever else had a hand in this. He had nothing to lose, and nothing else to live for; his heart had just been torn from him and he could feel nothing but hate.

Pure, cold hate. This hate would be his constant companion; the driving force in his life until he could watch Michel Boudreaux die a slow, agonizing death.

Chapter Six

Pam Chapman and Jessica Shirazi sat by the fireplace of the Mormon Lake Lodge's restaurant. It was a warm, friendly place with good food, delicious aromas and décor that harkened back to a century before. They had been chatting about the town's new library for about twenty minutes when Pam finally fell silent and began staring thoughtfully into the flames of the hearth.

"What are you thinking about?" Jessie asked.

"Hmm? Oh nothing special," replied.

"You sure?"

"No." Pam shrugged.

"Then what is it? Or is it a secret?"

"I'm not sure I should say, since Gina's a friend of yours," Pam said.

"Actually, she's a friend of my dad's," Jessie corrected. "I always got the impression she was checking me out; gave me the creeps."

"Gina doesn't go that way, Jess," Pam chuckled.

"Well, I know that now, but that doesn't keep me from getting weird vibes."

"Really?" Pam said. "I always admired her confidence. She always seemed to be so…in control." She sighed. "I wish we could have stayed friends, but it didn't work out."

"It doesn't have to stay that way," Jessie said. "Have you tried calling her lately?"

Pam fell silent once again; looked down at her coffee cup.

"What's wrong, Pam?" Jessie asked. "You still want Gary, don't you?"

The question surprised Pam. "Who told you that?"

"Oh, come on," Jessie laughed. "I think you should go for it. You don't owe Gina anything. You have every right to seek your own happiness."

"Not at the expense of another person, Jessie."

"You sound just like my dad," Jessie sighed. "Neither of you can bring yourself to try for something you want if it hurts somebody else."

"I can't imagine you'd disagree with that," Pam said. "You don't just go after something, knowing it's going to hurt someone."

"No, but this isn't that kind of situation," Jessie replied. "Gary is completely unattached now. All you have to do is get his attention."

"What do you have in mind?" Pam asked suspiciously.

"Nothing," Jessie shrugged. "I'm not good at that kind of thing."

"Well, that's a relief," Pam sighed. "I was afraid you'd want to paint me up and dress me like Tara did with Gina. And we all know how that ended."

"It wasn't Gina's clothes that got her pregnant, Pam," Jessie laughed. "It was a lapse in judgment. We all have them and we all face the consequences…and Gina's facing hers."

"True. Poor thing."

"Yeah."

"Yet…" Pam let the words trail off.

"Yet, what?" Jesse prompted.

Pam sighed, "I still wish it was me he wanted."

Jessica reached across the table, squeezed her friend's hand and searched for words to encourage her, but she could think of none. Pam was just too self-conscious to consider dressing nicer or getting her hair done in a new way. Yet that might well be what Gary liked about her. She was a real, sincere person; she was vulnerable. And if there is anything that attracts guys it's a girl who's vulnerable. It makes a man feel needed; makes him want to protect her.

"Listen," Jessie said. "Just talk to Gary. Don't pretend that you don't see him when he's around."

"Why can't that be as easy as it sounds?" Pam mumbled.

"Pam, you made out with him on top of your car—in *public*!"

"I know, but…"

"It's only hard if you make it hard. Believe me. I've watched my mom and dad do that for years."

"I thought your folks hated each other." Pam said.

"They never *hated* each other, no matter what they tell everybody else," Jessie smiled sadly. "My dad likes to pretend that they stayed together for my sake. But I could see he loved my mom. He was just too proud to show it. She hurt his feelings all the time. But I think that was because he just didn't give her the attention she needed."

"Really?" Pam was genuinely amazed by this revelation. Everyone who knew Jimmy and Corinda Stone was convinced that the best thing to happen to them was their divorce, because anytime either of them mentioned the other it was never in positive terms.

"Yes," Jessie nodded. "They don't think I remember how they were when I was little." She glanced around to make sure no one was listening then whispered, "They couldn't keep their hands off each other!"

"You're kidding!"

"I'm serious," Jessie giggled. "They didn't think I could hear all the noise they made at night. It wasn't until I was older that I realized what they were doing…"

"Eeww! TMI!" Pam recoiled.

"But that was a long time ago," Jessie sighed. "I think it stopped sometime around when I was turning like, eleven or twelve, something like that. They just stopped sitting close to each other when we watched TV. Mom didn't wait anymore for my dad to come to the table at breakfast; little things like that."

"Was that when they started arguing?"

"Oh, they argued all the time," Jessie said. Her eyes were moist as she looked at the fire. "Just, up 'til then they'd make up. After a while they didn't even bother. It was like they both knew things were dying between them and they didn't care anymore."

"How sad," Pam said. "I'm sorry to hear that."

"It was bound to happen," Jessie shrugged. "My mom's always been kind of, well…vain." She noted that Pam covered a smile at this statement of the obvious and tried not to smile herself. "Well, anyway, she was getting frustrated with my dad because he always wanted to just stay home with me and she wanted to go out and, I don't know…have him show her off, I think. That was hard on her. I felt guilty because I knew that she was jealous of all the attention he gave me. I remember once, right after we moved to Summertown, I woke up in the middle of the night and heard my mom crying. She was yelling at my dad so loud I heard it all the way from their room, which was on the other side of the house. She kept saying 'What about me? What about if *I'm* happy here? You always think about her. I'm your *wife!*'"

Pam held her hand. "I had no idea. But it's not your fault your folks split up."

"I don't really know that for sure," Jessie replied. "My dad and I have always been so close and we never really tried to include my mom in the things we did together. She had to feel like an outsider. In my heart I can't let go of it. It hurt my mom so much to take second place to me."

"You have some things to work out with her, then."

"Yeah."

"Start today then," her friend advised. "She won't be around forever. I know. There isn't a day that goes by that I don't think about my mom. If my dad isn't talking about her something else reminds me of her. Don't waste time thinking about it; go talk to her."

I'll try," she said.

"Don't try," Pam replied. "Do it. If I have to talk to Gary, the least you can do in return is have a serious talk with your mom and tell her how much you love her."

"Deal," Jessie agreed with a little bit of hesitation. "But only if you promise me something: if you and Gary start putting on another show, I want a video of it. I missed the last one and the copy I found on the internet is way too grainy."

Pam's face went white and her jaw dropped open. "It's on the internet?!"

"Yes," Jessie said, surprised. "It's been on there for most of a year. Nobody told you?"

"I didn't see anybody stopping."

"It didn't look like you weren't paying any attention to anything but Gary," Jessie grinned. "But it looks like the person who took the video was a little bit down the road and zoomed in you guys. It's still pretty popular. I think it's up to about sixty-five thousand hits."

"Oh, my *God*," Pam moaned. "I've been a porn star all this time and I didn't even know it."

Chapter Seven

Jerry Salyers was ecstatic. His latest client wasted no time in choosing where he wanted to live and of all the places available in Summertown, he chose the Cransky home, a split-level cabin with large bay windows that faced both north and south, an A-frame roof over the living room that needed to be re-shingled and plumbing that leaked in multiple places because the pipes froze up in the winter. The fee offered by the owner to rent it was much higher than any other home in town because it had been on the market for almost a year. The owners were going to hand it over to the bank if they didn't rent it soon. If that happened, home values in that part of Summertown would have taken a hit, and he was one of only three agents that made a large part of their living selling and managing properties there.

The house didn't get many viewings because of its location. It sat on top of a bed of granite, about five feet or so above the tops of the trees below, exposing it to the winds that swirled around the hills, which during heavy storms could be so strong it would uproot young trees. There were no neighbors on either side and the plumbing would freeze every winter due to their exposure above ground. The owner had inherited the house from his father who had built it from a kit, with no building experience but passed away before he was able to retire and move in. Jason told the agent he would love a place he could fix up a little. Since the owner had already told Salyers that if someone makes an offer he'd consider it and the rent being asked was already much less than most other places in town it was a no-brainer to simply make a low-ball offer to buy it.

No brainer, alright, Jerry thought. *It takes someone with no brains to choose a dump like that to live in.* But he closed the deal and turned over the keys with a smile on his face, still amazed at his good fortune in having this sucker land in his office.

Jerry was sharing this tidbit of information later that afternoon with Orin Nielsen at the café when he noticed Gary Callan sitting in his "office" booth.

"We got lucky with the Cransky house, Gary." Jerry said with a big smile. "Your newest resident, Jason Hadley, just *bought* that money pit. So, that's one less I have to push, and one less you have to check four times a day."

"So I heard," Gary replied. "That sure makes it more convenient. That place is way up on the hill and we have to park our car at the bottom of the driveway and walk up. I wonder what made him buy it."

"He says he wants something to fix up that has a nice view," Jerry shrugged. "I tried to tell him the problems the place had, but he didn't care."

Gary nodded, but he knew Jerry better than that. At most, Jerry probably gave him the full disclosure statement but downplayed it by telling him it could all be fixed with a hammer and a wrench, then pointed out the privacy advantages, the view, everything he could to sell it. "And he still wanted it, huh?" he said. "How about that?"

"Yep," Jerry grinned. "He wrote the check for the full amount and the papers have been filed. It won't take very long at all for the purchase to be finalized and then it'll be his problem, not ours."

"I guess so." Gary shrugged.

"Wait 'til I tell Deanne," Orin said laughing. "She'll just about fall out of her chair. She's been saying they'd have to tear that house down because it's such an eyesore. She'll die laughing when she hears this."

"Just don't tell her where you heard it," Jerry said. "I don't want anyone thinking I spread stories." He got up, put a twenty on the counter and told Ken he was covering Orin's bill, too. "I'll see you again sometime, Orin. Good talking to you." He walked out the door, almost skipping down the steps. This was a very good day.

While Jerry Salyers was crowing about his easy sale, Jason Hadley stood on the deck of his new home. The north-facing deck gave him a full view of Summertown with the single exception of the higher-end homes on the north face of the hill to the east. He could see every vehicle that entered town, whether it was on the main drag at Lake Mary and Pulliam Rd or at the north entry at Babbitt Parkway. That was the biggest draw of this place, next to the fact that there were only two homes separating this lot from the one he had bought years ago. It would be very easy to acquire those and begin work on his hotel. The second biggest advantage to this place was the absolute privacy; well worth the effort it was going to take to whip the house into shape. No one could enter town without his notice, but he could easily leave unobserved from the south side, just about any time after sundown.

And he was certain that was going to be very useful, very soon.

Chapter Eight

It was getting cold in the morning and the heater in my office was just not putting out warm air the way it used to. I was about to call our local handyman, Archie Dzuznich, when the door opened and Carol, my secretary, greeted my daughter Jessica and her husband Tom in her usual, cheery "Oh, how nice to see you!" that was reserved only for everyone who walked through the door.

"Hey, Papi," she greeted me with a kiss on the cheek. "We came down for Tom's monthly family meeting and decided to come a little early so we could check up on you."

"Well, I'm glad you did," I said. "But nothing's changed since we talked on the phone two days ago. I'm still pretty much all healed up and still running; up to two miles now. Tara and I are still on the verge of killing each other…"

"Papi," she sighed. "I told you, you need to end it. I know you love her. I do too, but she's not the same as she was before. She's turned into someone I don't even recognize and she doesn't care how you feel anymore. You said that yourself. You've already tried marriage counseling and it isn't working. It's time you started over."

"Well, I'll think about it."

"We'd better go," she said after looking at her watch. "Tom's dad said it was important, so we don't want to be late."

As they left, I wondered about the reason for the family meeting. The Little Creek Café was a popular place because the food and the coffee were good, the owners very friendly and the restaurant was very conveniently located. Their family meetings usually were done over the phone and were only a few minutes or so long, so for them to all meet in person there must be something important to discuss.

After a couple more hours of mind-numbing work, I decided to stop at the café before going to the Town Council meeting scheduled for 3 o'clock. As I walked the three blocks of storefronts I breathed in the cleansing chilled air and felt the icy breeze on my cheek and smiled. I loved autumn here almost as much as the spring. The hardier summer visitors finally packed up and headed back down to the desert from which I had escaped several years before, and left the rest of us to hibernate in what was always a beautiful, forest-lined hamlet that turned into a winter wonderland every time it snowed which, according to the weather forecasts would be frequently for about the next four months. I was looking forward to cross-country skiing with Gina. We had both agreed last year that it's easier and more fun to ski in the snow than to try running through it. I walked in the front door of the café and found Ken at the counter, much to my surprise.

"I thought you had a family meeting right now," I said. "I was going to sneak some real coffee while you weren't looking."

"We finished already," he replied, ignoring the opening I gave him for our usual banter. "Jessie got a call from the hospital asking her to come in. Apparently there was a big, multiple car accident on the forty and they needed the extra help. She asked me to tell you."

"Oh, wow," I whistled. "This time of year, it inevitably happens. The roads get icy and people just keep on driving at seventy, thinking nothing's going to happen."

"Yep."

He poured coffee into my Stone of Summertown mug. He'd had it made as a kind of joke playing on my last name, but it also referred to the rock I had in my hand when I tried to take out the guy who shot his son, Jhoon in the woods a little over a year ago. I was shot once with a rifle and I almost died, while the shooter did die from several well-placed bullets fired by our local police. Despite the fact that I was completely out of commission through most of it, I was hailed as a hero. I was glad when most of the attention began fading away, because I really didn't deserve it. I was just glad that Jhoon survived, considering he had been shot, too. After it was over, his girlfriend committed suicide, leaving him with a broken heart. He enlisted in the Air Force a few months later and was now assigned to a Special Operations Squadron.

"So, what's up?" I pried.

"Oh, just thinking of opening another business," he said casually. "Now that Chad has his own car, I was thinking of opening a pizza delivery business. The Campbells only have theirs open during the summer, which leaves an opportunity for us to make a little money the rest of the year."

"Hmm, what does Min think about it?" I asked. Ken's wife was very particular what they did with the business if I heard right. "Is she happy with it?"

"Oh, yeah. It was her idea," he shrugged. "She says that we could use a little space. I guess she's tired of having me around all day." He seemed genuinely hurt by that.

"Ah. Well, Ken, you have to remember that most of your life together, you were in the service and you only saw her and the boys at night and on weekends. And what about those trips... What are they called?"

"TDYs?"

"Yeah, TDYs. You had to go out of town, sometimes out of country, for weeks at a time. That made it easy to miss you. For the last few years, you two have been constantly together, with no break from one another. It was bound to happen that one of you would want a breather. It could have been you, but it turned out to be Min."

"Yeah, well…" he wasn't convinced.

"Don't worry about it," I said. "I'm sure that once you've got the pizza place up and running, you'll have just the amount of space you each need, and a nice little stream of income to boot."

"OK," he said. "We'll see how things go." He leaned over the counter then and said, "How about you? Are things improving with you and Tara at all?"

I knew he would get around to that.

"If only they were," I said. "She doesn't think there's anything wrong with her. She claims that I'm the one who's changed. I'm 'not the man I was when we married.'"

"I'm sorry, brother," he said. He shook his head sadly. "Min misses her. It's just so hard to understand how things can go so wrong so fast."

"Yeah." I looked at my watch and saw that I had five minutes to get to the Trailer. "Well, not that I want to end such a cheerful conversation, but I'd better head over to the meeting."

"The vote for the library?" he asked. "I thought that was a done deal."

"It is," I said. "This is about..." I turned and looked around the place to make sure there weren't any eavesdroppers—better known as Summertown residents—around. When I saw we were out of earshot of them I said, "This is to discuss Ray's request for more deputies. It's going to be a tough sell with Pedro."

"Yeah, it will," he nodded. "Good luck. I hope it goes through."

I took the short stroll over to the Trailer thinking about Ken and Min. If this was the worst that would happen in their marriage, I was sure they would be fine. But it obviously bothered Ken a lot. He must never have dealt with this kind of thing before. I'd dealt with it on multiple occasions with both Corinda and Tara and even though I learned to let it run its course it still hurt. I only hoped that Ken would adjust soon, because it pained me watching him carry the hurt around.

As I entered the Trailer for our scheduled meeting of the Town Council I felt a kind of negative energy, flowing through the room. Pedro Mendoza, the mayor of Summertown, was leaning on his elbows, staring down at the proposal submitted by Ray Brandt. Bill Gravattini, a retired car salesman from El Paso and senior council member, looked up from his copy of the same report and nodded a greeting to me. We still had two council members out; one of them, Mr. Sanderman, was unable to attend because he had a doctor's appointment. He was in his late eighties and had heart trouble so it was understood that he wouldn't always be able to attend. And as much as we liked him, this particular session was going to go a bit easier without him.

"Where's Todd?" Bill asked impatiently. "We need to get this underway if we plan on getting done before midnight tonight."

"He's walking over," I said. "His car won't start." This brought a chuckle from the others; the town's auto mechanic can't get his car started.

"How's Gina doing?" Pedro asked. "Feeling any better?"

"Yes," I said. "She's improving faster than I expected. I just saw her at the café this morning, joking around with Min."

"Good," he smiled. "She's a trooper, that one."

"Yeah, she is." I didn't tell him she'd been crying when I stopped by her place earlier. That would have just sparked another rumor that Bill would have done his best to spread around town. He and I never quite got along.

I sat in my spot, across from Pedro and scanned through the proposal. It had a lot of "cop-talk" that went on and on for about three pages, listing crime stats for the last two years, vehicle accidents, the cost of our contract with the Sheriff's Department, etc., etc. Then he came to the investigation of the multiple homicides last year and how much time and expense was tied up with that due to our not having a better staffed and equipped town police department. Cutting through the fluff, I could see Ray was basically saying that things were getting ugly and the Marshal's Office needed extra help. I mentioned this to Pedro who nodded.

"Yeah, that's the message I got, too," he grumbled. Pedro had remained the mayor of Summertown because he kept municipal expenses down. Now, for the first time since he took on the part-time office, he was being asked to add a permanent expense to the village's tight budget.

"Well, you may not like hearing this, Pedro," I said, "but I have to agree with him. Ray and Barry need help. They really don't have much experience investigating these kinds of cases and continuing to rely on the Sheriff's Office for our police patrols is getting expensive because even though we share the patrol contract with Mormon Lake, for the most part they're seasonal and they really have just one main drag. We're more densely populated all year round and we have several more streets—and the size of our business district has grown some in the last ten years, so we've been paying most of the cost. It just makes sense to take the money we're spending on a county contract that only gets us intermittent patrols and use it on augmenting our own police department. Then, we can offer a contract to Mormon Lake and free up a county deputy to work somewhere he'll do more good."

"That does make sense," Pedro conceded, to my surprise. "The contract with the county is our second-biggest expenditure. If we were to end it—or at least cut it, say, in half—we could conceivably pay for at least another full-time deputy. Especially if, as you suggest, we offer patrol service to Mormon Lake. If we don't get proactive and start taking responsibility for the safety and security of our own town and stop relying on the county for help, we could possibly even be annexed by a larger city. Flagstaff is already spreading out towards Lake Mary."

When Todd arrived a few minutes later, we filled him in on what we were discussing. A moment later Bill motioned to vote on it, I seconded and when the voting was done we had unanimously agreed to begin interviewing for one full-time and one part-time deputy.

"Now for the hard part," I said as a collective groan was heard throughout the room. This was the part of the meeting that we all dreaded: deciding how we were going to pay for these new town employees, as well as the equipment they were going to need.

"Yeah," Bill grumbled. "The hard part. Does anybody have any novel ideas for fund allocation that doesn't involve taxes?" Bill was a politician of the old school. He never voted for anything that would cause him to be voted out in the next election.

"No," I answered. I had spent yesterday afternoon researching that very question but could not come up with one single alternative short of going door to door, statewide, selling candy. "Ray has applied for, and received a grant to hire one officer, but we have to put up cash to match it. We can get a loan to cover the initial cost, but we'll have to get some kind of revenue coming in to cover the loan and to continue the services. We'll have to levy a tax of some kind. There's no way around it. Believe me, I've looked but I couldn't find any other means."

"Well, I'm for it," Pedro said, shocking us even more than he did a few minutes ago.

"What is *up with you?*" Bill said. He was as bewildered as I was. Pedro had always been rabidly anti-tax.

"I know," he said, raising his hands and shrugging. "I've always been against unduly burdening our residents with taxes...*But—*," he pointed a finger up and paused then continued, "The key phrase here is '*unduly* burden'. We need these new officers. In fact we need, probably, two more on top of that. As Jimmy just said—and he's our money man—we have no other way to fund necessary expansion of a needed service. Our tiny piece of state tax revenue barely covers sanitation." He stood up and began to pace around the little room, as was his habit. "We not only need these new deputies, but we also need that library. *And* we need to get at least an ambulance service set up inside town limits. Mormon Lake's fire station was established for Mormon Lake, and Happy Jack's covers too big of an area to have to respond to our calls. It's slowing down response times that one day is going to cost one of our residents their life. We are years overdue for a fire station of our own." He stopped behind Todd and put a hand on his shoulder. "Todd here has been asking for a property tax for the last five years and frankly, if we had listened to him—if *I* had listened— we wouldn't be having this meeting. We'd already have the funds in the bank to pay for these things. I say the time's come to listen to him and put it to a vote."

We all nodded agreement. In fact, I had always agreed with Todd, always voted for the property tax whenever he brought it up. The problem was, as mayor, Pedro held two votes to our one; and Karl and Bill agreed with Pedro regarding taxes, so the measure was voted down. But this time, the measure was put again to a vote and everyone including Bill—to everyone's surprise—passed it unanimously as required by town charter. This was going to be a tough sell to the residents, but a necessary move, so the deed was done.

"Now, on to our next order of business," the mayor sighed. "Bill?"

Gravattini cleared his throat, sat up and announced, "A formal complaint has been lodged against the principal of Summertown School for indecent public behavior."

The room fell silent as everyone stole glances in my direction. It took considerable restraint on my part to remain silent and hear the complaint.

"Apparently," Bill went on, "Gina Albright was at the Little Creek Café recently, having a sex-related conversation with two men. When Ken's teenaged son, Chad, entered the room Gina proceeded to grasp her bosoms and shake them in a titillating fashion—that's what it says in the complaint," he added when a few members let out involuntary snorts of laughter, "...she proceeded to shake them."

"Who is it that claims to have witnessed this?" I asked, trying to keep my temper in check.

"The complaint is anonymous," Bill said. He had a smug expression that I wanted to slap off of his face. "They said they were concerned about your reaction when this was brought up at the Council meeting. From the look on your face, I can understand why."

I ignored the implication. "I don't care what 'they' claim to have seen. I was sitting right there next to her and she did *not* shake her 'bosoms' at Chad Shirazi."

"I'm sorry, Jimmy," Todd replied. "But it isn't just a matter of what happened at this point. It has to do with whether parents are confident in Gina as an example of the moral standards they're trying to raise their kids by."

"Now, Jimmy, I know you're close friends with her," Bill said, "but we have to bow to the will of the residents. We're here to do their bidding, not ours." He sat forward in his chair and looking me in the eye asked, "And what part in this conversation did you play? You just told us you were there."

"Why yes, I was, Mr. Prosecutor," I replied. "Do I need to seek legal representation right now? Are you going to read me my rights? What's the penalty for having an adult conversation with two people of legal age?"

"There's no need for sarcasm, Jimmy," he said coldly. "You know perfectly well that it's part of our job as Town Councilmen to remedy any problems concerning Summertown, including its school."

The only reason Bill Gravattini was on the council was because he had political aspirations beyond Summertown. That and no one else wanted the job in his part of town. I was sick of listening to his lectures on civic duty. All he really wanted was to kiss peoples' backsides and hang onto his position so he could spend the pittance the town paid us on a PR guy who was always testing the waters for a shot at the County Supervisor election.

"You know, Bill…" I started, then changed my mind. I ignored him and addressed Todd and Pedro. "It isn't just the blind will of our residents that we have to consider, but doing the right thing. To persecute someone who's done an excellent job holding our school together and who continued to act as both administrator *and* teacher during her pregnancy and afterward, all on unsubstantiated hearsay is wrong. She doesn't deserve this crap, no matter how far up the asses of the 'Poison Tongue Club,' as Mr. Sanderman refers to them, Bill's head might be."

"Now, that's out of line!" Bill protested.

"Shut up," I barked.

"You know, there just might be a need for a recall election," Bill said threateningly. "Somebody here seems to have a pretty sordid private life…"

"Shut up, Bill!" Pedro cut him off. "There will be no talk of recalls. Now, sit down and be quiet if you don't have anything constructive to say."

"I see you've closed ranks against me," Bill replied. "So I'll not dignify this meeting with my presence any longer." He threw his papers into his fancy leather briefcase, which never had much in it, and headed for the door.

"That's the first thing you've actually *done* to dignify this meeting, you weasel," I said. "Hurry up and go. And leave the door open so we can air this place out. I'm getting sick from the smell of bullshit!"

He stopped in mid-stride, glared at me, then walked out the door and slammed it behind him. The room fell silent; the rest of them avoided looking at me.

"I'm sorry," I said. "I don't know what got into me."

"Hell," Todd chuckled. "You didn't say anything I wasn't thinking."

"I move we vote on this right now and end the meeting," Jack Tandy said. It was the first time he had uttered a word. He was a quiet man of sixty five or so, who had spent thirty years as a journeyman surveyor. He was a big help when it came to land use and boundaries and he was blessedly silent in all matters of the stupid like this.

"I second," Todd said.

"All in favor?" Pedro asked.

With all present agreed, we voted. The proposal to bring Gina's case before the town in a referendum vote was unanimously shot down. But while this attack on Gina's character may have failed, I had a feeling there were going to be more. And there was a fair-to-middling chance that one would eventually succeed.

***

"That's great news!" Ray said into the phone.

He'd been awaiting an answer from the Town Council regarding his request to hire another deputy. Finally, just as he was about to sit down to dinner at Corinda's house, he got the call he'd been hoping for.

"I can't believe you approved *two,*" he laughed. "I only requested one. I really appreciate that, Jimmy. Oh, yeah. She's been calling me for the last couple of weeks asking if I'd heard anything; she can start as soon as the funds are allocated, no problem with that. OK. I'll talk to you about it tomorrow at the Café. Have a great night. Bye."

"So, you got the council to hire your girlfriend, huh?" Corinda said as Ray hung up the phone and headed to the dining room table. "That detective from the sheriff?"

"No," Ray replied. He had a feeling this conversation would come up sooner or later. "I requested another deputy, and they agreed to hire *two* more officers." He hoped that she would at least pretend to be happy for him, but she just stood there waiting for him to explain his hiring choice. "Cindy Noe just happens to be an excellent police officer. And she is not my girlfriend, you are."

"Not for long, I'm not," she countered. "I won't be the other woman. I have to have a man who will only be with me."

"Cindy is just a friend—"

"So *you* say," she cut in. "When a man fools around, he doesn't just admit that he is seeing another woman…"

"I'm *not seeing Cindy*…"

"You see what I mean?" she interrupted again. "You could just tell me the truth." She began to cry.

"Are you questioning my honesty?" Ray demanded.

"No," she whimpered. "I think you want her but don't realize it."

"That's not what you said a second ago. You said I was fooling around. That means you think I'm being dishonest. And I will *not have that*. Do you understand?"

"Well, what am I supposed to think?" she threw up her hands in frustration. "You're always talking about her…"

"Yesterday was the first time I ever mentioned her name to you," Ray said incredulously.

"Why? You wanted to keep her a secret?"

"No, of course not," he replied. "Her name just never came up because…"

"Because you didn't want me to know about her!" she accused. "Because you know you have so much in common with her and you have nothing in common with me."

"I'm not in love with her. I'm in love with you…"

"Right now you are," she said. "But I think if you see her every day, you'll want her more."

"Why on earth would you think that?" Ray asked.

"Because you're both police officers and she's smart and I'm…stupid," her voice caught and tears welled up in her eyes. "She can do all that police stuff and all I can do is cook and style hair…"

"Corinda, stop," Ray commanded. He had reached the end of his patience and it was time to take command of the situation.

"I was going to give you this under more romantic circumstances. But, since you want a guarantee that you're the one I want, here it is." He opened the box and showed her a gold ring with a single, half-carat diamond mounted in the center. "Babydoll," he said tenderly, "you've been so patient waiting for this. Do you like it?"

Corinda gasped at the sight of the ring. It was beautiful; much larger than the one Jimmy gave her when he proposed so long ago. The thought of Jimmy sent a strange shiver through her body. What was it about him that bothered her at a moment like this?

"I love you, Ray," she said as tears began to flow. "But I can't marry you until I can receive the blessing of the Church. I must be sure that my marriage to Jimmy is ended in the eyes of the Church."

"Sweetheart," Ray replied, "Jimmy's remarriage ended your marriage to him, if your living with Nerville didn't."

"Why did you bring that up?" she said indignantly. "Are you saying that I destroyed my marriage by acting like a whore?"

"No, of course not," he said. "I'm saying that however the marriage ended…"

"Whether it was me committing adultery or Jimmy committing *bigamy*…

"Where are you getting that from?" Ray demanded. He knew he couldn't win this argument but he wasn't going to give in.

"You just said either Jimmy ended our marriage by marrying Tara or I did by living with someone else."

"Well…are you going to deny that you lived with Nerville for three years?"

"No, I won't deny it," she snapped at him. "But I didn't think that you would ever throw it in my face!"

"Oh, for God's sake."

Ray closed the box containing the ring and slipped into his pocket, then walked to the door, took his coat down from the hook on the wall and headed outside without a word.

Chapter Nine

"I'm so sick of having my life scrutinized by everybody in this stupid place!" Gina shouted. She had waited until we had reached the east side of Tubman Wash. I figured going for a long walk would be the best way to discuss her current standing with the community.

"I know," I said. "But it comes with the job, you know that. They're never happy unless they have someone to crucify."

"Yeah, but I don't have to subject myself to it if I don't want to," she said. "I really don't have anything keeping me here." That stung, but I kept my mouth shut. "Maybe I should go somewhere I won't stand out so much."

"As the old saying goes, 'No matter where you go, there you are'. Moving somewhere else will just put you in the middle of another set of problems. You can't get away from them, especially as a school principal."

"Jimmy, you know that it has more to do with me than with my job," she said. "I could choose another career, but I'm not going to be something that I'm not. And no one has any business telling me what I can or can't do as long as it's legal. I deserve to be happy, with or without some board's approval."

"I know."

"Don't you think *you* deserve to be happy?" she asked.

"As much as any human has 'a right', so to speak," I replied. "But it's God who allows man his rights. What we call rights are merely privileges bestowed on us by God— so, as far as that goes, I suppose I probably 'deserve' happiness, more or less..."

"Jimmy, cut the crap," she interrupted. "If God exists, He wants us all to be happy. And, because He wants it for you, you deserve to be happy, whether you like it or not."

"What do you mean?" I bristled. "'You don't think I would like to be happy?' Do you not remember that I was happy when Tara...?"

"Don't mention her," she commanded. "I'm talking about you, no one else. And yes, I'm beginning to think that you may not actually want to be happy. Maybe you think it'll make you holier, or that you have to serve some kind of penance or something. I don't know why really, but there's something different about you these last few months. There's something going on that you're not talking about."

"I didn't think it showed."

"I know you better than most. I can tell when something's bugging you."

"Well," I hesitated. I was afraid of how she'd see me if I told her what I'd done, even if it was twenty years ago, but I knew she'd keep asking. And in my heart I really didn't want to carry this secret around with me forever. "I've been having bad dreams for the past couple months. They're usually about something that happened a long time ago." I waited for her to reply, but after few seconds of silence I gave in.

"I'll tell you what happened," I said. "But remember, I was a lot younger then. It took a long time to put that night behind me and move on."

She still said nothing. She simply looked at me and waited for me to start talking. I let out a deep sigh and closed my eyes, thinking back. How good that day started, and then to end as it did...

Port-au-Prince, Haïti
November 1992

I had just gotten out of the little Daihatsu pickup that belonged to the "Lespri Bondye" mission and started to walk toward the large food wholesaler in downtown Port-au-Prince when I was approached by a young girl of no more fifteen. She was wearing what all the other young girls and boys wore: filthy clothes. She had a dirty, once-pretty blue cotton skirt with floral patterns and a t-shirt of some unknown color that had been covered in dirt and mud so often that there was no washing it out without destroying the shirt. Her shoes were the same clear, red plastic sandals that all the others wore; they were cheap, waterproof and they kept her from stepping on the sharp rocks and nails that were often found on the streets of the crowded markets.

She was a very pretty, fresh-faced girl despite her condition. I guessed that she had probably been sent to town by her family in order to make money to send back so the rest of them could eat. She didn't seem to have been here long; those that had been working in the capitol tended to have a much warier gaze and smiled less. She didn't have anything in the basket on her head, which she deftly balanced there without needing to hold it with her hands. So, she was a porter who was looking for a job.

"Bonjou, Blanc," she greeted me. Blanc, which meant white, was a standard greeting to those seen as a figure of authority, whether white or black. The young people would either call me Blanc or Direk or Djékta, which meant the same thing: director, boss. At first, I tried to get them to call me by my first name, but after a while, I gave up. "Bezwen poté?" she asked.

"Oui," I responded. I negotiated a price for her helping me carry the cases of food I was there to buy, and she followed me into the big, block building that had been painted a bright yellow some decades ago but now that paint was faded, dirty and peeling, the plaster cracked and broken in multiple places. This was the rule, rather than the exception among the buildings along Boulevard La Saline, the main street downtown that outlined the bay.

The owner, a tall, thin, friendly man in his forties was joking with a customer while his employees filled her order and packed her goods in boxes. He saw me enter and he greeted me in English. I smiled and answered, amused at how obvious it was where I came from. There were French, German, Israeli, Canadian men but everyone who knew English would address me in English.

"How can I help you, sir?" he asked in Arabic-accented English. Many of the "*commerçants*" in Haiti were of Mediterranean and Middle Eastern descent, their grandparents having been displaced from their homelands and coming here to reestablish themselves in what they saw as virgin territory.

"I need this order filled," I replied as I handed him a long list given to me by the director of the mission. "Can I get all of this here, or do I need to go several places?"

"I can fill this order here. My cousin has a store on the next block and he can send me the quincaille—the, uh, housewares. I give it to you at my cost, since you're buying so much, and it's for the mission."

"Thank you, that's very kind," I said.

I was always touched by the generosity of Haitians, whether they were middle-class or the poorest of the poor. In a place where misery was everywhere you turned, folks would give of their meager supplies to help someone in greater need than they were. And I knew that even this man, who owned this business, was hurting, too. When the Haitian army exiled the popular president Aristide the year before, the OAS and the UN both decided to place an embargo on all non-essential goods. That meant only basic food items, medicine and the like were available. There was no gasoline or diesel fuel allowed in, which sent the price of fuel through the roof and raised the price of all goods as well. The world was starving Haiti out because of the actions of a few men. And yet the Haitians still shared with one another.

"'Sa-ou vlé, ti fi?" the man asked my porteuse.

"She's with me," I answered for her. "She'll be carrying this for me."

The man laughed and shook his head, then shrugged and gestured with his hands as if to say, "It's your funeral."

"Is there a problem with this girl I should know about?" I asked.

"One of my employees caught her trying to steal a can of milk last week. So you'll want to watch her. If they steal once, they'll try it again."

"Thanks, I'll watch her," I replied politely. I hated when people pointed at a kid and basically said, "They're no good. Stay away from that one." But I could also see his side. He bought and sold wholesale, so his profit margin was very small. If someone stole just one bar of soap from a case of twenty-four, he lost his profit on that case.

When the order was complete, which ended up being eight large boxes, taped and tied up expertly by the store workers, the total weight added up to about three hundred pounds. I looked at the little girl I'd hired, then decided to go out and hire one more person. But she would have none of it.

"Pa gen danjé, Blanc," she smiled, waving a dismissive hand. "M-ap poté-l. Pa bezwen lòt moun."

Well, her telling me not to worry and that she didn't need help didn't keep me from worrying, but I watched and let her try anyway. She rolled an old rag into a donut shape, put it on top of her head to serve as a cushion, and then squatted down so that the two men lifting the first box could set it on her head. After a moment of shifting and replacing it, the box sat, stable and in place as she stood up, holding the sides of the box to keep it from falling, and followed me out the door to my truck. I gave two men, clad only in cut-off pants five gourdes each to help load the truck and to guard it while we went back and forth. I couldn't believe this little girl was carrying all this weight on the top of her head, but she did. All three hundred pounds or more sat in the back of my truck when it was over and this little girl just sat on the tailgate, smiling like she had when I met her a couple of hours ago. I suddenly wanted to hug the stuffing out of her and take her home to Phoenix with me. *Yeah, that's a smart move* I thought. *Bring a nice young girl home to give her a better life, then have her live with Corinda and me.* I stopped myself right there, the thought of subjecting a child to my domestic warfare negating any possibility of my adopting the girl. It was bad enough that our daughter, Jessica, was growing up listening to us argue over just about everything.

After I paid her and the two young men for their work, the two left but the girl remained and asked if I needed help unloading the truck. I ached to give this girl a better place to live than this place, with its streets that overflowed with sewage every time it rained and never knowing if she'll be robbed, raped or killed...or all three because those who would protect her couldn't watch her all the time and there were far too few policemen down here.

"Monté machin-nan," I told her.

She got up into the bed of the truck with the cargo. To sit in the cab with me would have caused people to think that I had picked her up for other purposes. We rode along the bumpy, dusty, crowded road to the highway, Route Nationale #2, and headed south toward Miragoane. Just about a half-mile down, I turned left onto an even more poorly-maintained road than the highway and weaved and bumped along until we arrived at the Lespri Bondye mission.

I had been asked to come along on a mission trip three years before by a work buddy at my accounting firm, who went every year and said it was one of the most fulfilling things he'd ever done. Curious, I agreed. I figured it would give my wife and me a break from each other for a couple of weeks. It wasn't like the movies, where two people who don't know each other well get married because of a baby and eventually fall in love and everything is perfect. We got married because she got pregnant, and it had been a terrible mistake for both of us. So, she didn't have any problem with my going. It was great, except it was almost unbearable not seeing my Jessie for two whole weeks.

The mission was comprised of one block-walled, tin roofed building that served as the chapel and school; one block-walled, thatch roofed storage building and a wood and tin dormitory that housed children and young unwed mothers. A corrugated sheet metal bathing enclosure stood next to the dormitory and its walls were high enough to give the residents privacy that they didn't have at the community water fountain, where most people bathed, filled their buckets and did their laundry.

I drove up to the chapel building and called Pastor Jacques, who came out, along with the rest of my mission team and emptied the truck before the little girl was able to arrange the cloth on her head. I couldn't help but chuckle when I saw the bewildered look on her face when she turned toward the truck and saw that it was empty.

"Sak pasé?" she asked suspiciously. Yes, she had every right to ask what was going on.

I thought for a moment how I was going to word my reasons for bringing her to the mission…like I didn't have an hour to think about it on the ride over. I decided that frankness was best, but I wasn't sure my command of the language was sufficient to get my point across so I called Pastor Jacques again.

"I was hoping that I could bring this girl to the mission to live, Pastor," I said tentatively. "I saw her downtown and couldn't help but want to get her out of there…"

"Jimmy," he said with a sad, knowing smile, "I understand. You want to take them all to a better place. If you could, you would take them all home with you. I know.

If I had a place for them all I would have every one of the children that people bring me here and feed and clothe them all and bring them to know what Christ's love is." He sighed and looked sadly into my eyes and said, "But I cannot take them all, Jimmy. I do not have the money to care for them all."

I could hear his words, understand what he was saying, but I couldn't allow it to be true. The moment I saw this girl, I knew that she was going to end up either a victim of some indescribable abuse, or a prostitute, or pregnant with the child of a man who she'll never see again. I had to do something.

"If it's a matter of money, Pastor, I'll pay for her," I said before I stopped myself. I hadn't even talked it over with Corinda but I was sure she would understand. As awful as it was being married to her, she was a good and compassionate soul.

"Are you certain, Jimmy?" Pastor Jacques asked, skeptically. "Everyone who comes here pledges to pay for a child's food and clothing but when they go home, few continue to pay beyond a few months. When that happens, we have no choice but to send them home." He looked at me with a piercing gaze, deadly serious. "Are you sure that you will continue to pay for this young girls expenses? This is not a responsibility taken lightly."

"Yes, Pastor Jacques," I replied. "I swear that I will always pay for this girl's needs as long as she's in your care."

I saw a smile break on his face. Not the sad one that he had a moment ago, but one of apparent amusement.

"Do you know your young friend's name, Monsieur Stone?"

He caught me there. I had never asked her name. All I saw was a young girl who needed a chance at a better life.

"I never thought to ask," I replied sheepishly.

He laughed heartily at that one. "You know, Frere Jimmy," he said, grabbing me by the shoulder affectionately, "your heart is bigger than your brain. That is both a blessing and a cross to bear."

I dearly loved this man, along with his sweet wife, a woman who accompanied every worship service by playing her accordion, which she played quite beautifully, as far as accordion playing goes. The sacrifice that these well-educated people made on behalf of their parishioners was far greater than any of them knew. Yet he and his wife never gave it a second thought. For them, following God's leading was far more important than making the big salaries that they were more than qualified to earn.

That evening at dinner in the pastor's home I was told that the girl accepted the invitation to stay. She had told the pastor's wife that she had come to Port-au-Prince a few weeks before because her mother had passed away and her father went to the Dominican Republic to work in the fields. While he was gone, she and her two older brothers were left alone. Her eldest brother was an abusive teen who had begun running with the "attachés", a group sanctioned by the military government to act as civilian aides to the police. What they really were was a group of gangs that prowled the streets at night looking for trouble and when they found none they would go to the local police station and hang out with the cops. There was very little patriotism to be found in these groups, which were breeding grounds for the same kind of leadership-through-fear that the country had tried to end back in 1986.

"So, did she give her name?" I asked.

"You brought a kid here and you didn't even ask her name?" laughed Trip Harvin, the mason of the group.

"It never occurred to me to ask. It was just at the last minute that I decided to bring her up here. I just couldn't stand to leave her in that mud and crud."

"Her name is Meprise," Pastor Jacques said.

"That's a pretty name," Ted Linelli said.

"It means 'ignore,'" the pastor replied. "Or perhaps 'ignored.'"

"Why would someone call their child 'ignore?'" Trip asked.

"It could be any reason," pastor said. "Her birth may have brought joy that would help them forget the loss of another child; perhaps she was unwanted and her mother or father wished to forget her…although that is unlikely, since her parents cared for her most of her life."

"Well, it's a very pretty name, regardless of its meaning," Ted said. "How old is she?"

"Thirteen," Pastor replied.

"Thirteen!" I said in surprise. "She's so strong! I couldn't believe how much she moved. She didn't look like she could carry all that stuff, but she did."

"Yes," Pastor agreed. "She is a strong one. And a very respectful girl, too. I believe we can teach her without much trouble. She has already made friends here."

"Great!" I said. "That is a big relief."

"Yes."

Just then we heard a knock at the door and there she stood, dressed in a clean blue dress, her hair washed and covered in the colorful hair-ties that all the school girls wore. It was only then that I saw just how young she was. She was so absolutely adorable I couldn't help but smile.

"Merci, Parain Jimmy," she said with as broad a smile as I'd ever seen. She called me Godfather, a common title for a benefactor.

"De rien, chéri," I replied. And at that moment it really did seem like nothing at all. Seeing this one child so happy from this small gesture on my part just warmed my heart.

"M-ap voye lèt, lè m'apwen ekri, d'ako?" she said tentatively.

"Mais oui," I answered eagerly. Of course I'd love to read letters from her—after she learned to write, as she said. I told her to have the pastor write letters for her, until she was able to do it herself, and include pictures so I could see how she grows. As I turned and walked back to the table, my eyes started to get misty.

"You want to take her home with you, don't you?" Trip said. "I know the feeling. Every time I come down here, I want to adopt at least a couple of these kids and take them home with me."

"Yeah," I replied. "This is my third trip and I still have a tough time leaving these kids to grow up in poverty."

Just then, a loud cracking sound, like gunfire rang out from the front of the mission. I ran out before the others could catch me and sprinted in the direction of the shots. I heard a vehicle speed away, toward the highway and the sound of wailing from several children. When I arrived at the scene, I found Madam Jacques, the pastor's wife on the ground, a small red stain growing larger just above her left breast. She was motionless and as one of the girls tried to rouse her she began to moan. Just then, the pastor arrived and knelt beside his wife and spoke comforting words. The rest of the mission team came up and we carried her over to the truck, and after laying down a blanket, set her down gently and helped Jacques in so that he could sit with her as we drove to the hospital next to the naval base. I could have gotten us there in a few minutes if we had been in the U.S. but in Haiti, with the roads in a constant state of disrepair, I was dodging potholes and animals, slowing down when I came to a long rough patch for fear that shaking Madame Jacques might cause the bullet to move and do more damage. It seemed to take forever just to get to town.

Just as we entered Miragoane, the pastor rapped on the window of the cab and motioned to pull over. We got out along the side of the road and walked back to see what was wrong, but we knew what it was. Pastor Jacques was cradling his sweet wife in his arms and in a broken voice, tears streaming down his face, was singing a hymn that I didn't recognize but I understood the words, "All to You, Lord, all to You. I give You everything Lord…" Ted, who had ridden with us climbed up into the bed of the truck and wrapped his arms around the poor man. Just then, something snapped inside me. All I wanted to do at that moment was find whoever did this and tear him apart.

"Pastor," I asked as gently as I could, the blood in my veins growing cold and my voice shaking in rage that I was barely holding in check. "Who would do something like this? Is there anyone who would ever want to hurt your wife?"

He looked up at me and sobbed, "TiZo."

"Who?"

"He is one of the attachés around here, bullies that are always bothering the girls."

He stroked his wife's hair and face, took a ragged breath and went on, "He came here a few days ago and wanted to take Marie-Claire to the bar to dance. Denise knew what he really wanted and told him to leave our girls alone." He began weeping again, but managed to finish, "He said he would come for her. He said he would make her pay for getting in his way…" he broke down completely then and buried his face in his wife's neck. Ted held him tight and spoke soothingly to him, trying to console him at this most inconsolable time.

I had no idea what I was going to do, but I knew whatever I did, this TiZo coward was either going to die or he would never, ever be able to walk again. I began to walk toward town before the others could realize I was gone. It was only about a half mile further and I had a good guess where I might find this punk, since there were only a couple of popular bars in town.

I entered the first bar, which was nothing more than the back room of a private residence with light bulbs strung across the rafters and a tape player cranking out festive Haitian Kompa music as a handful of couples, mostly dressed in the flashy Caribbean floral styles of the working class danced close together. I walked over to the long, tall workbench that served as a bar and asked the attendant if TiZo had come by. He looked at me suspiciously and said that TiZo never came there; he preferred the Hotel Lambi, where he could find a prostitute if he wanted. This was "a respectable place", the man said. I apologized for offending him but he waved it off and smiled. I turned and headed out, walking as fast as I could to get to the Lambi before Ted and Pastor Jacques could catch me, because I was sure that by now they had realized I was gone and figured out what I was about to do.

"Mais oui," the clerk said when I asked if TiZo was in.

"Where is he?" I asked in Creole. "I don't know him. I was told that if I needed a gun I should talk to him."

He looked at me for a full minute, giving me the going over from head to toe, trying to judge whether or not I was trustworthy. When I handed him $20 American he nodded and pointed upstairs and said, "Trente".

I headed upstairs to room 30 as casually as I could, trying to keep my anger in check and to think clearly. It was at the ended of the hall, to the left and an ancient, stainless steel fire extinguisher was hanging on the wall opposite. *This'll do,* I thought. I took the extinguisher down, held it with both hands like a battering ram and slammed the base of it into the door just above the doorknob. It didn't give way until the third try and by that time TiZo already had his gun in his hand and was pointing it at me. But I was following the momentum of the big steel extinguisher and just swung it sideways, sweeping across his arm and knocking the gun out if his hand. Then I stepped into a backhand swing and cracked the base of the canister across the right side of his skull, dropping him like a bag of rocks. Then I threw the extinguisher to the side and pounced on him, straddled his chest, pinned his arms under my knees, and began hammering my fists into his face over and over until I was sure that I had rendered him unrecognizable even to his mother. As I ran out of steam, the sounds of screaming started to work their way into my consciousness. I looked up and saw three women in varying conditions of undress, huddled together on the bed, staring at me in fear. I stood up and raised my hands in surrender, trying to assure them I meant no harm. That was when I suddenly felt or heard, I'm not sure which, a high-pitched gong sound in my head and a short, dull flash of light then everything went black. In the moment before I lost consciousness the odd notion occurred to me that now I knew what they meant by 'seeing stars'.

***

"Damn, Jimmy," Gina whispered. Her eyes were wide as she stared at me. I wondered what she was thinking, but was afraid to ask.

"Yeah well, like I said, it was a long time ago," I said, as if that made everything OK.

"How did you get away from there? Who hit you?"

"A cop, probably. I spent the night in jail, then some guys from the embassy bailed me out and put me on a plane back home. They told me I was 'no longer welcome in Haiti'."

"They deported you?"

"My visit was cut short. Permanently."

We walked in silence for a while, Gina glancing at me from the corner of her eye every few minutes. We topped the rise located about a half-mile southeast of the trailhead and we could see the valley below ringed in golden aspens and patched here with icy sheets, there with dormant grass.

"So, how are you doing now?" Gina asked, breaking the silence.

"Depressed, I guess." I shrugged.

"What you need is a good roll in the sack." Her little joke caught me completely off-guard.

"Gina, you have got to get a grip on yourself…"

"That's all I've been doing. But going solo only satisfies for so long…"

"*Gina!*"

"*OK! I'll stop*," she held up her hands in surrender. "So, how are you and Tara getting along?"

"Same as the last time you asked which was…yesterday?"

"That's too bad."

"Yep." So much for snappy conversation.

"How about Ray and Corinda?" she asked.

"Oh, pretty good I suppose," I said. "Ray doesn't talk about it much. At least not with me."

"Yeah, it would be a little weird, talking about your girlfriend with her ex."

"Yes, it would. I wish him all the luck in the world with her. I think they can make each other happy, if she'll let him."

"*They* can make each other happy if *she'll* let him?" she said quizzically. "You mean Ray has nothing to do with it?"

"Sure he does," I said. "But Corinda could screw that up with no effort at all. She'll need to keep her big mouth shut and just let him make her happy, without questioning everything he does and griping when things don't always go her way."

"Like everybody else in the world?" she said, a grin forming on her lips.

"Maybe," I sighed. "But twenty years of it, non-stop, gives me a little better idea of just how much Ray will have to endure. I only hope she's managed to let that go."

"Oh, well," Gina shrugged. "It's not your problem."

"Thank God."

Gina took my right arm in hers and leaned against me as we walked down toward the frozen meadow. Her presence was the only soothing thing I had to enjoy lately, so I just soaked it in and tried to let go of painful memories. Yet that brought with it another problem: I had become emotionally dependent on Gina and I missed her when we parted. Worse, I was catching myself fantasizing about her in the middle of the day. I'd always found her attractive, but I never thought of her as anything but my good-looking friend. She was my buddy. But the more time we spent together as my private life declined, the more I started noticing the lovely young woman she was. I started stealing glances at her face whenever she looked away. I was finding myself daydreaming of holding her and staring into those blue eyes...

Then I'd snap myself out of it and cuss myself out for committing adultery in my heart. The kind of thoughts I was entertaining betrayed Tara's trust as well as Gina's. I had a problem and reflecting on my sins and saying prayers weren't helping like they used to. I needed to stay away from Gina and get my head and heart straight. But by now the very idea of not seeing Gina was too painful to even consider.

Chapter Ten

Tara Stone stood on a stepladder in her classroom, stapling new posters about personal hygiene to the cork board. Gina had asked her to take over the Sex Ed classes for the junior high and high school after Charlene Muir was killed by her husband. *Just another straw on the camel's back,* she told herself.

She was not having a good day at all. But that was to be expected, since she couldn't recall having had a good day in quite some time. She'd been off her medicine for about two months because she never had a chance to sneak in to Flagstaff and have a session with her psychologist; and he told her she had to do that before the pharmacy would refill her prescription. Spending all that time taking care of Jimmy when he got shot was so hard to take. She never wanted to care for another man after she got rid of Jared. That was why she stayed alone for eight years before she let Jimmy into her life.

It was great the first two years, even though he dropped everything anytime Jessie said she needed him; it made her a little jealous. But then she started seeing things in him that were very similar to that douchebag she divorced, like drinking until he was half blind at the wedding rehearsal dinner then going around making out with every woman he saw. If he'd been any drunker, he'd probably have tried to do it with his own daughter. And he had the nerve to be jealous of her at the reception when that hot groomsman, Lonny—what was it? Whatever his last name was, Lonny had made her feel sexy again, after years of being made to feel like an old woman, being married to a guy eight years older than she was who already had a teenage daughter and was always talking about how he looked forward to grandkids. How insensitive could he get? He knew she couldn't give him children after what Jared had done to her.

She stopped and took a breath. Her moods were going way overboard in both directions. She couldn't be happy without being ecstatic. She couldn't be unhappy without either being depressed or angry, sometimes both. She had to get her meds as soon as possible. She'd been off of them for weeks now. Jimmy couldn't know she was on psych medication. He didn't even know she had borderline personality disorder. Nobody did. That was the reason she came to this town eight years ago; to start over without the stigma.

She was lucky to find a place that had only a charter school, and a poorly managed one at that. They looked at her resume but never did any more than a cursory background check. And the state just checked her criminal background and found nothing. So, all she had to do was find a shrink nearby, take her meds regularly and stay as mellow as she could and she would be fine. But as life started getting more complicated, and the more she saw that she was married to another skirt-chasing jerk, the harder it was to stay even-tempered.

She was so distracted thinking about this that she didn't hear Peggy Turik come in. Peggy was a nice young girl of twenty-two, just out of NAU and working as a substitute teacher at Summertown School in hopes of being hired full time. Her only negative trait was a habit of playing practical jokes. And the moment she saw Tara Stone facing the wall, completely oblivious to her presence, she couldn't resist sneaking up behind her very quietly, reaching up and simultaneously grabbing her by her sides and yelling, "Boo!"

Tara screamed and instinctively swung her arm at the sound, catching Peggy hard in the nose and knocking her to the ground. Tara tripped rushing down the ladder and fell across Peggy, landing with an elbow digging into the girl's stomach. The result was dramatic: all of the air in Peggy's lungs was knocked out of her, then she began to wretch violently, sending the lunch she had just eaten into the air and onto herself and her intended victim. Tara scrambled up from her landing spot and out of shock, she began to scream profanities at Peggy, who was still trying to gulp in air between convulsions.

Moments later Harold Chapman, Gina Albright and Mr. Gershon, the custodian came rushing into the room.

"Who screamed?" Harold demanded. "What happened?" On observing the condition of the two women and seeing Peggy on the floor, he rushed to stand between them. "Tara, you need to step away now," he said as calmly as he could.

"I didn't do anything!" Tara snapped, still very high-strung from the shock.

"Mrs. Stone," Mr. Gershon said firmly. "You need to do as Mr. Chapman asked, please, and calm down right now."

By this time, Peggy had managed to catch her breath and had rolled into a sitting position. She waved at the others to get their attention.

"It isn't her fault," she sobbed. "I startled her and she just threw her arm out…"

"What the hell did you do?!" screamed Debbie Smith from the door. She had just run from the other end of the school when she heard that a fight had broken out in Tara's room. Debbie was Peggy's best friend, graduating with her from college and applying at Summertown on the same day. "I knew you'd go off one of these days," she said, bringing her face within inches of Tara's. "We all did. Why didn't you go get help like you were told? If you had, you wouldn't have attacked Peggy!"

Tara was taken aback. They all thought she was crazy?

"That's right," Debbie said. "You'd better back off before I rip every hair out of your head, *bitch*!"

"Debbie, that's enough!" Gina commanded. "Go to the teachers' lounge, please."

"I'm not going anywhere until *this* chick gets away from Peggy!"

"It's not her fault!" Peggy shouted to be heard, slapping her friend on her leg to get her attention. "She didn't mean to. I startled her and it scared her. She fell off the ladder and we both landed on the floor."

Debbie stood silently, allowing this to sink in, then began to calm down. After a minute, she sighed and turned to Tara.

"Look, I'm sorry," she said, unable to look Tara in the face. "I overreacted. I just…"

"Thought I finally went crazy like you were all expecting," Tara cut her off. "So, that's what you all think. That's what you're all saying behind my back."

110

She began to cry. Harold reached out to comfort her but she batted his hand away and ran out of the room, choking back sobs.

***

Ray Brandt and Gary Callan sat at their favorite booth in the Little Creek Café, going over their daily briefing which, on most days, consisted of what gossip was going around and what the real story was. When he started working in Summertown, three years ago next spring, Gary almost didn't take the job when Ray told him he would be expected to stop rumors from spreading, often by telling the real story as accurately as he could. Being a shy person by nature, engaging people on anything but a law enforcement-related issue was a tough job for him. But as time went on, he became more comfortable with the people and them with him. Now, "rumor control" was a regular part of his duties. And for good reason, as Summertown had its first murders last year as a result of the effects an ugly one had on a young girl. When that was over, two teachers, the girl, her mother and her step-father were dead and two Summertown residents were in critical condition. If that was all the motivation they had for keeping the gossip under control, it would be enough. But the fact that it never stopped; in fact it barely slowed down since these things happened, showed that gossip was a community pastime that could not be rubbed out but could only be reined in to reduce the damage it caused.

"The word is, Jimmy and Tara are close to a domestic violence call," Ray said. "I'm pretty sure it's the Nielsens that have started it, as usual. Their house being across from the Stones gives them an unimpeded view and on a quiet night they can probably hear shouting if the Stones are arguing." He leaned forward and said in a low voice, watching to see if anyone was listening, "And the incident at the school this morning worries me. It was a misunderstanding according to the other teacher, but Tara's reaction was way out of character for her."

"Yes sir," Gary replied in his usual professional voice. Even though Ray was his closest friend, when they were on duty Ray Brandt was either Sir or Chief or Marshal, never Ray. "What about the rumor about her going off on Mr. Olsen?"

"That, I'm afraid, is apparently true," Ray grimaced. "Mr. Olsen called me over yesterday to report it. He showed me the security tape of it and she was definitely screaming. And she threw a pack of gum at him..."

"What!"

"I wouldn't have believed it either, but it was on tape. Olsen said she came in to pay for gas she pumped then she got a cup of coffee, then she put a pack of gum on the counter. Olsen says he told her he had to raise the price a few cents. When she looked and saw it went up...just a second." He pulled out his note pad, "from 80 cents to 85 cents, she 'went berserk', quote-unquote. Actually, she had to build up to it from what I saw, and it looked like Olsen added some fuel to the fire by mouthing off to her, but she definitely did go off on him. And she didn't just toss the gum on the counter. She drew it behind her ear like a pitcher throwing a baseball and just let it fly. Missed Olsen but knocked a bottle of vodka off the shelf behind him." He laughed a little at the memory. "I think it scared him because he's so used to being a jackass to everybody and nobody standing up to him."

Gary shook his head. Tara Stone used to be so nice and Mr. Stone was so in love with her. Her behavior started to change around the time of Jessie's wedding. No one could understand it, but she just kept getting more erratic. She needed help and she needed it soon.

Over at the counter, Pam talked to Chad, read a newspaper and waited. She didn't have to wait long. Within twenty minutes Ray and Gary came in and sat at their usual booth. Pam had been waiting all week to run into Gary. She had hoped that she would just accidentally bump into him but as luck would have it, five days passed and their paths never crossed. Finally, she gave in and went to the café, where she knew he went for his morning coffee.

She sat there, pretending to read the Arizona Daily Sun while mentally rehearsing what she would say when she got up the courage to approach their booth. Finally, when she saw them take a break from their briefing she got up, paid her bill and acted like she was about to go, then "noticed" them sitting there and walked over.

"Hi, Gary," Pam began just a little perkier than necessary. "How have you been? You look good."

"Hello, Pam," Gary grinned nervously. "I'm doing fine. You look well. I was glad to hear you're starting a library."

"Yeah, well. I needed a challenge." She stood there an awkward moment and tried to think of something to keep the conversation going. Drawing a blank, she waved and said, "Well I guess I'd better go. I don't want to interrupt your meeting."

"Don't go on our account," Ray said. "Have a seat. We haven't seen you in a long time and I, for one, want to know what you've been up to."

"Oh, well…"

"Scoot over, Gary and let our new librarian sit down," Ray said with a grin.

"I really don't want to impose if you're in the middle of something," she said tentatively.

"No, no. We were just hanging out, getting some breakfast," Ray assured her.

"Yeah, nothing important," Gary nodded.

"OK," Pam smiled. As Gary moved over toward the wall she sat down, careful not to sit too close to him.

"So, you've decided to stay, have you?" Ray began. He was prepared to carry the entire conversation if necessary.

"Yes," Pam replied. "My dad practically begged me to move back in with him. We're very close."

"That's good. I was close to my parents, too." Ray looked over to Gary and added, "You still see your folks every Sunday, don't you Gary?"

"Yes."

Ray waited a moment to see if his friend would elaborate, then went on in order not to lose what little momentum there was in the meeting.

"And you're OK with not having a lot of nightlife, Pam?"

"Sure," she shrugged. "I'm not a partier. I like reading and doing projects at home."

"Hmm," Ray said. "A librarian who likes to read. Who'd have thought?"

"Yeah, I'm a rare commodity," Pam grinned.

More silence. After asking about the library and getting another one-sentence response, Ray took a riskier tack.

"So, I guess this is the first time you and Gary have actually been in the same room since I found you two wrapped around each other on the hood of your car."

Both Gary and Pam went pale, then crimson, practically at the same time. After a very awkward minute in which they avoided eye contact and searched for words to say, Pam began to stand up.

"Don't go anywhere," Ray said in that practiced way he had that was gentle, yet left no room for argument. "I just figured it was time to get it out in the open. I've watched the two of you this past week, looking for each other but trying not to *look* like you're looking for each other...and when you finally meet, you're all smiles but can't think of anything to say. So," he spread his hands palms down on the table, "now it's out in the open."

They sat in silence for about another minute.

Ray said, "I'm not going anywhere and neither are you, so you might as well just start talking."

Gary cleared his throat and said with eyes glued to the table, "I'm, uh...I'm sorry I did...what I did that day, Pam. My behavior was completely unacceptable."

"I started it," Pam murmured so softly that they could barely hear her.

"I can't tell you how much I regret what happened," Gary continued. "Is there any way you…"

"What do you mean, you regret it?" Pam said, visibly hurt. "Was it that bad?"

"No, no, I didn't mean it like that…"

"You already apologized, Deputy. And I accept it." She got up from the booth, her eyes suddenly moist. "I'm sorry, I've got to get over to the Trailer; the new library building is being delivered today."

"I know," Ray said. "Gary will be heading over to direct traffic there to make sure there are no tie-ups on the street."

Gary looked askance at his chief. The only time there was a tie-up here was during the Summertown Days Hoe-Down in July. This time of year, almost no one was on the streets.

"Gary, give Pam a lift over to the town hall," Ray instructed. "You walked over here, didn't you, Pam?"

"Yes, but that's fine. I like to walk…"

"Oh, it's no trouble," Ray said. "We don't want you catching a cold out there. It's freezing right now." He looked over at his deputy, who was trying unsuccessfully to mask his anger towards him. "Gary, that won't be a problem will it?"

"No, sir." Gary replied, looking daggers at his boss.

Pam wanted to walk out, but she knew that would have tongues wagging all over town. She was embarrassed enough right now not to add that humiliation.

"Thanks," she said.

The drive over, which lasted all of one minute, since the town hall was only a block away from the main drag, was perhaps the longest minute Gary recalled ever living through. He mentally rehearsed half a dozen lines that he thought might soothe Pam's feelings. But none of them were any good. When they pulled up and parked in front of the Trailer, he noticed that the lot was empty save for the stem wall that had been prepared as the foundation for the new building.

"When were they scheduled to deliver it?" Gary asked.

"Not for another hour," Pam said. "I was just going to go inside and do some work in the conference room."

"Oh. OK."

"Thanks for the ride."

"Not a problem." He looked out the driver's side window and remarked, "It looks like it's going to snow. I hope the delivery doesn't take long."

"Me, too."

"Do you have keys, or do you need me to unlock it?"

Pam winced. She thought she could just get out of the car and be free of this uncomfortable situation, but the trailer was empty. "Could you open it? I thought somebody would be here, but I'm obviously wrong."

"Not a problem."

Gary escorted her to the front of the trailer, opened the door and stepped in to turn on the lights. He was just about to reach for the switch when Pam grabbed him by the shirt, shoved him against the wall and wrapped her arms around his neck as she delivered a deep, passionate kiss. It would have ended there if Gary hadn't decided to reciprocate. Then Pam reciprocated right back. The reciprocation continued until they lost track of everything but each other.

The new library was delivered, put on blocks and had the utilities connected before the two of them emerged from the town hall, straightening their clothes and awkwardly trying to think of something to say to each other…until they heard muffled laughter and looked around to see that the small crowd that had gathered to admire the new library were finding them much more entertaining. Several people were standing around in the parking lot, looking at them and laughing; a couple of them made mocking "shame on you" gestures.

"Oh, no," Gary said.

Twelve yards away, Ray Brandt stood with his eyes closed and his head bowed, shaking it slowly.

"I'm dead," Gary mumbled.

"How am I going to tell my dad?" Pam said, mortified.

"You don't have to," Gary said, pointing to their left. "He's right over there."

"Oh, God."

Chapter Eleven

"Well, hi, sweetie," Margie McGrady greeted Tara cheerily as she entered Old Smokie's Tavern. "I don't recall seeing you at our humble establishment before." She looked at Tara's shirt and gasped. "What happened to you?"

Tara looked at herself in the mirror and only then realized that there was a big vomit stain on the front of her white blouse, just above the waist that covered the whole right side.

"Somebody puked all over me," she said in disgust. She went to the restroom and rinsed it out as well as she could, then came back and sat on a stool. "Give me a double," she said.

"Of what, hon?" Margie asked. She could see Tara had been through it today.

"Surprise me," Tara grinned mirthlessly.

"Hey. I know you," a dark-haired, handsome young guy said as he walked over to her from the pool table to her left. "You're the good-lookin' lady I was dancing with at

Tommy's wedding. Funny I should see you here, today of all days." He sat down next to her and leaned in toward her.

"Why is today so special?" She asked. *Yeah, 'today of all days' is right. Think of the devil, and here he is.*

She could smell his cologne and feel his eyes burning through her. She was getting excited but knew she shouldn't be. She lived in a fishbowl; she was a married teacher at the only school in town. But she didn't care anymore. She was sick of having to live for everyone else. She wanted to feel the intimacy that Jimmy didn't give her anymore; even when he tried, it wasn't enough. She was sick and tired of not getting what she wanted, and she was sick of pretending that everything was OK.

"I came to pound your hubby into dog meat," he said simply, like someone would have said they were going to visit friends. "I waited so he could heal from the bullet he took. I don't want anybody saying I kicked a cripple's ass."

"Well, I hate to disappoint you, but he isn't here," she said, trying to sound cold, wanting to feel the desire to protect her husband, but all she could think of at that moment was how this guy turned her on, and how he made her feel special. Like he wanted her in a way Jimmy didn't, or couldn't.

"No?" he said, with real disappointment in his voice. "Damn. I've been looking forward to this for a long time.

See this?" He turned his head to the left to show her the scar on the right side of his face that curved from the corner of his mouth up about an inch along his cheek.

She could see that his nose had changed since Jimmy hit him that night. She touched it and felt a surge of electricity shoot through her. There was something rugged about him now. The scar and the ridge across the middle of his nose made him even more attractive than before.

"Yeah, your old man's friend did that," he said, watching her face as she ran her finger over the bump that wasn't there before that night last year. "When I'm done with old Jimmy, I'm gonna find his fat buddy and see just how much he likes getting the same treatment he gave me."

When she didn't respond, he smiled and moved closer. He brought his lips close to her ear and whispered, "You don't seem very worried about your husband. Is there some trouble in paradise?" He began brushing his fingers down her arm, then he laid his hand on her leg. When she didn't protest, he slid it up her thigh and kept it there.

Tara was beginning to have a hard time breathing steadily. She kept her eyes locked on the glass in front of her then, realizing she hadn't drank any of it, she downed the whole thing in two swallows. Tequila burned its way down her throat, complementing the heat she felt just about everywhere else. She knew that she had only two choices.

She knew the whole town would be watching her, whatever choice she made. And she knew that no longer mattered to her.

Lonny grinned. He saw that she was nervous. He knew she wanted him and he liked the idea of taking Jim Stone's lady and making her never want her husband again.

"When is he coming home?" he asked.

"Does it matter?"

"Not really."

***

Ray sat in his office, leaning back in his chair with his feet up on his desk. He looked across at his deputy and said nothing; he just stared, stone-faced. He kept this up until he was satisfied that he had sufficiently unsettled the young man for him to listen carefully and quietly to what he was about to say.

"Do you know why you're here, Gary?" he asked in a flat, inflectionless voice.

"Yes, sir, I do," Gary replied, swallowing hard. "I'm being terminated."

"Do you think that you deserve termination, Gary?"

"Yes, sir," he responded, looking down at his boots. "I disgraced the uniform."

"Do you have any idea the number of complaints I've received about this incident?" He held a hand up before Gary could answer. "Have you any idea just how embarrassing it is to drive up to a call about loud noises in a municipal building and see my *deputy* leaving said building with the new librarian, both with satisfied smiles on their faces after doing the wild monkey tango on the Town Council's table?" He stared hard at his deputy for what seemed like an eternity. "*Do you?*"

Gary stiffened but remained silent.

"This," Ray took a small stack of papers that were stapled together and tossed it across the desk to him, "is a written reprimand—a *Final* Written Reprimand. I trust you know what that means."

Gary was awe-struck at the leniency the marshal was showing. He was still trying to think of what to say as Ray continued.

"You will sign it; go out to the common area and make a photocopy, then hand the original back to me to be filed. You will then get your horny ass out of my office, go home and put your uniforms away. I didn't tell you to bring them in, by the way."

"Yes, sir."

"You will receive notice of your two week suspension as soon as I can get Noe scheduled to cover your days. That's suspension *without pay*, by the way."

"Yes, sir." Gary didn't even blink at the punishment. He was still recovering from the news that he was still employed.

"And you will spend some of that time actually getting to know the young woman that you were just playing ride-the-wild-pony with while *on duty*. Do you understand?"

"But…"

"Are you actually going to *argue with me?!*" Ray shouted and started to stand up.

"No, sir!" Gary leapt to his feet, grabbed the reprimand and ran out the door.

The instant he entered the common area, which all the rooms in the building opened to, he was confronted by four members of the Town Council standing in a semi-circle. Mayor Pedro Mendoza stepped forward, one hand behind his back.

"Deputy Gary Callan," he said gravely.

"Yes, sir," Gary replied nervously.

"The members of the Council are especially impressed by how you've gone out of your way to make our new librarian feel right at home."

Todd Webb choked back a laugh.

"Why, Mr. Webb here was just commenting on the big smile she had on her face after her meeting with you here. That kind of extra attention to duty cannot go unrewarded." The mayor brought a small, gift-wrapped box out from behind his back and gave it to him. "This is from the members of the Town Council."

"Uh...thank you."

"You're going to need a second ammo pouch for that," Ray said from the doorway behind him as Gary opened the box.

"Yessir," Gary mumbled in embarrassment.

"Now, we mean this, Deputy Callan," Mr. Mendoza said. "You be sure to carry them at all times."

"Yes, sir...thank you, sir...I guess." Gary walked out of the building as quickly as he could, his face red for the second day this week, as he stuffed the box of condoms he'd just received into his back pocket.

The occupants of Town Hall had the grace to wait until Gary had driven out of the parking lot before laughing themselves hoarse.

Chapter Twelve

I sat on a picnic table along the north side of Upper Lake Mary, alone with my thoughts. I looked out and was captivated by the panorama that lay in front of me. The water shone sky-blue with silver sun-sparkles in those places that didn't have thin sheets of ice floating on the surface; the forest that rimmed the lakeshore was deep green with white speckles, the ground spotted here and there with snow; a hawk glided across the water in search of dinner—it was beautiful and I was happy to be there. How many times had I driven by here and not taken notice? I was taken in by the wonder of it all, here at this little lake. All the problems with my health, my marriage and my business faded into the background as I looked on the spectacle of God's perfect handiwork. I wanted this moment to last forever, even though I knew it was just one moment of many, in which I got a little taste of the paradise to come. One day this would be even more perfect than it was now, when every square inch of the earth would be made a paradise. Until then, God gives us little tastes of it while we endure the imperfect world we currently live in. I sat there and soaked it all in until Carol called me and reminded me of my two thirty appointment.

As much as I dreaded going back to the office I drove back to town, only to get another call from Carol as I pulled into the lot, telling me that my 2:30 had cancelled. Oh, well. I headed over to Old Smokey's for an early afternoon beer before heading back to work. That was the nice thing about being in business for myself; I didn't run the risk of getting fired if I came back from lunch with beer on my breath. Of course, I was going to get stern looks from my teetotaler secretary, but I'd survive.

"Jimmy?" Margie greeted me with surprise. "What are you doing here?"

"And hello to you, too," I replied. "Is there something wrong with getting a beer in the afternoon?"

"No, no," she smiled nervously. "I just didn't think you'd be in here anymore after the doctor told you to quit drinking. What'll you have?"

"A Guinness, please."

"Coming up," she smiled, but there was something about her mannerism. She seemed anxious about something.

"Margie, what's wrong?" I asked.

"Nothing," she laughed. Margie was as bad as I was at lying.

"The truth," I said suspiciously. "You're hiding something. What is it?"

"I beg your pardon," she said with a just-slightly-too-forced indignation. "Are you implying that I'm hiding something?"

"That's what I just said. And if you weren't so busy trying to think of what to say next, you'd have heard me." I was about to ask if she and Pat were having problems when she shrugged her shoulders and huffed.

"Look, Jimmy," she said raising her hands. "I'm not getting involved with your marriage problems. So…"

"What marriage problems?" I asked in surprise.

"Jimmy, just sit down and have a beer, OK?"

"Margie, please tell me what's going on," I begged. The hair on the back of my neck was standing up as my mind ran through all the possibilities.

She huffed again and threw her arms up in surrender. "Tara left here a couple hours ago with some guy, honey. I'm sorry."

My chest suddenly got very tight and my blood went cold. I tried to calm down but I was losing control. I grabbed the edge of the bar and gripped it as tight as I could.

"Who was it?" I asked quietly, trying to avoid shouting at her.

"He looked familiar, but I didn't know him," she replied nervously. "Jimmy, don't do anything stupid. She's not worth going to jail for…"

"Don't tell me she's not worth it!" I snapped. "She's my wife! She's worth everyth—"

"Jimmy stop!" she barked. "She's not worth giving up your freedom for. She went with him of her own free choice. He didn't force her. Nobody who'll do that…"

I couldn't hear anymore because I was rushing through the door. I got into my car and sped down the seven blocks to my house, pulling up behind the racing-yellow mustang parked in my driveway. I walked straight to the front door and fumbled for my keys, then unlocked it as quietly as my shaking hands could manage. As I walked into the living room I found clothes strewn in a trail leading to our bedroom, where the door was left wide open.

They didn't even know I was there. They were grinding and moaning, grunting like a couple of animals. Her legs were up in the air and he was giving her commands and saying filthy things and she was moaning louder. I stood there frozen in place, everything going glassy and surreal. I wanted to walk out but I couldn't. I just stood there for what felt like forever, yet they never noticed me. I really don't remember much after that. One moment I was standing there in the doorway, the next I was sitting on top of Lonny

Jarrette and punching him over and over again. I remember being pulled off of him by somebody and thrown on the floor, then somebody was sitting on my back and shouting at me. I have no idea how long it took for me to calm down enough to somehow come to my senses but when I did, I was face-down on the floor of my bedroom with my hands cuffed behind my back and Ray was kneeling down next to me. I heard Cindy Noe's voice from the hallway and some guy whimpering. My hands were hurting and my jaw and face were aching; I was having trouble seeing out of my left eye.

"Are you listening to me, Jimmy?" Ray asked.

"Huh?" was all I could say. My mind was still fuzzy.

"I asked you what happened here," he replied.

"I…I don't know."

"What do you mean, you don't know?" his voice didn't change from the gentle but firm tone he always had. "You did a lot of damage here. Don't you remember any of it? Do you know why you did it?"

That was when I started crying and didn't stop until we were about halfway to Flagstaff with me sitting in the back of Ray's police car, on the way to jail. I saw everything clearly then. I saw that my life as I had known it up until that point, like my marriage, was over. Worse even than that, I saw that after all these years, the angry monster that I had thought was long gone, was still alive and well inside me.

***

The young man smiled as he looked through the scope of his new toy. *No*, he thought. *Not a toy. A tool. A tool of the trade.* He had been practicing with the weapon for days now, making sure that he would be ready when the call came, and the results of all that practice were visible through his scope; he had written a perfect letter A with his bullets, on the trunk of a Ponderosa pine, two hundred meters away. Any day now, he would get his first job and with it, membership in the exclusive community of professional assassins. He knew that it was nothing like the movies. He knew that this was something done silently, secretly; that he could never talk about what he did. He was a rifleman and that was all. But that was enough. He'd always wanted to feel the rush of excitement that he knew accompanied the act of killing someone. He'd spent so much time playing games, target shooting with various guns from his large collection, joining chat room discussions, dreaming of being a professional killer. If he hadn't come across DaggerB543, he would still be fantasizing about this.

It was Dagger who encouraged him to risk it all. DaggerB543 was the real deal, he could tell. Somebody who spoke from experience and knew what it took to succeed in this business. It was Dagger who encouraged him to pick up one of the best sniper rifles ever made: the Dragunov Tiger SVD. It took a lot of searching and a lot of saving, but he finally found one, at a price he could just barely afford. It was beautiful, a real Russian art piece with original wood stock, 10-round magazine, all metal parts blued perfectly and polished to a shine. It fired a big, 7.62x54mm round and it left a bruise on his shoulder after the first day of firing it. After that, he took a wad of rags and some duct tape, and made an extra-thick shoulder pad, which helped not only to absorb the recoil, but also to fit his long arms more comfortably. He was ready now. All he needed was the job.

He got up from the ground where he had been practicing from the prone position. It was time to go home and wait. Dagger said the call would come. He (or she?) told him that the word was out, and it was just a matter of time.

Chapter Thirteen

"Poor Jimmy," Corinda said, shaking her head. "I knew that woman would drive him to do something terrible one day." She poured coffee into Ray's mug and watched him pick at the eggs and chorizo she had just served him. "You're not hungry, are you, querido?"

"No, I'm really not," Ray mumbled.

The incident at Jimmy's house took only a couple of hours to clear, but Lonny Jarrette had sustained significant injuries to his body; he had to go to the trauma facility in Flagstaff, where the ER doctor told him there was possibly irreparable damage to his reproductive organs and he needed reconstructive surgery on his face. Ray had a terrible feeling that Jimmy was going to be on the hook for a fortune in medical and punitive damages when this scumbag sued him. And a lawsuit was all he was going to win, since it would be clear to any jury that Jimmy acted out of passion and could probably be acquitted due to temporary insanity.

"I just feel so bad for Jimmy," he said. "Nobody saw this coming with Tara. Sure, *you* always knew there was something wrong with her, but nobody ever thought for a moment that she'd bring a man to her own home to cheat on Jimmy."

"I know," she sighed. "We were married for twenty one years and I never thought of doing that to him. As much as we despised each other at the end, I couldn't imagine sleeping with another man when I was married." She looked down at the table and was drawn back in time to several years before. "And then I met poor little Nerville. I can't believe I fell for him. He was always wearing his security guard uniform with the shirt hanging out, he never wanted to get his teeth fixed, and he was so—fat. And yet I stayed with him for three years. He really was sweet in his way." She thought about that silently, then pulled herself out of her reverie and continued, "But I wasn't…*with him*—until I had left Jimmy. Only a *whore* will sleep with another man while she's still living with her husband."

Ray didn't reply. The memory of seeing Nerville's battered body lying in Corinda's bed was still vivid; his face a sickly bluish hue from being choked to death by the man Corinda took home with her after Jessie and Tom's wedding reception. Yet as gruesome as the sight was and as traumatized as Corinda was from it, she never seemed to show any sense of loss or grief. She never talked of Nerville, yet she mentioned Jimmy frequently, even if it was in derogatory terms. Ray tried to dismiss it, but he still had a nagging suspicion that the girl he wanted to marry still had feelings for her ex-husband.

"Well, I sure hope Jimmy can find a good lawyer," he said. "He'll need one for the criminal case against him. And he'll need a good one when Jarrette sues him. He'll be lucky to get out of this with the shirt on his back. And Tara is sitting at home free as a bird when she caused it all. I'm afraid she's going to either hurt someone or get hurt before I can do anything about it, and there's been enough of that here in the last couple of years to last a century."

Corinda got up from her chair, walked around to him and sat on his lap. Then she put her arm around his neck and rested her head against his. "You need to get your mind off of all this, querido."

"I'd like to, but I can't," he grumbled. "This is something I'm going to be dealing with for a while. And when it's over, I'm pretty sure I'll be wishing I'd done things differently somehow. 'Cuz no matter how you look at it, nobody involved in this is going to come out of it unscathed."

"I certainly hope not," Corinda replied. "The Jarrett boy can't have children now. And Jimmy was hurt so bad, too. And you just said he's going to probably go broke paying for everything. I hope Tara gets her teacher's license taken away."

"She most likely will," Ray said. "And if she loses her license, she'll probably have to leave because she won't have a job."

"Good," Corinda said. "Maybe then we can get some peace and quiet."

"I don't recall Tara ever being a problem until now," Ray said dubiously. "In fact, until Jarrett came along, she was great. Let me ask you something. Could you be just a little bit jealous of her?"

Corinda stared at Ray in amazement. "Jealous? How can I be jealous of *her*?"

"Well…"

"She's chubby; she has to dye her hair that red tint to cover the dingy brown of her real hair; she's *crazy*…"

"She left Jimmy when he needed her and then he still took her back…"

"And why is that?" she demanded. "She treats him like a leper and he still loves her. He should have told her to go back to Iowa."

"Indiana."

"Indiana, Iowa, wherever," she snapped. "She shouldn't still be here."

"Well, looking at it that way, tell me; why are *you* still here?"

This question surprised Corinda as much as the first one did. All she could do was shrug.

"My salon, maybe?"

"Maybe? You're not sure?" Ray was beginning to fear that his suspicions had been well-founded.

"Well, I don't have anything else that I can do to make a living," she shrugged, uncomfortably.

"You don't think you could have sold this salon and bought one in Phoenix, or somewhere else?" he probed.

"I suppose so," she conceded. "But Jessie was here, and she wouldn't have gone with me…"

"Are you sure of that?" he pressed. "You told me that she was living with you at first, but Nerville made her uncomfortable."

"Yes, but…" she suddenly threw up her hands then dropped them to her sides in exasperation. "Why are you interrogating me?"

"What? I'm not…"

"Yes, you are!"

"I'm sorry," he replied sincerely.

"That's not an answer. *Why are you asking me all these questions?*"

"If I tell you, I don't want you to be angry with me."

"I'm already angry," she snapped.

"I shouldn't have brought it up. I'm sorry. Just forget it."

"No!" she commanded. "You are going to tell me why you're questioning me like a criminal."

"I wasn't questioning you…"

"Tell me why, Ray," Corinda demanded. "I'm not going drop it. I'm not going to forget it. There's a reason you asked me all these questions, now tell me *why*."

"Alright," he sighed in surrender. "I just want to be sure you're not still harboring any romantic feelings for Jimmy, that's all."

Corinda's jaw dropped. She stared at him in shock for a full minute before speaking and when she did it was with a trembling voice.

"You would doubt my love for you?" she asked, her eyes fill with tears. "How can you question my love?"

"I just…Honey, you were married to Jimmy for twenty years…"

"I know how long it was, Ray," she said. "And all that time, he only had time for Jessie. Do you know what it's like to be ignored by the one person that should always care about you? I had to compete with my own daughter, Ray. That hurt me bad."

"It still hurts, doesn't it?"

"Of course it does," she replied.

"And being with me doesn't make it go away."

"That kind of hurt doesn't go away, even after you meet the right man. Just because you can't heal the hurt I got from Jimmy doesn't mean I still love him." She sat in the chair next to him and put her hand on his. "You make me happy now. Don't try to fix what happened in the past because that will just waste time that we could be spending making each other happy now."

"OK," Ray said. He kissed her cheek. "You're right. I'm sorry I brought it up."

They sat silently together until Ray had to leave for work, each lost in their own thoughts. They both knew nothing had really been resolved in the conversation. Ray still had his suspicions about Corinda. But now, unfortunately, Corinda was beginning to wonder, too.

Chapter Fourteen

Miragoane, Haiti
November 1992

I awoke in a dank, putrid-smelling room occupied by several other men, all of them wounded in some way. Through bleary eyes I looked around and saw a metal bar that ran from one wall, traversed the room, and was bolted to the other. A man was hanging from it at the far end of the room, by his wrists which were handcuffed. His face was swollen so badly that his eyes were closed. Blood trickled from his left ear and whelps had formed all over his bare torso. *I knew it,* I thought. *Jail. I'm in jail in the worst place in this part of the world to be in jail. Now what do I do?* I sat up and suddenly realized what a bad idea that was, as my ribs ached horribly and my head throbbed so painfully I thought it was going to split open. I lifted a sore and swollen hand and felt around on the back of my head to discover a large lump at the base of my skull. Fortunately, there were no cuts that I could find.

I could hear voices shouting down the hall but they echoed so much off the cement walls that I couldn't make out what they were saying. A few minutes later there was silence, followed by the sound of feet approaching. It was the captain of the police for this district, followed by a white guy, about fifty, around five-ten, slightly pudgy, gray crew-cut, wearing a baggy, flower-print shirt and cargo pants; and a young man in his twenties, either mulatto or light-skinned black, square-jawed, greenish eyes that stood out for some reason that I couldn't quite figure out, military-cut black, tightly-curled hair, built like Bruce Lee only about fifty pounds heavier, wearing a polo shirt under a safari vest, an oversized fanny pack in front and BDU-style tan pants. U.S. Embassy, it looked like.

"Mr. Stone?" the middle aged guy said.

"Here," I replied half-sarcastically since I was the only white guy in the cell.

"Mr. Stone, I'm Robert Shultz. I work at the American Embassy, and this is Reno Chatelaine, one of our security men." He pronounced it "reh-*noh*", like the French car. "We're here to escort you to the airport."

"The airport?" I asked, confused. "But I'm here to help at…"

"The mission down the road," he finished for me. "I know. And I'm sorry, but I'm afraid you're no longer welcome in this country. You see, Jim—can I call you Jim?" he asked. I shrugged and nodded. "Jim, most countries don't take kindly to foreign visitors killing their citizens."

The words hit me like a truck at high speed. "*Killing?*" I gasped. "*I killed him? Oh, my God.*" My body began to shake; I could feel the blood leaving my face and my stomach turned to knots. I wanted to throw up.

"You weren't trying to kill him?" the guy named Reno asked looking at me skeptically. "You crushed the man's face."

"Reno, please," Shultz said. He turned to me, put a hand on my shoulder and said gently, "That may not have been your intention Jim, but that was what happened. If it weren't for your friends from the mission, we would never have known and you probably would have disappeared without a trace. These guys don't play nice with people that kill one of their own, justified or not. I'm sorry, but now you have to make a choice. You can either leave with us right now and let us escort you onto the next flight out of here, or stay here in jail until they decide to kill you and dump your body somewhere. That's it. You have no other alternatives."

Three hours later I was on an American Airlines flight headed to Miami, seated in first class, next to a reporter for some obscure newspaper so as to avoid being seated next to any Haitians. The coach section was packed with people, as it always was. Many of them had saved for years to pay for the visa and the ticket that would give them a chance to either find work or buy goods that would improve their prospects in the world. They sat shoulder to shoulder, mashed together yet cheerful. They helped each other with their bags, kept one another's children entertained through the three hour flight. It was an adventure they all were sharing and morale was high. While I, on the other hand, sat weeping, each sob sending a spasm of pain across the sides of my chest. How could I have been so full of rage at another human being that I would hunt him down and beat him to death? What kind of monster was I?

***

Flagstaff, Arizona
Present Day

I sat in a holding cell at the Sheriff's Office in Flagstaff for eight hours until Ken could bail me out. A short, stocky female Sheriff's detention officer escorted me to a window down the hall where I was given the personal items they took from me when I was brought in that afternoon, then she walked me further down the hallway and stood with me at the exit which opened with a loud click, presumably after someone watching us on camera pushed a button. Ken stood there, looking confused. I thanked him for bailing me out, but that was all I could muster at that moment. I just walked out to the parking lot and got into his car. He never asked questions, he just drove the car and allowed me to tell the story when I was ready. When we got back to Summertown he suggested I stay at his house for at least a couple of nights, and since I couldn't go home with Tara still there I gratefully accepted. I slept on their couch that night, woke up the next morning and went to the bathroom and surveyed the damage.

My hands were still swollen from punching Lonny. My left eye was almost swollen shut from, I think, Lonny slugging me. I'm not sure who scratched my face up; it could have been either one of them. Tara had told Cindy Noe that she kept trying to pull me off of him and that was probably where I got all the whelps and bruises around my neck. I looked like hell and I deserved it. I cried, cussed Tara out, then swore I'd find Jarrette and finish him off. When I was finished blaming them I started blaming myself for the whole thing. I wasn't attentive; I didn't try hard enough to satisfy her. I didn't treat her the way she wanted to be treated. I finally walked out the door and went for a walk, ending up at my office. I had called Carol earlier from Ken's place and told her not to bother coming in today because I probably wouldn't make it, so I had the place to myself. I had plenty of work to do and if I was lucky I might get lost in it for a while.

Chapter Fourteen

"Well, honey," Harold Chapman said to his youngest daughter. "It looks like you've overcome your shyness."

"Oh, Daddy," Pam sighed. She leaned over on the couch until she could bury her face in her father's shoulder.

"Pammy," he said, putting his arm around her. "There are some things we experience in life that seem so awful at the time, but a few years down the road nobody will remember them."

"Not here," she said, raising her head to look at her dad. "You know they'll remember this for the rest of my life."

"No they won't, honey. Don't worry."

"What makes you so sure they'll forget this?" She asked. "You know what the people are like around here."

"They can't hold it against you for the rest of *your* life, because they're not going to live that long. The people around here are old; they have one foot in the grave already. In ten or fifteen years, they'll all be dead and the story will die with them. Then you can start fresh."

"Daddy, you are such a piece of work," Pam laughed.

"Yeah, that's what your mother always said." He smiled. "So tell me," he said, "when are you going to give Gina a call? Now that you've spent some 'quality time' with her ex, you two have that much more to talk about."

"Oh, yeah," she said with mock enthusiasm. "We can start a club. We'll call ourselves Gary's Girls and the initiation is to bang Gary Callan!"

"What a choice of words," Harold replied.

"I'm sorry," she sighed. "I'm just trying to joke about it because if I don't I'll cry."

"A better word would be 'screw.' Or maybe 'hump.' Or how about 'doin' the nasty'?"

"Daddy!"

"What? I thought you wanted to lighten the mood…"

The doorbell rang and Pam answered it. *Speak of the devil,* she thought.

"Hello, Gina," she said tentatively. "It's nice to see you. Want to come in?"

"Sure," Gina said, trying to act as if nothing had happened between them. "Sorry I'm so late in welcoming you back. Things have been a little crazy lately."

"So I hear," Pam replied. "I'm so sorry to hear about the baby…"

149

"Please," Gina interrupted her with a raised hand. "I'd rather not talk about it. I'm getting better though, so don't worry about me."

Pam smiled slightly and nodded. "How are you handling being down another teacher?"

"The same way we were handling the staff shortage earlier: bringing in temps. The Town Council just released more emergency funds to hire an extra substitute."

"That's good."

"Yeah," Gina nodded. Then she winked and added, "So, I hear you've joined the 'hussy club'."

"I knew it," Pam moaned. "They're going to cancel my contract and somebody's going to take my job in Payson and..."

"Take it easy," Gina said. "Nobody's even hinted at that."

"That's right, honey," Harold put in. "If you go, what would they talk about?"

"They'd think of something," Pam retorted. "As long as the Nielsens are running their store in the middle of town, there will always be a steady supply of gossip."

"And the Olsens," Gina added. "And the Holloways, and the Purskis..."

"Exactly," Pam said.

"How's Jimmy doing?" Harold asked. "Ken told me he had to go bail him out last night. How's he feeling?"

"I don't know," Gina shrugged, worry written all over her face. "I haven't been able to see him yet. When I called him this morning and asked about what happened, he just said, 'Don't worry about me, sis. I'll be fine.' That man just pisses me off sometimes."

"I know what you mean," Pam said, throwing a look in her father's direction.

"He was going to get his substitute teacher's license so he could cover a few classes for me while I go to see my mom," Gina said. "I guess that's out the window."

"Can't he still do it?" Pam asked. "He's back home now. They aren't going to arrest him again, are they?"

"It wouldn't matter, honey," Harold put in. "Jimmy's got felony assault charges hanging over his head. The State won't give him a license to teach."

"Oh, that's horrible," Pam shook her head. "I hope his CPA isn't at risk."

"No," Gina replied. "I think that's safe. The state won't license someone with a violent crime record to teach because, obviously, they don't want to endanger children. But a CPA? What would he do? Rubber stamp somebody to death?"

Harold snorted a laugh. "You never know with Jimmy these days." This brought an uncomfortable silence to the room.

Finally, Pam broke it. "So, what brings you to our humble abode?"

Gina looked confused. "You're dad invited me." She turned to Harold and said accusingly, "You said she asked if I could come over."

"And now you're here," Harold grinned. "So, why don't you two sit down and talk? I'll get coffee started."

"You think you can get away with pulling this by making me coffee?"

"Well…it's really good coffee."

She would have continued the banter if Pam hadn't suddenly wrapped her arms around her and given her a big hug.

"I'm so glad you came," Pam said. "I'm sorry I—"

"Don't say it," Gina said. "It's all in the past, and all for the best. Gary and I were not a good fit and if that thing with you and him hadn't happened we might not have done anything about it until it was too late."

"In that case, you're welcome," Pam smiled.

"Don't make me slap you."

***

I was in my office trying to work on a client's quarterly tax documents with only one functional eye and six swollen fingers when Todd and Pedro came to visit. They took one look at my face and both winced.

"Jimmy, are you alright?" Pedro asked. "I heard something happened at your house last night and Ray had to take you in to Flagstaff to be interviewed."

"I'm OK, Pedro," I said. I knew some screwed up version of the story was probably making the rounds by now. After all, it was a whole fifteen hours after it happened.

"Good," he sighed in relief.

"Well, I hear the other guy is in a lot worse shape," Todd said.

"Yeah," I said. "It wasn't exactly my finest moment."

"We came as soon as we heard about it," Pedro said. "Todd figured we should hear your side of it before it got distorted from the retelling."

"Not that it's *anybody's* business but mine,' I growled. "But since you guys are friends, I'll give you a general idea of what happened." I told them the story, leaving out the more lurid details, knowing they could figure those out themselves.

"Ah, Jimmy," Pedro said sadly. "I'm sorry. Is there anything I can do for you?"

"A new place to live would be nice," I said, half-joking. "I'm staying at Ken's right now and I hate being a burden on them."

"Well," Todd said after a second, "I do have that one townhouse on the east end that's still vacant. I can't afford to rent it at a discount, but you can move in right now if you want. Just give me $700 a month, including utilities."

"I'll take it," I said. "And thanks."

Three hours later, Ray stood by as Ken and Chad helped me pick up my clothes, computer, filing cabinets and the only piece of furniture that I had brought into the house with me from before; my recliner. Tara had gone out somewhere so that we could get it done with a minimum of conflict. It was very uncomfortable for the guys and I felt bad for them. Then we drove through town, several people watching our little caravan go by. Ken's big pickup carried most of the office furniture and the chair, Chad had all of my clothes and personal items in his car. I followed in my little sedan. It took minutes to unload it all, then they each shook my hand and wished me luck and left.

I closed the front door of my new home and turned to look at everything. All that I owned after twenty-three total years of marriage took up only two thirds of one room. I thought about the mess I was in with Lonny Jarette and Tara. It's amazing how your life can be changed so completely in just a few seconds. Standing there, thinking of all my problems was only getting me more depressed. I had to get out of there.

I headed down to Old Smokie's, which was mostly empty at that hour, and ordered a tall Jack Daniels and water. I don't usually drink hard liquor, but this time I made an exception. I wanted a good, healthy drink of something and I wanted it now.

"I heard you had a skirmish at your place, but I had no idea just how bad it was," Margie said shaking her head in wonder. "I'm trying hard not to say I told you so."

"Yeah, I know."

"Are you all right?"

"I'll feel better once I have a couple of shots of JD."

She gave me a look that got on my nerves. "Didn't your doctor tell you not to drink liquor anymore?" she asked.

"You know, I'm a big boy," I said. "I make the decisions about what I can and can't have, and I live a mile from here. If I have too much to drink I can just walk home. So, don't mother me."

"Don't get snippy with me, boy," she shot back. Margie and Pat had owned bars the entire 43 years of their marriage. This was their "hobby bar" which they opened after they retired to Summertown and realized that full retirement wasn't for them. Margie was a thick, sturdy woman of old Irish lineage who had a ready wit, a warm heart and the famous hot Irish temper. If there was one thing this sixty-something-year-old lady would not take, it was any lip from a customer.

I pushed my stool back and turned to walk out. I was in no mood for an argument and I knew who was going to win this one if I stayed around. But Margie just reached across the bar, grabbed me by the sleeve of my shirt and pulled me back.

"Sit down, Jimmy," she said in a gentler, but still motherly tone. "Don't waste good liquor."

"Alright," I conceded after thinking about it for a second. "I'm sorry, Margie. I don't mean to take my frustrations out on you."

"I know, honey. Things just get kinda tense sometimes, don't they?"

"Yeah."

"So, tell your bartender about it," she said, leaning forward on her elbows after filling a tumbler with what looked almost like a 50/50 mix of water and whiskey and sliding it in front of me.

"Isn't that a little cliché?"

"Hell no," she gruffed. "If Pat was in here right now, it would be his job. We're the only therapists this town has right now." She winked, "And when a licensed one gets around to hanging up their shingle, we'll still be more popular."

I smiled a bit and nodded in agreement. "You got something there."

"So, let's have it out," she said again.

"I really don't want to talk about it now, Margie," I said. "I came here to get my mind off of it all."

She nodded and winked. "OK, change of subject." She waited until I had my glass up to my lips to say, "Now would be a good time to start taking Gina out."

I half-gagged on my drink but managed to choke it down. I stared at her, trying to think of something in response. I saw the mischievous twinkle in her eye turn into a knowing grin on her face.

"It's obvious that you have a soft spot for her, Jimmy."

"She's way too young for me, Margie…and I'm married," I protested. "Why on earth would you even suggest such a thing?"

"Methinks thou dost protest too much, m'dear," her smile widened.

"No, I protest just the right amount," I replied. I knew I should have been cleverer but I was too busy being utterly mortified. If Margie could see it, who else could?

"Everybody knows you have a crush on Gina, Jimmy," she said, confirming my fears.

I felt so ashamed. How can a man my age…?

"You're human, Jimmy," she said gently. "You have to stop beating yourself up all the time. You haven't had good luck when it comes to choosing wives, but a lot of people can say that. Why do you think you have to be the example to everybody around you?"

"What do you mean?" I said defensively. "I don't have any illusions about myself, Margie."

"You have one," she said. "You have the illusion that you have to be perfect all the time. The 'hometown hero' who everybody looks up to."

That really got under my skin. I'd had to live down that day in the woods, trying to convince everyone that it was entirely an act of blind rage and not heroism. And to have someone tell me that my head was getting too big for my own good…

"Let me clear something up for you, Margie," I said. "I don't think of myself as anything but Jimmy Stone, paper-pusher. The most heroic thing I've ever done is live with Corinda for twenty years so my daughter would grow up with two parents in the same house. I do not now, nor have I ever thought of myself as a hero, a role-model, a prophet or anything but an accountant. Now, if your therapy consists of accusing your customers of having enlarged egos, then I'll just stick with drinking at your bar in silence."

"OK," she said, hands up in surrender. "I'll leave you alone with your self-loathing." She turned and walked toward the other end of the bar, adding over her shoulder, "By the way, Gina's thirty four, so you wouldn't be robbing the cradle; and no one would blame you for divorcing Tara after all she's put you through."

"The vows were for better or worse," I replied. But in my mind I was thinking, *Thirty-four? Why didn't I know that?*

"I know you're a good Catholic," she nodded, walking back over to me. "So am I, you know that. We're at mass every Sunday, just like you. You know as well as I do that adultery is grounds for divorce." She reached over and patted my hand maternally. "Jimmy, I'm your friend, so I'm going to tell you what you *need* to hear, not what you *want* to hear: you need to get a divorce. Tara committed adultery, she's mentally ill—only God knows what's going on in that head of hers. You don't deserve to live the rest of your natural life with that. For your own good—for your own *safety*, divorce her. It's perfectly acceptable in the eyes of the Church."

As she spoke the words began to drive the reality of it

all home. *Divorce.* I started bawling like a baby. I couldn't help it; the whiskey was going to my head and I wasn't able to hold it in any more. I hadn't told anyone that I had already decided to divorce my wife, because I was still trying to think it all through. But Margie's words made me finally realize that divorce was not only inevitable, it was the best option under the circumstances. My attorney had assured me that it would be short and simple, since we didn't have children together and I was willing to take on all the debts that we'd incurred during our marriage. Then I'd be free to live the quiet life I'd had before I met her. I thought of that—what I'd lost when this...*illness* showed itself—all the joy we had in our life together, the romance; always so happy just to be together...

Margie stayed there with her hand on my shoulder as I sobbed, gave me napkins to wipe my face when it got too soggy and then after a few minutes of letting me get it all out, she shook me by my shoulder.

"All right now, boy," she said. "Let's get a little Guinness into you. That always cheers you up." She took a glass from the rack that was mounted above the bar and went to the tap and filled it. "We're going to keep these coming for a while, and bring you some chips and just hang out. Don't worry about walking home. Pat's around somewhere; he'll drive you home when you're ready."

"Thanks, Margie," I managed to say. I knew that my next lab test was going to be the subject of a serious lecture from my doctor, if I didn't land in the ER before then. But I didn't care. All I wanted at that moment was something to dull the pain and if drinking myself numb worked, I was willing to pay the price.

***

The rifleman made his way to his post unnoticed. It was hardly difficult since no one in this area ever paid attention to what happened on this side of the highway, in the middle of the night. He'd hiked three miles, following the coordinates given to him by his client. His feet had gone numb from the cold; he blew into his gloves to keep his hands warm. The heavy gun case slung over his shoulder was growing heavier with every step. He found the tree that he was told looked like three trees growing out of one root, he searched each of the trunks and found the RFID tag nailed to the bark as described then he passed his cell phone over it. The number that came up on the smartphone's screen matched the one given to him in the encrypted email that he'd received. The email said that his client arranged the perfect position so that he would remain completely invisible until the job was done. Everything up to this point went exactly as planned so, feeling confident, the young man strapped the climbing spikes to his boots, adjusted the night goggles he'd been wearing and slowly, carefully worked his way up the tree, passing thick branches that took time and energy to get over. He looked at the other two trunks as well, thinking he may have gone up the wrong one. The higher he went, the less sure of himself he became. Did the message say that the position was already prepared, or simply chosen? Was he supposed to bring his own stand and equipment? He reached up, waving his hand in search of something that would tell him where he belonged when he heard the sound of fabric sliding against his glove. He climbed another step and could see the camouflage pattern on a teardrop shaped bag of some kind, fastened to two branches, just big enough to accommodate him. With a sigh of relief he stopped a moment to rest, then he climbed up to what he could now see was a mountaineering tent, rolled carefully into it and pulled the entrance closed. Judging by how far he had climbed and the number of branches he had passed, he was sure that with the camouflage mesh surrounding him, he was virtually invisible to anyone who wasn't looking very carefully at this particular tree, and even then they probably couldn't see him. It was cold at this hour of the night and as the wind whistled through the branches of the tall pine he shivered and cinched his field jacket tighter around him and pulled the jacket's hood over his balaclava-covered head. One thing this big Russian gun had going for it was that it allowed him to use heavy winter gloves, or he might not be able to pull the trigger. If all his jobs were like this, then he was going to make a lot of very easy money. He'd trained for too long and had sighted-in the rifle's scope too carefully for there to be any question that he would hit precisely as planned. For now, all he had to do was lie back and wait for the right time.

***

Reno leaned back in his seat and tried to sleep as the airliner passed over the Gulf of Mexico. He looked out the window and thought about his sister and her husband. Robert had been the love of her life. Reno could only try to imagine what that was like. All his life, as many women as he had loved—or thought he'd loved—he never found that one soul-deep connection that Mireille had found with Robert. Tears began to well up in Reno's eyes. They were the most perfect, happy couple he'd ever seen. And Soraya was the light of their life. *She was the light of my life, too,* he thought to himself. Never having had children of his own, he lavished affection on his niece, buying her gifts whenever her parents permitted it. Her bright smile and playfulness was the reason he made the four-hour trip from Port-au-Prince to Thiotte every other weekend. Now she and her mother and father were in Heaven, far away from the place where they were so savagely, brutally...

He squeezed his eyes shut, trying to block out the images that were forever burned into his memory. The blood...on the walls, on the floor, on the ceiling was the first thing he saw when he entered the room. When he...

Stop! he commanded himself. *You can't think of that now. You can't do anything to change what happened. You can only make the murderers pay, and that is what you will do. Starting tomorrow, you'll search and find the filthy animal who made this happen and you're going to kill him.* A small, nagging voice in his head told him to have the murderer brought to justice. But he knew this would never happen because he could never connect the man to the crime. Not in Haiti, even with the improvements that had taken place there; corruption was still rampant, especially in the provinces. *And even if I were certain he would go to prison, I could never be sure he would remain there. No. I promised myself that I would hunt him down and that is what I am going to do.*

He had it coming, Reno was certain of that. He was the one who recruited Reno for this assignment when he was perfectly happy working the security detail at the embassy.

Another seven years and he would have been able to retire and start his own agency. But *Tonton* told him it was a matter of Haiti's national security and it was his duty. Two years of training followed by six months establishing his cover as a dirty cop assigned to the U.N. mission in Haiti and two more years playing the part of liaison for the Jacmel Quartier of the Police Nationale d'Haiti to the U.N. mission known as MINUSTAH and he was on the verge of breaking the network wide open when Michel Boudreaux pulled the floor from under him. Two years of careful infiltration and intelligence gathering ended up being two years of unknowingly passing false information to MINUSTAH. How stupid could he have been? All that time, he had wondered why there weren't more arrests. *Tonton* always blamed someone else for the failures; always praised him for his professionalism.

For seven long weeks Reno had lay in a hospital bed in Miami. He would have bled to death had police officers and UN soldiers not arrived a short time later to investigate reports of gunfire at the house. A UN helicopter took him to the Hôpital de Canapé Vert where he was stabilized. The police officers were advising him that he was under arrest for the murders of Captain Boudreaux two other police officers when two officials from the U.S. Embassy arrived with documents authorizing them to take custody of the prisoner an American citizen. By the time the nervous officers phoned in to their headquarters and learned that the U.S. officials had no authority to remove a prisoner from their custody Reno was safe behind the walls of the U.S. Embassy, then spirited onto an Air Force transport plane and taken to Miami. Two bullets he was still carrying were removed. The first, and the one that concerned the doctors most, was lodged near the spinal cord, just below the rib cage. It was in a very delicate spot that could very well render him a paraplegic if the surgery were not performed by very capable and experienced hands. The other had sliced through his right lung before it stopped, deep in the latissimus dorsa muscles. The other two struck his left shoulder and forearm and had passed through without doing extensive damage. As soon as he was able to walk the full length of the outer garden twice, without a walker or leaning on someone he signed himself out, ignoring the doctor's plea to remain longer. He'd done enough physical therapy for his shoulder to get a reasonable amount of its use back. The arm ached terribly but he was determined to get himself into fighting condition before he started his search for Tonton Djé.

"*Tonton*," he said to himself with disgust. How could his father have called that man his friend?

When he caught up with him, Reno was going to beat the truth out of *"Uncle Jay"* Hadley. And then he was going to kill him.

Chapter Sixteen

Jason Hadley sat at what had become his favorite stool at the Little Creek Café, listening to Ken Shirazi talk about his travels in the service. When he saw a chance to cut in he took it.

"So, tell me," he said. "How long have you known Jimmy? Chad sure seems to idolize him."

"Oh, you saw that, huh?" Ken laughed.

"Yeah," Jason smiled. "I guess every young fellow needs someone to look up to."

"Yes." Ken paused for just the tiniest of moments but Jason could see that he'd just hit a nerve. "His Uncle Jimmy is quite a guy. None of us really knew how selfless he really was until he took on Don Muir."

"It's hard not to appreciate something like that, alright," he nodded. "So, you two are close, huh?"

"Oh, yeah," Ken shrugged. "We don't talk about everything, like we use to, though."

"Really?"

"Oh, Jimmy is family," Ken said quickly. "I love him like my own brother. We just don't have the same lives anymore." He looked down at the counter, forlorn, "He's been through so much that a...kind of a *different* side of him seems to show itself sometimes. Some kind of defense mechanism, I guess. He tries to hide it, but..." he shrugged.

Jason nodded sympathetically. He saw that the subject was a difficult one, so he changed it. "So, are you thinking of expanding this place?" he asked. "You seem to be doing such good, steady business that adding some more space to the dining area would seem to be a good idea."

"No," Ken replied, shaking his head. "We're too much at the mercy of the weather. It can really snow heavy out here and then no one but the dedicated coffee addicts come in. For Jimmy not to come for coffee, it takes some serious weather," he laughed.

"A real coffee hound, huh?"

"Oh yeah," Ken said. "After the hospital let him come home, they told him he couldn't have more than one cup every couple of days, because he'd lost a chunk of his intestines..."

"He was hurt that badly?"

Ken nodded. "The doctor said it was a miracle he survived. The bullet tore him up real bad." He tilted his head, "Of course, having Gina Albright around didn't hurt."

He smiled. "She's cute—well, you've met her—and she shows more concern for his well-being than his wife does."

"Yeah, that'll make a man think of straying…"

"Oh, no," Ken said. "Jimmy would *never* break his vows, no matter how bad things got. Then again, now that Tara's broken them herself, who knows?" He pointed a finger at Jason to accentuate his words, "But he would never have severed the marriage himself. He's a strong Catholic Christian and no matter how many people tried to get him to leave her in the last several months, he refused."

Jason mentally noted the label "Catholic Christian". So many Protestants ostracized their Catholic brethren for praying to saints, that they were careful about who they considered a Christian, despite a shared belief in the same God, Messiah and Holy Spirit. *If only they were as careful about their own beliefs.*

"He's a rare one, alright," he said.

"He is," Ken replied proudly…but did Jason detect the slightest tinge of jealousy?

"Well, you sure picked the right one, first time out," Jason said. "Min is—if you don't mind my saying—a very lovely woman."

"I don't mind you saying it, as long as noticing is all you do," Ken said with a wink. "I've always known that she was the most beautiful girl that ever walked the earth."

"I envy you, Ken," Jason said. "All the years I spent running around and I never met a woman that could make me want to settle down and raise a family, especially one like you have."

"Yeah, God has really blessed us. That's for sure." He said it sincerely.

"Yes, He has," Jason agreed. "Well," he shrugged, "It's too bad what happened at Jimmy's house, anyway. It's a heavy blow to come home and find your wife in *your* bed with another man. He doesn't deserve that."

"No, he doesn't," Ken agreed. "And what makes it worse is that she got to stay home while he went to jail. And he still has a lot more to deal with."

"You mean, legally? Yeah, a criminal trial can be a scary thing."

"A big cup of my favorite beverage, please, Mr. Shirazi," Ray said as he walked to the counter and sat down. "I feel the need for something hot and bitter to charge me up."

Ken and Jason looked at each other and smiled.

"Alright, spill it. What did you hear?" Ray asked.

"Well, apparently," Ken replied, "the Town Council is giving out free contraceptives to employees of the Marshal's Office."

"Very funny," Ray said. "Have your fun if you must, but leave Gary alone."

"Sorry, Marshal," Ken grinned. "I can't promise that."

"Ken," Ray said with his famous poker-face, "have you ever been Tasered?"

Ken leaned in, smiled and opened his mouth to speak as a small spray of red suddenly erupted from the left side of his head and a coffee pot on the shelf behind him shattered. Reflexively, he put his left hand on the wound then looked at it; blood was running down his fingers. Only then did they hear the gunshot.

"Ken!" Ray shouted in alarm. "Get down! Everybody on the floor, *now!*" He barked. He jumped over the counter to check on his friend as the frightened customers scrambled to follow orders. He turned to Jason, who had already begun helping the older customers to get to the floor.

"Jason, go back and make sure Min and Chad stay put!" he commanded.

Hadley nodded and went immediately, keeping his head down to avoid being the next victim. Ken sat with his back against the ice machine, his left hand pressed against his head to stop the bleeding. He waved off Ray's efforts to help.

"I'll be fine," he said. "It just creased my scalp. Damn that hurts!"

"Paul One to Paul Two, 10-33!" Ray barked into his radio. "10-33, Shot fired, one man down at Little Creek Café! Respond immediately!"

A short pause was all Gary took. "10-4, Paul One. I'm en route. Any descriptions available?"

"Negative," Ray replied. "None of us saw a damned thing! The shot must have come through one of the front windows."

"10-4. Searching the perimeter now." It seemed like an eternity, but it was really less than a minute before Gary was back on the radio. "No one visible in the immediate area, Chief...wait—I see movement across the highway...I'm responding now. Subject is armed and on foot, running northwest from the far end of the park." He was breathing hard, the adrenaline taking effect. "About two hundred, two-twenty yards out." The sound of the patrol car's motor screaming up to redline could be heard inside the café. Then the thudding and bumping of the Crown Victoria muscling its way over the poorly maintained road and through rough brush, dodging the trees as the deputy gained on the shadowy figure that he could now see was carrying what appeared to be a long-barreled assault rifle and was wearing camouflage BDUs and a ski mask. Gary got as close as he could then he drew his weapon, veered right, braked hard, opened his door and took aim.

"Stop now or…!"

The figure spun around and fired a pistol from the hip, sending the shot wide of the mark and hitting the searchlight ten inches from Gary's face. Gary, who saw the weapon come up before the shooter fired it, returned fire almost simultaneously. He placed two rounds into his assailant's torso which brought him down, but then the killer got back up and threw himself toward a tree only three feet away. Gary fired four rounds in a row, aiming for the head. He missed twice but landed two rounds, one through the assailant's neck and the other under the left armpit, dropping him just short of the cover he'd sought.

Before leaving the car, Gary pulled the clip from his gun and performed a tactical reload, putting in a fresh magazine. Stepping out of the cruiser he took one hand off the gun to reach up and radio the marshal for backup, which was all the distraction the hard-dying suspect needed to get off one last shot which found its mark, dead center of Gary's chest, knocking him back. Gary fired instinctively, this time putting a forty-caliber round through his enemy's head, ending the firefight once and for all.

"999!" he coughed into his shoulder mic. "999! Officer down!"

Ray was there before Gary finished the transmission. The moment he heard Gary take off in pursuit, he had run to his own car and followed. He was just getting out of his vehicle when the final showdown took place next to the tree. He ran to the deputy, who had fallen against the front wheel of his patrol car. He kept his gun on the shooter as he looked over at Gary and asked him where he was hit.

"Center—of my chest," Gary coughed.

"I don't see any blood, son," Ray said, trying to keep his own heart from beating out of his chest. He looked over at the body of the shooter and asked. "Is this guy dead?"

"Yeah."

After seeing the hole in the man's face and the red and grey spattered behind his head Ray asked facetiously, "You sure?"

"I am now," Gary tried to laugh but when he did, he started coughing uncontrollably, causing him to wince with pain and grab at his chest.

"We have to get you to the hospital," Ray said as he pulled open Gary's shirt to check his wound. He let out a big sigh of relief. "But your vest did its job; the bullet bounced off your trauma plate."

Ray went to take a closer look at the shooter. Gary shot as trained and hit him several times; the guy should have gone down the first time.

He felt around on the killer's chest and discovered that telltale hard square over the middle of the chest. A ballistic vest! If Gary hadn't kept shooting until he was down this bastard would have killed him and gotten away. He fought the temptation to kick the body a couple of times.

"This piece of crap was wearing a vest with a trauma plate on it," Ray said. "And look at all that camo." He pulled out his cell phone to call in the Coconino County Sheriff's Office; he needn't have bothered, since they were monitoring the channel and two units were already on their way.

A paramedic unit and ambulance from Happy Jack got there and Ray had helped Gary onto a stretcher and into the ambulance just as the Sheriff's Department arrived and fanned out across the area to search for any possible partners the dead man may have had. Evidence technicians took photographs of the scene and were beginning to pick up empty cartridges and lay down markers when Cindy Noe pulled up in her Hyundai Tucson. Today was supposed to be her first day off since starting with the department but it was clearly not going to turn out that way. She was a fit, rather masculine woman of forty-one with short, dark brown hair combed to the side and today she wore a pink polo shirt under her ballistic vest, which looked rather odd when one saw the Colt .45 automatic strapped to the hip of her tight blue jeans.

"*Son of a*—"Cindy stopped herself mid-sentence and regrouped. When she spoke again she was all business, "What do you need from me, Ray?" she asked.

"Thank God you're here," Ray said. "Could you go and interview the folks at the café and see if you can find any witnesses? I have to watch over things here and I need a cool head handling the scene in there." He was clearly stressed. This was way too close to home for him.

"You got it, Chief," she nodded. Without another word she got back in her vehicle and headed across the street.

Damn it, she thought.

It had been three years since she was involved in a shootout at a meth lab outside Williams that resulted in one dead suspect and three critically injured deputies, but the memory of it was carved into her psyche so deeply that the feel of the gun brought back all of the anxiety and near-panic of that frightening 30-second horror show. It didn't matter that she was one of the lucky ones that came out of it unscathed. Watching her friends go down, seeing the shooter's head snap to the side and brain and blood splash out of his skull when she fired the fight-ending headshot marked her for life. She spent three years trying to overcome the trauma, only to realize she was losing the battle. Summertown was supposed to be where she could finish out her career without the likelihood of such a thing happening again.

Snap out of it, Cindy, she thought. *You have people depending on you.*

It was nearly sunset when the last of the Sheriff's Office personnel left the scene. Ray and Cindy sat on the hood of his patrol car and drank a cup of coffee that Pedro brought to them from the back office of his store.

"So, tell me, Bubba," she patted Ray on the arm. "How are you holding up?"

"I'll be OK," he said. "I just have to clear my head and kind of distance myself enough…"

"You can't distance yourself from this, Ray," she said. "Gary's in the hospital. Ken was shot by somebody we haven't even ID'd yet; lucky for him, the guy had bad aim. And it happened *in front of you.* Let me walk you over to the crisis counselor. You need to talk to…"

"I've dealt with this stuff before," he waved her off. "I just need to clear my head. I'll go over to Smokie's when I sign off for the night. A beer and some mindless conversation is all I need."

"Did you hear anything I just told you?" Cindy said. "I know you've been in some bad fights before. But this one is too personal not to talk to a counselor about it."

"Maybe," he said.

"No maybes, Ray," she said, putting her arm around his shoulder and shaking him. "Let's go talk to him. He's over at the café talking to witnesses right now."

"OK," he sighed. He was in no mood to argue anymore.

"Then you can go get your beer. If Corinda can't pick you up, call me and I'll take you home."

"Thanks. You're a good friend, Cin."

"Everybody needs somebody to take care of them sometime…or however that song goes," she smiled.

"And who takes care of you these days?"

"My two cats and my cable TV subscription. That's all I need."

"Uh-huh," Ray said. "That's what I said, too."

"Well, I'm doing just fine right now," she said dismissively. "If another Ray or Corinda comes along, I might change my mind."

That made Ray grin a little bit. Cindy was always making people wonder which way she "swung"; she liked watching them try to figure it out. Even he didn't know, but he really didn't care. She was Cindy; a good detective and great friend. And he was going to be utilizing her detective skills for this case over the next few weeks.

Chapter Seventeen

The wind was cold and the streets were covered with a thin sheet of ice from the sprinkling of rain that had fallen the night before. The sky had only a few light-gray clouds floating off to the east and the sun gave everything on which it shone a bright, crystal-white glow. It was a beautiful day, and I sat enjoying it from the comfort of my office as my daughter walked in the front door.

"What are you doing sitting in this moldy old office?" Jessie asked as she sat in a chair across from my desk. "It's gorgeous outside. You should be taking a walk around the square, bundled up to your neck the way you like."

"Too much work, baby girl," I shrugged. "I have to keep up on the paperwork that other people don't want to do themselves."

"Yeah, yeah, yeah. I've heard that excuse for as long as I can remember. But you always manage to take breaks. I was just down at the café, having lunch with Gina and Pam, and everybody kept asking me where you were. They said they haven't seen you down there in days. I didn't think you could go without Ken's coffee for more than a day at a time."

"Like I just said, I have too much work." I knew she wasn't going to let it go, but that didn't mean I had to spill my guts to my little girl. I still had some pride.

"How are you doing, Papi?" she asked. "You getting lonely up there yet?"

"No," I lied. "It's pretty relaxing, actually. It's nice to come home from work and not have to walk around on eggshells, afraid that something I say or do might start a night-long argument."

"I guess there is that," she shrugged. She knew me too well. "Your face is healing up pretty well," she said. "Your eye looks less like it was hit by a baseball bat than the last time I saw you."

"Yeah, it isn't sore anymore. It's definitely easier working with two working eyes."

"You know you couldn't have stopped it, don't you?" she said, slyly catching me off-guard with the question.

"I know," I replied after a moment. "I just...I don't know..."

"You wanted to be there for Ken. I know."

"Instead, I was at Smokie's getting so drunk that Pat had to drive me home. Busy feeling sorry for myself while somebody was trying to kill my friend."

"Papi, get a grip," she snapped. "You couldn't have done anything to change what happened even if you were there. You're not Superman. The last time you ran in front of a bullet you almost died. And I do *not* want to lose you. Don't you want to hold your grandbaby when it's born?"

"Of course, when the time comes…"

"The time is coming in about seven months," she grinned.

"What are you saying? Are you…?"

"Pregnant," she smiled. "Seven weeks."

I jumped out of my seat and wrapped her up in my arms, and shouted so loud that Carol spun around in her chair to see what happened.

"I'm going to be a grandpa!" I shouted as Carol squealed with delight. My mood changed immediately as all my dark thoughts of the last couple of days disappeared. "What did Tom say when you told him?"

"I haven't yet," she smiled. "I wanted you to be the first to know."

I started to tear up at that. She was still my little girl. Of course, I wasn't going to let Tommy find out that she told me first, but knowing that she did warmed my heart so much I had to wrap her up in my arms all over again. Then, like a stroke of lightning, a thought hit me.

"I've got to start a college fund…"

"Papi, we have plenty of time to worry about that stuff," she laughed. "We don't even know if it's a boy or a girl."

"You can never start too early," I said.

"Will you stop being an accountant for just a minute? Can you please just enjoy the news before you have to get all money-crazy?"

I stared at her as if she had just uttered a dirty word.

"I beg your pardon," I protested. "I am not money crazy."

"You're always worrying about money and work. You need to get out of this office and start socializing." She reached over and started fiddling with my shirt collar and added, "Gina and Pam were asking about you." She was watching my face for some reaction.

"So they've made up? I'm glad." I was going to keep my poker face as long as I could.

"Yep. And Gina told me a new pool has been started." She had a mischievous twinkle in her eye that I knew all too well.

"I wish they'd quit with the pools," I muttered. "Who started this one going?"

"She didn't say. But she did ask me to tell you that you'd better head into the city and start updating your wardrobe because you're going be getting lots of offers."

"Oh, no…Oh my *God.*"

She reached over, grabbed my hand and managed to hold herself together long enough to say, "*You're it!*" before she fell apart laughing. I guess the look on my face had something to do with it. No wonder I suck at poker.

***

Gina stayed at the cafe long after Pam had gone. She was deep in thought about her life and her choices in men. It was true that she tended to let her sex drive cloud her judgment when it came to dating, but she wasn't so air-headed as to let that problem remain unsolved. *Just because I'm a little heavy doesn't mean somebody wouldn't find me attractive and interesting.* She had worked hard to drop the ten pounds she lost since starting her diet and she was noticing results. *I don't know why I worry about it,* she smiled to herself. Jimmy always told her the right guy would come along, she just needed to be patient. She knew he was right, but it's easier said than done when you have a huge, dark void in your life and the way you used to soothe the pain is to find somebody to sleep with. The intimacy always helped her ease the pain and keeping it casual kept things from getting serious, then going sour. And they always went sour. The only relationship she ever had with a guy that got better the longer she was in it was her friendship with Jimmy.

At the mention of his name a light bulb seemed to go on in her mind. Jimmy. Why not Jimmy? *He cares about me more than any guy I've ever known. He knows I'll do anything for him. He was there when I lost the baby and he never left me.* She smiled at the thought of sleeping with Jimmy Stone, partially because it would give them both a welcome jolt of pleasure, part because it would piss off Tara. *Jimmy needs some tenderness after what she did to him. He needs somebody who'll take it slow with him and let him know he's still attractive.* And he was attractive, to her at least. There was a certain something about him that made her feel safe and cared for. And his face was so…masculine. He was once a real cutie, she could tell. But now his features were…just—*manly*. The look in his eyes told you he cared. He didn't have to say a word. His deep-set green eyes, his broad, not-quite-flat nose; his chin was square and his mouth curled up a little at the ends, giving the hint of a faint grin. His dark brown hair was going gray at the temples. His chest grew more V-shaped the more he worked out. His chest…

Alright, that does it, she said as she realized that her breath was getting heavy. *I'm going over there right now, and I hope to hell I don't embarrass myself.*

***

"We have positive ID on our shooter, Bubba," Cindy Noe said the moment Ray answered the phone. "And it's a strange one." She paused to let his mind clear, since she obviously woke him up.

"OK, I'm ready," he said in that gravelly voice he had whenever he woke up. He didn't sit up, but his eyes were open at least.

"The name is David Corbett. Ring a bell?"

Ray sat bolt upright. *"Corbett?"* In all this quiet country, that man was one of the few truly violent and hateful. He was a member of a militia called Purity in Arizona, a group that's opposed to Nazism, Socialism and just about everything else but Libertarianism, yet espoused racial segregation in the state through peaceful means first, but by force if necessary.

"I take it you're familiar with him," she said.

"Just from the news briefs we occasionally get from DPS and the FBI," he replied. "Let me get dressed. You can fill me in when I get to the office."

Thirty minutes later he was looking over Cindy's shoulder at the computer monitor on his desk as she scrolled through the file on David Corbett.

"He was kicked out of the Purity in Arizona militia because he was dealing meth, according to the FBI," Cindy said. "As a matter fact, he was starting to build a network when his supply was cut off, right about the time you killed Don Muir."

"What a coincidence," Ray mumbled.

"Isn't it though? The militia kicked him out about three weeks before the shootout here. CCSO is going over everything in his place, looking for anything that can prove motive."

"When did you find out?" Ray asked.

"A couple hours ago," she said. "I figured I'd give you an extra hour's sleep before I woke you up. The reason it took so long is he didn't have a criminal record—believe it or not…"

"He didn't have a CCW?"

"No one in PIA has a concealed carry permit," she replied. "They don't believe the state has a right to tell citizens what weapons they can carry or how they can carry them. Anyway," she continued, "no DNA record, we couldn't get a good photo because Gary's bullet took half his face off. There were no dental records that we know of, which isn't surprising since he was a meth user and his teeth were almost rotted out of his mouth. We finally hit paydirt when his fingerprints got a positive ID through the Navy."

"Navy, huh? What did he do there?"

"Let's see," she clicked a tab on her computer and read, "Culinary Specialist Basic."

"He was a cook."

"Apparently so," Cindy nodded. "He went in on March 5th 2002, was discharged June 3rd 2005. OTH; "Other than Honorable" Discharge. It looks like he was basically kicked out around his third year in. It doesn't say why."

"This guy was a real screw-up," Ray said. "A cook in the Navy—not exactly a job that requires intensive combat training—and he manages to get booted out, then he kicks around doing God-knows-what, joins PIA somewhere along the line, then starts selling drugs and gets kicked out of PIA—a group *full* of screw ups. It takes effort to be kicked out of a group of your own kind."

"And he was a slob," Noe added. "Not that you didn't notice that at the scene, but he was sloppy with everything; his clothes, his weapons…Sheriff's office had to send the rifle down to Phoenix because it was so caked with crap from being fired without cleaning that they couldn't show positively that it was fired at the scene…"

"Yeah, I read that in the email."

"But this morning we got another notification that Phoenix PD has to send it to the FBI. They can't prove it was the weapon used, either."

"No residue on his gloves?"

"Sure," she said. "But they can't tell how recent it is because Corbett never washed them. The same goes for his jacket, the ski mask, his vest...Damn, Ray. When they pulled that vest off of him I thought I was going to puke."

"How did he get his hands on that kind of firepower?" Ray mused. "A Dragunov is no AK47, it's a gun made for sniper operations. It's got a big cartridge. It's expensive."

"Not as expensive as an AR15 or any of its variants," Cindy replied. "With a little luck and the right contacts, a person can get their hands on one."

"I suppose you're right."

She searched through the stack of files on her desk and pulled several sheets of paper out of one.

"Which brings up another interesting finding," she said as she handed Ray the document. "The guns—all three of them—were on the list from that sting operation that went bad awhile back, Operation Fast and Furious."

"What!"

"That's right. These guns made their way over the border, then somehow came back and were sold by one of Corbett's connections, who is known to also supply PIA members. So, now we have probable cause to search every single member of the militia, as well as have the feds come in and help with the investigation."

"Good," Ray said. "Ken's been pretty shook up from it. This will help his morale a little, I think."

"I hope it helps you, too, Ray," she said. "This means you probably weren't the target. He'd never had a beef with you; you never had contact with him. That shot was placed exactly where Ken had been standing at the moment Corbett pulled the trigger. At the distance he had set himself up, the bullet probably took about a second to travel from the muzzle to the target. If Ken hadn't leaned in toward you at the last second his brains would have been sprayed all over the back wall. I'm convinced Corbett was aiming at him. Remember, Ken's Iranian."

"American with Iranian parents," Ray corrected.

"He *looks* like an Arab. But that's just one of a few things that could have made him single him out. Ken has a Korean wife; their kids are mixed-race; Ken's a non-white who owns a business in Corbett's stomping ground..."

"That's true. But how about Jason?"

"Hadley? You think an old missionary could have been the target?"

"Probably not," he allowed. "But we need to keep ourselves open to all possibilities until we're sure. He was seated close enough to the path of the bullet that we should keep him in consideration."

"Well, you read my interviews of witnesses on the scene," she replied. "He knows of no one who would want to kill him. And he hasn't been here long enough to make any enemies around here."

"Well, I suppose just a cursory check on his background should suffice, then."

"Will do. And by the way," she turned to look at him, "are you taking the meds?"

"Yeah. They're just for sleeping."

"They workin'?"

"Yeah. I'm able to sleep the whole night now and I don't remember my dreams."

"Good," she said relieved. "Getting enough sleep helps a lot."

"Yeah, I guess."

"What's wrong, Ray?"

"Nothing. Nothing you can fix, anyway."

"Try me," she said. "You and Corinda having problems?"

"Why do you ask that?" he replied defensively.

"Just a guess. I'm right, aren't I?"

"We'll work it out," he said dismissively. "It's just a minor thing."

"I know you better than that, Ray," she said more gently. "If you really thought it was a minor thing you wouldn't be bothered so much by it."

"All right, detective," Ray relented. "I'm having second thoughts about marrying Corinda."

"What! Why?"

"I don't know if she's over her ex-husband," he said, simply.

"Did you bring this up to her?"

"Yes, and she got very upset about it."

"I'll bet," Cindy chuckled.

"You laugh, but it wasn't funny at the time. She told me that Jimmy hurt her feelings by ignoring her all the time—and that got me wondering…" Ray got restless at this point and started pacing around the little room. "What if I'm not as attentive as she wants me to be? This is going to be my first marriage. What if I'm too set in my ways and turn out to be a rotten husband? Will she dump me for the first guy that showers her with compliments?"

"You don't like being tied down, do you?" Cindy declared with a certainty that irked Ray.

"That's not true," he chaffed. "I've been waiting for someone like Corinda to come along."

"When is the last time you stayed overnight at her place?"

"Corinda wants to wait 'til we're married," Ray mumbled, unable to meet his friend's gaze.

"Really? Hm."

"What do you mean, 'Hm'?"

"Well, Bubba, neither of you is a virgin," she replied. "And she lived with that pudgy little guy…Nermal?"

"Nerville."

"Nerville," she choked back a laugh. "She lived with him for a while, and don't tell me that was a sexless relationship. And that guy she took home with her the night…"

"Yeah, yeah, I get the message," Ray said, gruffly. "I'm good enough for her as a boyfriend, but not a lover."

"That's not what I'm saying at all," Cindy laughed. "She's holding back for a reason, but there's no way she thinks you're not good enough for her. I've seen the way she looks at you. You're her knight in shining armor. Maybe she doesn't think *she's* worthy of *you.*"

"That's ridiculous."

"Have you shown her how much she means to you lately?"

"I bring her flowers every few days," Ray shrugged. "We went to that nice restaurant in Flag a few nights ago; the one on Milton…Picazzo's. I'm taking her to meet my brother in Phoenix next month…"

"Do you tell her she's beautiful?"

"Not anymore," he replied. "The last time I did, she thought I was trying to get into her pants."

"Are you serious?"

"She thought I was trying to seduce her," Ray nodded. "She said that if I can't wait until after the wedding, then I didn't respect her."

"Damn, Ray," she shook her head in amazement. "I don't know what to tell you. I'd hate to think you're right, though. I hope she just needs the extra time."

"Me, too," he sighed. "But my gut says I may lose her."

"Well," Cindy said after a long pause. "If she causes you this much frustration and stress, maybe she isn't the one."

Ray said nothing. He just stared at the floor and thought about what his friend was saying.

"I know how easy it is to be drawn into a relationship with someone who has everything you think you want," she shrugged. "The problem is, what you *think* you want may not be what you *really* want, or what you actually *need*." When Ray didn't reply, she said, "Hey c'mon, Bubba. It isn't the end of the world. Who knows? Maybe I'm just talking out my ass and everything is going to work out."

"Yeah, well…"

"Come on," Cindy said, wrapping an arm around Ray's shoulder and walking toward the door. "Let me buy you a cup of coffee and we can plot our course on this case."

"All right," Ray nodded. "You're right. I can't be wasting time worrying about my love life when there's an investigation underway."

Cindy began to say that wasn't what she meant, but decided to let it go. Ray needed to work things out for himself.

***

Jason Hadley walked out of the little Chinese restaurant on Flagstaff's Beaver Street, feeling the pleasant satisfaction of a well-made dinner of Kung Pao washed down with two glasses of good plum wine. He took his time strolling through the shops in the downtown area before he headed to his appointment at the New Age bookstore situated between two coffeehouses along Route 66. It was cold, as usual for early December and the fluffy, grey clouds in the sky hinted at the likelihood of snow. The thought of a fresh, clean, white covering over everything in sight made him smile. Christmas decorations were up everywhere. Although times had definitely changed, the colorful garlands, the lights, the Christmas trees in the windows of the small stores along with the winter weather brought him back to his childhood on the Upper Peninsula of Michigan. It was a pleasant memory that he savored all the way to the front door of the bookstore. When he entered the shop, he went from happy reminiscing to cold-as-steel business.

"Hello," he greeted the young man at the makeshift counter constructed from three old bookshelves fastened together. "I'm here to return a book. It was mailed to me last week, at the Little Creek Café in Summertown."

The man looked at him carefully, his face expressionless. He stood about six three and weighed maybe one-ninety, give or take ten pounds. His face was broad and his nose aquiline; his hair was dark-brown and long but well-groomed. He wore a black t-shirt with a large marijuana leaf emblazoned on the front. Jay could see the smallest spark of fear in the young man's eyes, which told him that he had found the man he was looking for. He placed both his hands on the counter and leaned in.

"You are the one I speak to about that, aren't you?" he prompted.

"Yes, I'm the owner," the man replied, recovering quickly.

"Good," Jay smiled affably. "Where should I bring the merchandise?" When he received a blank stare from the young man, he added, "The title of this book is 'Dragunov SVD'."

That caused a very slight break in the man's poker-faced disposition.

"I'm sorry," the store owner said cautiously. "We don't do returns. But I can offer you store credit."

"No," Jay laughed. "The quality of the merchandise was shoddy. I want my money back. Unless, of course, you would like a free sample of *my* product."

A long silence was followed by sudden deference on the part of the store owner.

"OK, no problem," the man smiled. "I understand. But I'm afraid I'm going to have to keep 50% as a restocking fee. We did, after all, deliver on time. And we do keep such orders confidential."

"Ten."

"…Thirty five."

"Twenty five."

"Agreed."

"When and where?"

"At my office, out west of town. That's where I keep my funds."

"You don't like banks?"

The young man smiled. "I'd have a hard time explaining that stream of income to the IRS."

"Yes, I suppose that would be tough," Jay grinned.

After arranging a meeting time and getting directions to the man's office Jay turned and headed out. What he had anticipated to be a very tense discussion turned out to be a suspiciously easy meeting of minds. And giving him directions to his "office"?

This kid must take me for a fool, he thought.

Chapter Eighteen

Reno lay on his bed in the small motel room and stared at the ceiling. His resolve to hunt down his family's murderers had not faltered, even when Pastor Jacques came to see him as he languished in a hospital bed, impatient to be released. Pastor Jacques was the only person that Reno could trust here in the U.S., and the only one who could understand what he was going through.

"Reno, you *must not do this*," Pastor Philippe Jacques insisted. "It will only make you equal to the man who did this horrible thing. You must make your life a tribute to the love you had for your family by forgiving their killers and serving others who have suffered similar loss."

"I *can't* forgive them!" Reno said. "How can you even suggest…"

"Because God demands that we forgive those who hurt us," Pastor Jacques replied simply. "It is the only way to keep hate from destroying us. If it were not for forgiveness I would not have been able to go on."

"You're a far better man than I am, Pastor," Reno said. "Because I simply cannot…*will not*…forgive these animals."

"I am no better than you are, Reno," the pastor replied. "I have simply lived according to my faith in Christ, who has always kept each promise He has made. I didn't want to forgive TiZo," he said. "But God demanded it of me. It took far longer than one night to release the pain, but God gave me the strength to heal. It is God who empowered me to forgive. Left to myself I would have tried to kill TiZo myself."

"He would have killed *you*, Pastor," Reno replied.

"Very possibly," Philippe nodded. "And that would be preferable to living without my Denise. But God had other plans, and I would not be able to continue with them if I had not learned to forgive the ones who took her away from me. You must reach that place also."

"One day maybe, but not yet," Reno replied.

Philippe Jacques sighed in resignation then held out his hands in surrender.

"You'll not give up until you've found the man you think is responsible, will you?"

"No," Reno said. "If you won't tell me where Jason is, I'll find another way to hunt him down. I'd sooner die than let him live after what he did to my family."

"Reno," the pastor said wearily, "you are *wrong*. Jason Hadley is not responsible for your family's murder."

"How do you know?"

"I simply do," Jacques shrugged. "I know the man. I am convinced that he is incapable of such a thing."

Reno Chatelaine barked a mirthless laugh at his friend's words. "I probably would have thought so as well," he replied, "if he hadn't been the one to assign me to mission that kept me sending false information for two years. And then, when they no longer needed me, they tried to kill me while a group of their friends were violating Mireille...and Soraya. And torturing Robert..." he stopped himself before he lost control.

Philippe said nothing. He knew even before he came here that there was no convincing Reno that he was on the road to his own doom. But he knew what was expected of him—to at least try, regardless how futile he knew it to be.

***

It was approaching sunset when Jason Hadley pulled up to the gate of the home of Brent Carval. Jason chuckled at the thought of how upset the kid was going to be when Jason called him by name. Poor Brent had gone to such lengths to keep his anonymity. The place was described as a little trailer out west of town. It turned out to be a triple-wide mobile home on a fenced one-acre compound located twelve miles west of town in a remote, heavily wooded area off Fort Valley Rd. It was wisely placed among the trees, yet on a rise high enough to spot approaching vehicles from a distance of about a half-mile. The problem with the location—for the owner—was at about two hundred yards from the compound the forest blocked the view of the road. It was just common sense to figure that Carval had taken a few precautions in that department. And for that reason Jason decided to do some pre-meeting scouting.

From his place among the trees, in the middle of the house's blind spot, Jason almost laughed out loud. The owner of this place obviously thought technology was going to protect him. The gate was automatic but it had a biometric hand scanner to access it. There were two cameras mounted on opposite sides of the gate, one aimed at the outer path and the other aimed at the interior drive. There was a pole from which electricity was brought to the house and on that pole was a Lexan-encased security camera.

So much gadgetry, he said to himself. *The only thing it's going to do is slow me down a little. But I have all the time in the world.*

Chapter Nineteen

For the twenty-second day in a row, I pondered the possible reasons anyone would try to kill Ken. I knew he'd had a long and well-travelled career in the service. Could this Corbett guy have been someone he knew from there who held a grudge? It wasn't impossible, but it certainly seemed unlikely. At least the shooter was no longer a threat. Hopefully, that would be the end of it.

The end of it…the end of my marriage…

Here I go again, I thought. *All I need is an excuse and I'll start feeling sorry for myself again. Don't start crying, Stone, for God's sake. Get your butt up from this chair and do something to occupy your mind.*

I had been sitting on the front porch of my townhouse and watching the clouds float across the sky, feeling the chilly breeze nip at my hands and face. Before I could stand up, I spotted Gina strolling up the hill. *Wonderful,* I thought. I did not need her here, the way I was feeling. She didn't need my crap with all that she had on her plate, but it was too late to hide.

"Hey, Sissy," I said with a smile I didn't feel. "What are you doing at this end of town?"

She just looked at me and said, "Have you just been sitting out here, depressing yourself?"

"Yep," I said. "I'm so low maintenance I can do that on my own."

"Then let's go inside where it's warm and I'll try to cheer you up," she said. "It's the least a friend can do."

"Well…"

"Come on," she coaxed. "What's the matter, Bashful? You chicken?"

"Chicken of what?" I laughed a bit too readily.

"Of being alone in your apartment with a woman."

"Of course not," I lied. "It's just that you're having this issue with the school and if somebody sees…"

"Let me worry about that," she said, putting her hand up to stop me. "I might just leave this town anyway."

"What? Why?" I tried to sound more concerned for her, than selfishly afraid of losing her.

"Because there's too much crap going on around here," she said with a shrug. "I don't think it's healthy that the kids in town are sent to a school where their parents think the principal's a slut. Would you have wanted to raise Jessie in a place like that?"

"I don't think it would have affected Jessie if people thought you were a slut," I joked.

She looked at me stone-faced. "Let me in. I have to pee."

Realizing I had no excuse to do otherwise, I obeyed. I had to get her out of here fast before I started blubbering.

"I'm sorry I'm not good company right now," I said.

"Yeah, Ken told me."

"Did he call you?" I said, making no effort to mask my irritation.

"We talked about you when I was at the cafe this morning," she said. "What do you expect? He's your friend and he's worried about you."

"Well, he shouldn't," I replied. "He's got too many other things to worry about right now to be wasting time on me. And so do you."

"Friends watch out for friends, Jimmy," she smiled. "You know that as well as anybody."

"Yeah, well I'm tougher than you think," I said unconvincingly.

"Bullsh—irts."

"Nice save, whatever bull shirts are."

"If you're so tough, why were you crying?" When I didn't reply, she reached up and wiped a tear from my face and held her wet hand up for me to see. "What's this, tough guy," she said gently.

"I don't know," I said, unable to come up with anything clever to say.

She wrapped her arms around me and hugged me tight then. "It's going to be OK, Jimmy. I promise."

"I know," I said. "I just have to get past this rough part and things'll get better in time."

"That's right," she said as she stroked my back soothingly.

"Thanks," I said, squeezing her and patting her back. I pulled away gently, hoping to avoid her noticing the effect she had on me. After months of having no desire for physical intimacy I was suddenly, embarrassingly aroused by Gina's touch. How I could be so depressed yet still be excited by her was a mystery.

"I'll be fine." I walked over to the kitchen, purposely keeping my back to her. "Would you like a drink?"

"Sure."

I could sense her following me as I went to the refrigerator and opened it, using the door to cover my embarrassment.

"What would you like?"

"To see what you're hiding behind that door," she replied with a twinkle in her eye.

"I'm not hiding anything…"

"Bullshit."

"I thought you didn't cuss anymore."

"I thought you didn't lie."

"Gina, please," I begged. "Let's just drop it."

"I don't want to drop it," she grinned. "I think it's cute."

"Oh, great. 'Cute', huh?"

"Yeah," she laughed. "You talk all the time about being all virtuous and pure, and all along, you're keeping a secret."

"I am not!" I replied, hoping that my indignation would make her drop the subject.

"Yes you are," she insisted. She took a step forward which brought her just inches from me and my door shield. "You're hiding a very dark secret."

I could feel the warmth of her breath, smell her perfume. I tried not to stare but she was too close.

"You're hiding the scandalous secret…" she grabbed the door and pulled it away from me before I could brace for it, "…that I turn you on." She pressed herself against me and stayed there. She didn't touch me, didn't say another word. She just looked up at me with a look of challenge on her pretty face.

"Why are you doing this to me?" I asked, trying to keep my composure.

"Because I want to," she said simply. "I like feeling wanted."

"You can do better than *me* wanting you," I said as I looked away and tried to think of anything but her. "You're my friend, Gina. My best friend, really."

"Which makes it that much better."

"No, it doesn't," I insisted. I tried to step back but she had pinned me against the kitchen wall and blocked my escape route.

"Jimmy, who can you trust to try their best to please you more than your best friend?"

"I don't want to lose you as a friend. And besides…I'm too old for you."

"I decide who's too old for me, not you," she replied.

"Then you're too young for me."

"I'm not a girl, Jimmy. I'm thirty-five."

"And I'm forty-eight. I'm too old to keep up with a girl like you."

"You're in great shape, baby," she said, running her hand across my chest.

I pushed her hand away and pleaded, "Gina, no. I can't do this."

"From the neck up, you say no. But from the waist down…"

"Gina…"

"Jimmy," she put her hand over my mouth, "nothing will ever hurt our friendship. What I'm proposing is a little interlude to just—make each other feel good. You know—clean out the pipes."

"My, how romantic," I chuckled nervously.

"If I wanted romance I'd join a dating website," she said. "I just want to screw my best friend." She grabbed my hand and tugged. "Come on. It'll cheer us both up."

"Make love to you so I can feel better?" I asked incredulously. "Are you listening yourself?"

"I've found that things work out so much better when I don't," she said. "And no one said anything about 'making love'. This is just sex. Don't make it anything more complex."

"Gina—"

"I'll count to three, then when I say go, we'll strip…"

"Wait—"

"*One-two-three-go!*"

"Oh, God…."

I could tell myself all day long that I wasn't going to give in, but I knew it was a lie. If only I had enough strength to resist. Of course, I never did, and that was the cause of most of my problems.

An hour later we were lying next to each other on my bed, talking about how fun it was and how we needed to do it again soon. Actually, it was mostly Gina doing the talking. I was too busy cursing myself for being so stupid. I had loved this little episode, but now reality had sunk in. I knew that sex enhanced loving relationships, but all too often it destroyed friendships. Yet, to my shame, I knew that if and when she came knocking on my door again, I'd probably be ready and willing.

"So, what do you think?" she purred as she rolled over to me and gently dragged her fingernails down my chest. Her hand stopped at the pink scar on my lower abdomen where the surgeon opened me up last year. She very tenderly ran her fingertip down the length of it and said, "Did the experience live up to your fantasies?"

"What?" I asked in surprise. "What fantasies?"

"The ones you've been having about me," she replied simply.

"Who told…?"

"Jessie."

"Jessie?! I've never talked to Jessie about…"

"It wasn't like that, Jimmy," she said, putting my chest. "She came to my place last month to tell me not to hang out with you anymore for a while. Apparently," she said with a wry grin, "she felt that I was causing problems in your marriage."

"I'm sorry," I said. "All I ever said to her was that Tara and I weren't really married anymore."

"She said you fantasized about me."

"I *never* said that," I insisted. "I told her that when both people in a marriage fantasize about other people, the marriage is in deep trouble."

"So, she just figured out on her own that you fantasized about *me*."

"Is that what this was about?" I asked.

"I don't know," she shrugged. She stroked my chest absently, considering the question. "Maybe, in a way," she said finally. "It's flattering. It makes me feel...I don't know...*special*. It's been a long time since I really felt *wanted,* the way you make me feel."

"You've been 'special' to me all along," I said. "Physical attraction doesn't make you any more precious to me."

"I know," she replied. She stretched her arm across my chest then and rested her head against my neck. "And that's the other reason it felt right. I knew you wouldn't turn your back on me after it was over. I know you'll always be my friend."

"I will," I assured her. "Even when it gets weird."

"Yeah, we'll get through that." She pushed herself up, patted my cheek and kissed me softly, then got up and began to dress. "I'd better take off. It's getting late."

"Really? What time is it?"

"Eight."

"Eight!? It feels like you just got here."

"Time flies when you're having fun," she smiled. She climbed across the bed, kissed me once on the forehead then hopped up and headed for the door. "Don't get up. I'll see myself out."

"Lock the door on the way out," I said. "You might as well take the spare key. It's on the kitchen counter."

"Really?" she smiled. "You're giving me the key to your place? My, my, Mr. Stone. Do you do this for all your conquests?"

"Is that what you call a girl who pins you against the wall and strips?"

"I could not help it," she said melodramatically, in an accent I think was supposed to be Russian. "Eet vaz yoor aneemal magneteesm. You mek me eensane vees deesire!" She ran over and pounced on me and began kissing me all over my neck and making tiger noises.

"Help!" I yelled in mock terror. "I'm being ravished!"

"Oooo, I like this game," she giggled. "But I really do have to go," she said as she pushed herself up and hopped off the bed. "We'll start there next time."

"Why, you're a shy little thing, aren't you," I said as she walked out the door.

"Oh yeah," I heard her say from the living room. "A shy little girl with *clean pipes!* Bye, Jimmy! See you later!" I heard the door close and the lock click into place.

I lay there until I drifted off to sleep, which didn't take long. When I woke up, the dial of my alarm clock read 3:43 a.m. I got up, walked into the bathroom and took a shower. If I had been twenty, it would have been invigorating— making love to a pretty young lady then waking up to a bracing shower the next morning. But I wasn't twenty. I was more than twice that age with two ex-wives...or one and a half...and an adult daughter carrying my first grandchild. I had made love to my closest friend, while she was merely having sex with me. I felt like the world's biggest fool.

Chapter Twenty

Brent Carval awoke to a sharp pain in his wrists. His mind was too disconnected to recall where his wrists were at the moment but he did know that it was his wrists that hurt. The pain brought him to consciousness and as he opened his eyes he discovered that he had a very bad headache that went from the base of his skull up the back of his head, then took up residence right behind his eye sockets. He looked around the dark room and recognized it as the living room of his home. The front curtains were closed, the only light was from the clock on the stove. He tried moving his arms and realized that they were bound to the back legs of the dining room chair he was sitting in. Another chair stood directly in front of him. He was bound to his chair at his waist and ankles. He couldn't see what was used to tie him, but it was very thin and it didn't stretch at all.

"You shouldn't squirm around too much," someone said. "The bailing wire your wrists are tied with could badly damage them. I've seen people permanently lose the use of their hands because they tried to break out of it."

"Who are you?" Carval demanded.

"I'm sorry. Did the knocking you out and tying you up give you the impression that I came here to answer *your* questions?"

"I'm going to cut out your heart and eat—!"

"That's very funny," Jason Hadley replied as he moved to the chair across from the bound man. "I would expect to hear that from someone who thinks he's going to be rescued. Is that what you think?"

"I have…"

"*Had,* Mr. Carval," Jason said. "You *had* two men waiting in the trees. You don't have them anymore. The thing with deer stands is, they work pretty well when you're hunting deer. Not so much when you're on sentry duty. They don't provide any cover when someone's shooting at you." Jason reached over to the table on his left and picked up a small wooden contraption that Carval hadn't noticed was there.

"You may have seen pictures of these on the internet," he said. When his companion failed to reply he continued, "This is a Montagnard crossbow, used by the Degar people of central Vietnam. As a matter of fact, this particular one is a souvenir from my time there. I took it off of a dead VC…you know what a VC is?"

A faint, frightened nod was all Carval offered. His eyes began to widen as he deduced what had happened to his buddies.

"These little beauties are powerful," Hadley continued. "You can drive a bolt—that's what crossbow arrows are called—from this into a mature pine tree and it would go all the way in. You'd never get the bolt back. Not only are they powerful, they're also silent...at least from the distance I fired it to kill each of your friends."

"N-no..." Carval groaned.

"I'm sorry," Jason said gently. "Were they close friends?" A nod from Carval prompted a sad grimace from Jason. "I hope it's of some consolation that they never knew what hit them. If they felt anything, it wasn't for long."

He stood up and picked up the roll of wire that he'd brought with him then walked behind Carval, who was straining his neck to see what was going to happen next.

"Unfortunately for you, Brent," he continued, "you won't die as easily."

The sound of wire wrapping around the back of the high-backed dining chair and scraping across the top of the chair behind his head made Carval's breath go ragged.

"Brent," Jason said. "For some reason, you've been under the illusion that you're the head killer in a deadly league of assassins. Yet, all you and your play-buddies really know—or, rather, *knew*—is old tricks that you probably learned by googling the word "spy"." He leaned over and whispered, "I'm the real thing. As they say, I've forgotten far more than you and your friends ever learned on the subject."

Brent Carval began to cry as he lost control of his bodily functions. Hadley looked down at the puddle on the floor under the chair, then looked at the terrified man with a faint paternal grin.

"That's all right, Brent," Jason said soothingly. "It's perfectly normal to react this way when you know you're about to be tortured."

Chapter Twenty-one

C hristmas in Summertown was a wonderful time. The whole town turned out to string lights on the huge Ponderosa pine tree that stood in front of Town Hall, helped in large part by crews from the nearby Century Link telephone line repair station, who brought their boom-lift trucks to help place the big, custom-made star at the top. It was a tradition started when the town was first established that each resident or family would bring one string of lights, then all of the strings would be connected and strung around the tree from bottom to top. Some years were easier than others, with many incompatible light strings sending residents to the nearest hardware store, usually in Flagstaff, to buy something that would work. These issues were avoided a few years later when the Town Council issued general guidelines for the kind of lights permitted.

This year, a truly white Christmas was expected as snowfall was higher than it had been in many years. Ray and Corinda stood by as the truck's boom lifted Gary, who was holding the huge, copper-plated topper, higher and higher until he stood suspended only a couple of feet from the tree top, the cold breeze causing the basket in which he stood to sway. I was pretty sure Ray was wincing a little as Corinda squeezed at his arm nervously. If memory still served, Corinda's nails were probably digging into Ray arm, right through her gloves and into his coat. Gina and I stood among the crowd of fifty or so. I held my breath, praying the boom stayed steady long enough for Gary to attach the star, and then get the heck down from there. I glanced over at Pam who stood with her dad and her sister, Doris, who had come with her two kids to join in the festivities. She had part of the collar to her light-purple snow jacket in her mouth, chewing on it nervously.

Last year was the first time Gary did topper duty and he got a little over-zealous. He leaned too far out from the edge of the basket and, having forgotten to fasten the safety harness to his waist, fell out into the tree itself. If the cherry picker crew hadn't sent one of their guys up to rescue him, Gary would have been spending the night on one of the upper branches. Outside of a few small scratches and a torn coat pocket, the worst wounds that he suffered were to his pride. When the phone workers got him down, he swore over and over again that he "would do it right next year".

And, true to his word, he did. The star was installed straight and true. Gary tightened the clamp at the base of the decoration to keep it attached, then signaled to the truck driver to lower him back to the ground. A moment later, the sun broke through the fluffy clouds overhead, sending its light bouncing radiantly from the many-faceted surface and causing us all to gasp at the beauty of it.

Then another light breeze nudged the star at just the wrong angle, pushing it sideways and snapping the center branch it was attached to. In a moment, the star went from object of beauty to dangerous projectile. It tumbled down the side of the tree, picking up speed as it went, until its base struck a large branch about two thirds of the way down. The star bounced away from the tree and free-fell toward the ground, sending us all scattering in fear. I was about ten yards away, pulling Gina along with me, when I heard it hit something metallic and turned to see where it landed. Ray was beside himself. Gary's head was in his hands. Ken burst out laughing.

The beautiful, custom-made, copperplate star that had decorated the town's Christmas tree was now decorating the Marshal's patrol car, its top point having impaled itself in the roof and shattered the brand-new light bar.

Mayor Pedro Mendoza went to Ray and patted him on the shoulder comfortingly and said, "I know what the town is getting you for Christmas, Marshal."

Doris appeared at Ray's other side holding her smartphone. After a minute or so spent tapping and searching, she held it up so that the others around her could hear the song that was playing: "Catch a falling star and put it in your pocket, save it for a rainy day…"

Ray could have used a few comforting words from his girlfriend, but Corinda was too busy trying to stand up. She had laughed so hard that she fell over onto her backside in the snow and was now having a heck of a time squirming her way back to her feet.

Soon, everyone was joining hands and singing along. When the song finished, they shouted for it to play again. I think we sang that song at least five times. When we were finished, we all crowded around Ken's truck where he had prepared gallons of hot cocoa and coffee to go with the various goodies we all brought to share. Well, everyone but Ray, who had finally lost it during the second round of singing and thrown his cap down and stormed into the Trailer, Corinda scurrying to keep up. He never came back out.

When Gary climbed onto the car and began tugging at the star in an effort to dislodge it, the marshal's voice bellowed from inside the trailer.

"Leave it alone, Callan!" he shouted. "With your luck, the car will explode!"

***

Christmas Day finally came in all its joy and splendor. The snow had stopped long enough to find its resting place everywhere the eye could see, decorating all of the trees with natural garlands of purest white, icicles stretching their way down from each tree branch and roof edge. The sky was overcast but the light's reflection from the snow gave me such a wonderful feeling I couldn't stop smiling. Then, as it always does, it got me missing my mother.

I grew up in Phoenix where I could count on one hand the number of times snow had managed to fall at all, much less remain on the ground. I still had pictures somewhere of the first time I saw it rest on a cactus outside my house. I was nine when mom ran into the house and awakened me early on a Saturday morning, camera in hand, and told me to put my coat on quickly and come outside. She got three photos before the tiny smattering of snow fell off the barrel cactus she had me stand next to, and melted as soon as it hit the ground. When she saw how disappointed I was that I couldn't play in it, she told me of her childhood and how cold, miserable and hungry she and her family were during the winter. I knew she was trying to make me feel better about living in the desert, but it only made me want to play in the snow that much more.

So, she bundled me up and we got into our little Datsun B210 and drove to Flagstaff, where I rolled and jumped and threw snowballs and even managed, with her help, to build a small, lop-sided snowman. When we got home I was exhausted, but I was smiling from ear to ear. Seeing how happy it made me, she decided that we would go see the snow at least a couple of times each year. Even though she complained each time we went, I could tell she enjoyed it, too, mostly because it made me so happy. As grumpy and domineering as she could be, she loved me very much and showed it. It makes me misty-eyed sometimes, just thinking about her.

I walked in the front door of the Shirazis' home and noticed that I was the last one to arrive. Ken was in the kitchen mixing his special recipe of egg nog, Min was carrying a platter full of cookies out to the living room where Jessie and Tom were sitting on the sofa and talking with Jhoon, who had gotten a short leave to come home for the holiday. He was always a healthy, athletic boy but after a year in the service working on a rescue helicopter, he had filled out into what could be described as a human action figure. I was especially happy to see that he had made peace with the terrible loss of his girlfriend and the events that surrounded the incident. He was happy and smiling, joking around with Chad just like he used to.

Even Gina had beaten me there. She was standing over at the tree, pretending to admire the many decorations that hung from it. But I knew she was missing her mom, too. She usually flew out to see her for Christmas, but with everything that was happening at the school, she just couldn't manage it this year. When she saw me come in, she smiled with relief. I walked over to her and we hugged tentatively, unsure of how we should act in front of everyone.

"Oh, for Pete's sake just kiss her, Papi," Jessie commanded. "We all know you want to."

Gina and I looked each other, embarrassed by the attention. Then Ken appeared with and sprig of mistletoe and held it over us.

"Now you have to kiss," Chad called out. "You'll be breaking tradition if you don't."

So we gave each other quick peck on the lips just to shut them up. Ken shrugged at the lack of passion but didn't say anything. Jessie was not so easily satisfied.

"Don't tell me you guys are just giving each other quick little pecks on the cheek when you're spending the whole day at each other's houses," she said.

"What I do in the privacy of my own house is my..." *Crap, I just made it worse.*

"Ah-hah!" she shouted triumphantly, "I knew it!" She slapped her husband's leg and announced, "I win the pool!"

Gina, who I thought was unable to feel embarrassment, turned away, her hands covering her face. I was flabbergasted.

"My own daughter?" I said. "The fruit of my loins?"

"Hey, let's leave your loins out of this," Ken said. "There are ladies present."

I changed the subject. "Where's your mother? Ken told me he invited her and Ray, too."

"They went to uncle Manolo's house," she smiled. Tommy chuckled and looked over at me knowingly as she added, "She's having Ray meet the family."

"Oh, that poor guy," I groaned. "He'll be lucky to get out of that inspection without being put through a full physical."

"They're not that bad, Papi," she laughed.

"I beg to differ," I said. "You weren't around yet when I was put through the Baca family inquisition. For a while there, I thought they were going to make me drop my pants, grab my ankles and cough."

"OK," Chad mumbled. "Now I've lost my appetite."

"I'm not sure that's even possible," his mother retorted.

"I guess that's true," he conceded. And he proved her right when we sat down to the table by eating two helpings of everything.

After dinner we gathered at the Christmas tree to exchange gifts. It was fun having so many people to share this day with, and I could see that Gina was beginning to loosen up as well. When all of the presents were passed out Ken instructed us to each take turns opening our gifts so everyone could see what everyone else got. It seemed to take an eternity going from one person to another, applauding their prizes, joking around, teasing each other...and I loved every minute of it. I had always wondered what it would be like to have siblings and now that I knew, I didn't want it any other way.

Chapter Twenty-two

The bell on the door of the Little Creek Café jingled and Min looked up from serving a customer to see Tara Stone walk in. She had dressed herself in a blue wool turtleneck and jeans and her hair was neatly brushed. She walked to the counter and sat down, looking straight ahead. No one had seen her in three weeks; the school had placed her on administrative leave pending an evaluation and when she admitted being under a psychiatrist's care for seven years her contract was put up for review. Now she was venturing out, apparently.

"Hi, Min," she greeted her nervously, unsure of the reception she'd get. "How are you?"

"Better than I was a few weeks ago," Min replied with a half-smile. She, too, wasn't sure how to go about this reunion. "How was your Christmas?"

"Kind of fuzzy," Tara replied. "I'm still getting used to my medicine. How is Ken?"

"He's doing good," Min replied. "It's hard. But God is good and He's giving us strength."

"Yes," Tara nodded.

There was an awkward silence, each woman looking down, each uncomfortable with the other's presence yet not wanting to lose the connection.

"So, besides getting medicine, how have you been doing?" Min asked finally.

"Oh, I'm OK, considering," Tara shrugged. "I ruined my marriage, I'm about to lose my job…stop me when I've depressed you enough."

"But you still have your health," Min grinned. "That's what Ken always says."

"Oh, yeah," Tara smiled wanly. "That's right. You can tell him everything is going bad. You could even tell him your house burned down with everything you owned and he'll still say that. 'But you still have your health.'"

"Tara," Min covered her friend's hand with her own, "you kept a secret from your husband, and it came back to hurt you both. I'm going to pray for your marriage, but you'll have to work hard to make things right. It isn't going to be easy."

"I know," Tara said. "It's really up to Jimmy, if he'll forgive me."

She had hurt him very badly with Lonny. She knew she didn't deserve his forgiveness after that, but maybe he'll understand when she tells him it was part of the episode she was going through. Maybe he would listen to her, as long as

Gina wasn't around to get in the way. She was after him. No woman every gets that close to a man without there being some ulterior motive.

"I'll try." She grabbed Min's hands and squeezed them. "I'll give you a call sometime and I'll fix you dinner at my place, OK?"

"Sounds really good," Min smiled.

As Tara walked out the front door, Min shook her head at the prospect of Tara and Jimmy getting back together. If they did, it would never be like it was before.

***

Gina and I lay on top of my bed in the sweet afterglow of lovemaking that, for me, was diminished somewhat by the heavy weight of guilt. I had come home that afternoon to discover her in my bed, waiting for me. I'd been trying to psych myself into telling her we had to stop doing this, but the moment I saw her under my blankets, her bare shoulders peeking out from them, the speech I'd been rehearsing vanished from my mind.

Oh, I definitely enjoyed myself. The adolescent high school pervert in me was soaking up the feeling of Gina and her body and her energy. The more into it she got, the more I was able to keep going and the less I thought about anything but her and her beautiful, soft body. Then she made up this role-playing game that started to weird me out.

"Let's do something different this time," she said. "Let's pretend I'm your stepsister."

"My *stepsister?*"

"Yeah," she said wickedly. "It'll be fun. Listen. I'm your step-sister and our parents are in the next room sleeping, and I…"

"*What?*"

"…and I decide to sneak into bed with you."

You get the idea. It was very strange and I felt…well, kind of filthy. And while filthy can be fun during sex, when it's over, you're—or at least *I was*—left with a rather empty feeling that all that lovemaking was done for the sole purpose of satisfying a carnal itch. It really wasn't lovemaking but rather, plain old casual sex. And it really bothered me now as we were lying next to each other, Gina with a satisfied grin on her face and me with my eyes glued to the ceiling, wondering what the hell I was doing. I would have kicked myself if I had enough energy left to raise my leg. Just then the doorbell rang.

"Who the…" I looked through the curtains at the front porch and saw my wife standing there. *Oh, my God.*

"Who is it?" Gina asked, looking at my terror-stricken face.

"It's Tara," I whispered frantically.

"So what?" Gina laughed. "You're separated. It's none of her business what we do."

That was true. Tara had no say whatsoever in what I did. I relaxed a little and nodded, "You're right. It's none of her business."

"There you go," she said then she gave me a peck on the lips. "Now go out there and get rid of her then come back to bed." She swatted me as I got up and put my pants on.

I closed the bedroom door behind me and went and opened the front door. Tara was standing there, shyly fumbling with her fingers and not quite looking me in the eyes.

"Hi," she said. "Can I talk to you?"

"Actually…I can't talk right now. I'm kind of busy," I said. "But we can talk tomorrow if you're free."

"You're just trying to get rid of me," she said sadly. "I understand. I don't blame you. I hurt you."

"Yes, you did," I replied shortly. "But I don't want to discuss it now."

"Please let me in so we can talk," she pleaded. "I don't want the neighbors to hear us discuss our private business."

"I can't right now," I said, my patience wearing thin.

"Why not?"

"Hey Jimmy, I'm going to use your shower, OK?" Gina said from behind me. "Look at this. You got me all sweaty." I turned and saw her standing there, wrapped in the sheet from my bed, posing for Tara who was now peeking past me to see who was in my apartment.

"I knew it," Tara said, contempt dripping from her lips. "She's been sniffing around you all year. And now she shows off her tight little ass and you're jumping into bed with her!" She tried to push her way past me but I shoved her out.

"Where do you get off saying that crap?!" I demanded. "I walked into our home last month and found you in *our bed* with another man! Just a minute ago you wanted to talk about our marriage and even though you acknowledged hurting me, the words 'I'm sorry' were never spoken. Now you're pissed off because I'm with someone else? You hypocrite! Get the hell out of here and don't come back! *Ever!*"

"She's just using you!" Tara insisted.

"I know!" I snapped. "She told me. She was honest about it, unlike somebody else I know. Just get away from me... *Now!*"

"What are you going to do when she finds out you can't give her what she wants all time, huh?" She yelled.

"Get...!"

"And how is it you can do it with her, but you couldn't get it up…"

"Shut up!" I shouted. "And get out of here before I call the marshal to get you out of here!"

As I stood there yelling at my soon-to-be-ex-wife, the neighbors along the other side of the street were opening their doors and looking out their windows.

"And what the hell are you looking at?!" I shouted.

This prompted all but the nosiest to close their doors, but I knew this was going to make its way around town before morning. Tara threw her arms in the air in exasperation and walked away toward the main road, sobbing. A twinge of guilt plucked at my heart as I watched her. She came to make peace and I didn't accept the terms.

"Look, babe," Gina said, wrapping her arms around me from behind. "Let's go shower off and then you can drive me home. Sound good?"

"'Babe'?" I said, welcoming the change of subject. "So 'Bro' is replaced by 'Babe' is it?"

"Yeah, it did sound kind of weird calling you 'bro' while we were doing it," she admitted. "Although it seemed to turn *you* on. You're nastier than I thought," she teased, which made me turn red. "Babe is better, at least in the bedroom. Is that OK with you?"

"Sure," I replied. "Is that what 'friends with benefits' call each other?"

"I have no idea," she laughed. "This is the first time I've tried it."

If I can just control the horny, idiot teenager that's taken over my body, I thought, *I may be able to keep my friend when the benefits end.*

God, I'm way too old to be this stupid.

***

Pam stood in the middle of the library floor, gazing at the pallet-load of books to be catalogued and shelved, trying to mentally talk herself into getting started on them when she heard a knock at the door. She looked through the window next to the front door and saw that it was Gary, dressed in his street clothes.

"Can I talk to you?" he said from out on the front landing.

Pam gave a heavy sigh and opened the door. "I have a lot of work to do."

"I'll help you," he offered. "I really need to straighten things out with you."

"Is that, you need to clear the air with me, or you need to straighten me out?"

"I came to apologize," he said simply.

"Alright," she said. She gestured for him to enter and as he did she followed him, but left the door open.

"You're going to leave that open?" Gary asked. "It's cold outside."

"I don't want anybody thinking we're doing anything unseemly in here," she explained. "Now, what is it you have to tell me?"

"I'm sorry."

Pam stood and gazed into his eyes coldly, considering his words. After a few minutes of silence she reached out and took his hand and spoke gently, but still firmly.

"Gary, I came home to work on this library because I want to be with you. But I want to have a real relationship. I don't just want to be a 'booty call.'"

"You're not a booty call to me," he insisted. "I'm attracted to you. That's all. I want to get to know you better because I like you a lot."

"Gary," Pam shook her head and smile slightly. "How can you know you like me when we've hardly ever talked to each other for more than a few minutes? I'm very attracted to you, too, but that isn't the only thing I'm looking for in a guy. I want to be stimulated by you mentally as much as I am physically."

"I want the same things," Gary smiled. "Can we go out tonight, go see a movie in Flag, whatever?"

"Yes," she agreed. "*If* we get at least two of these pallets finished today. There are more on the way and I want to get things started so that when the Friends of the Library group comes in tomorrow all they'll have to do is scan them and log them."

"You got it."

Gary took a box cutter and sliced through the shrink wrap attached to the first pallet and peeled it away from the books then carried a stack over to the folding table nearby where Pam showed the procedure for prepping them to be shelved. As she worked the data entry on her laptop, he printed and attached the labels with the card catalog number to the books' spines. Then he went to get another stack. This routine was repeated several times until the monotony of it started to make Pam's mind wander. As Gary walked to the pallet for the ninth time she watched him from behind and when he leaned over to pick up another twelve books took him all in. When he turned to walk back she quickly returned her attention to the computer screen, but not before he saw her looking. He returned to the table and remained silent as they processed another stack, then another until they finished the first pallet. He looked at his watch and saw that three hours had passed since they began. He got up, went to the next pallet and unwrapped it, then walked over and closed and locked the door.

"What are you doing?" Pam asked nervously.

"Taking a break," Gary replied as he walked to her with a purposeful stride. "I'm going to kiss you and I don't want the world watching."

"But we agreed…"

"That we want to have a relationship that wasn't entirely based on physical attraction," he finished for her. "But since we already know that there is a physical attraction, why not enjoy some innocent expression of that?"

"'Innocent expression'? You mean you want to neck?"

"Yes."

"No," she said flatly. "I told you I would go out with you if we finished these books. That's *go out* not *make out.* I don't want to be in a position where I might do something I shouldn't. Now, please open the door."

Gary nodded silently. It was hard for Pam to tell whether he was disappointed or embarrassed. Probably a little of both. But he reopened the door as she requested, then went back to working on the pallets of books. A couple of hours of monotonous labor later, Pam stood up from her place at the computer.

"Well, it's 5:45 and it's almost dark out," she said. "Do you still want to take me out?"

"Of course," Gary laughed. "Did you think I changed my mind after you shot me down?"

"Well…"

"Pam, I really do want to get to know you," he insisted. "I don't have much self-control with you. It's hard for me to admit that because I've always prided myself on my self-control with everything else…"

"Maybe you have self-control with everything but girls," Pam suggested.

"Maybe," Gary allowed. "But with you I…I can't explain it. I just…"

"I'm safe," she said. "I'm not pretty like Gina. You don't have to worry that someone else will steal me away from you. You feel confident with me and it turns you on."

The hurt look on Gary's face made Pam want to kick herself. She had spoken out of her own insecurity and in the process she'd insulted him.

"I never thought of it like that," Gary mumbled, his gaze now at the far wall, "Thank you for telling me what was really going on in my mind." He walked silently to the door, walked out and closed it behind him.

Pam stood and watched him leave, without speaking a word. As the door closed her inner voice was screaming, *Stop him! Tell him you're sorry! Tell him you just said it because you're afraid of getting hurt again. Don't let him leave!* But she remained rooted to the spot, unable to speak or move. All she could do was watch as Gary Callan walked out of the building, taking her heart with him.

Chapter Twenty-three

"Tara, why don't you go home?" Pat McGrady asked. "You shouldn't be in here drinking at all, much less pounding down as much as you are."

She'd had four shots of whiskey and two beers and was working on her third brew with no sign of stopping until either she passed out or he threw her out.

"I don't want to go home," she mumbled. "There's nobody to go home to."

"You probably should have thought ahead before you fooled around with that Jarrett kid," Pat replied. "You're lucky Jimmy didn't kill you both. I would have."

"Don't lecture me," Tara said indignantly. "You run a bar. It's a place where people come to get drunk. Your job is to keep pouring the booze."

"My job is whatever I decide it is in *my bar*," Pat said, his gaze boring right into Tara. But she was too inebriated.

"Whatever," she shrugged dismissively. "Anyway, Jimmy and I are even, now."

"How is that?" Pat asked incredulously.

"He's been sleeping with somebody else," Tara growled. "The bastard gets all high and mighty about something I did and he turns around and does the same damn thing!"

"But it wasn't in your bed, though. Was it?" Pat shot back. "He's living in that apartment on the hill, by himself and away from you." He turned to serve another customer as he added, "And frankly, I hope to hell he stays there because the way you treated him…"

"He's screwing Gina Albright!" Tara shouted loud enough for the whole bar to hear.

"Good!" someone at the table behind her answered. "He needs somebody that'll treat him right for a change."

"What did you say?" Tara asked, challenging the man. She turned and took a close look at him. It was Todd Webb, the mechanic.

"Hey, aren't you the town drunk?" she said with a smirk.

"Yep," Todd replied unperturbed, "But it looks like you're about to take that title away from me."

"What did you say to me?" Tara demanded. She wiggled down from her stool with some difficulty, swayed her way over to the old man then she grabbed his shirt and pulled at him.

"Let go, Tara," Todd said patiently. "You need to go home and sleep this off."

"I'll decide when I'm ready to go home," she said. She pulled her hand back, getting ready to slap him, but Pat McGrady grabbed her wrist, spun her around, planted his foot on her backside and shoved her toward the door.

"You're cut off, Tara," he said firmly. "Get your butt out of my bar and don't come back 'til next week."

"You don't understand," Tara insisted, her words barely intelligible. "I went to his house to make up with him and *she* was there! She was…"

"Looks like Jimmy traded up!" shouted somebody at the other end of the room. This brought a round of loud laughter.

Tara started climbing onto a chair and threw her middle finger up. "Hey, fu—"

"Get out of my bar!" Pat shouted. "Or do I have to call the marshal to get you out of here?"

Tara stepped back down onto the floor, turned and staggered out the door. She managed, miraculously to walk the five blocks to her house, stumbling only once. She fumbled around in her purse and found her keys then, after considerable time and effort she managed to get the front door open. As soon as she slammed the door behind her, she passed out on the carpet.

Later that night, Tara awoke from a deep sleep, feeling as if she'd been run through a washing machine and hung out on a clothes line. Her head hurt, her mouth was so dry her tongue stuck to the roof of her mouth and her eyes blurred from the goo that had built up during her sleep. She sat up from her place on the living room floor and rubbed her eyes until the they started to clear then laid back down and rested until her head quit throbbing just enough for her to be able to carefully sit up. It was dark. She didn't remember where or when she fell asleep but she did vaguely remember raising hell at Old Smokie's. She looked at her watched. The luminous dial read five a.m. An hour and a half before sun-up. She needed to rest some more, then later she could go and apologize to Pat. As far as Jimmy was concerned...

There she was lost. She didn't really want him back after he'd been with someone else, but the idea of Gina taking him away from her really burned.

Oh well, she thought. *I can't do anything about it now. Might as well go to bed.* She got up with some difficulty and wobbled her way to the wall, letting the light from the street light outside guide her down the hall to her room. She walked into the room, sat on the bed and peeled her hose off then crawled under the cold, scratchy covers and slept.

***

Pam walked in the front door to her home and found her father sitting at the kitchen table, grading papers. Harold looked up from his work and regarded his daughter with some concern.

"I was expecting you home a lot later," he said

"I know," Pam said. She was troubled for some reason and her father stood up and held his arms open. Pam took the hint. She let her dad hold her as she told him of the night's disappointment.

"I can't believe I said what I did," she sobbed.

"It couldn't have been that bad," he said.

"It was."

Pam repeated exactly how her last conversation with Gary went. When she finished, her father shook his head sadly.

"Sweetheart, you must have really hurt him."

"I know."

"What made you say such a thing? Why would you think it?"

"I don't know, Dad," she sighed. "I waited all this time for a chance to be with him and…" she shrugged. "You should have seen the way he looked at me. It was like I'd slapped him in the face."

"In a way, you did," he said. "Pammy, you need to make this right, whether you decide to go out with him or not. Then, you should take some time and try to figure out why you said what you did. Although I have my suspicions."

"Sam?"

"Probably," Harold said. "You were so in love with Sam, then just a few weeks before your wedding he tells you he's gay. That would make a lot of people very shy about getting involved again."

"Yeah," she nodded. "Maybe. The thing about Sam was that he never would have told me if I hadn't made him say it. He was so afraid of hurting me that he was going to marry me anyway, even though he would have been miserable."

"He loved you very much. He may still. Sexual attraction is only one part of a relationship, Pammy. This world we live in places too much importance in the physical, when it's the heart and the mind that really last." Harold looked toward the front window as if he were able to see through the thick draperies that were now closed for the night. "Your mother and I made love many, many times over the course of our marriage." He patted Pam's leg when he saw the look of disgust on her face. "I know, 'TMI'. But you see, as often as we made love, I really can't remember any particular one of those times. They were sweet, wonderful, they felt great. But the things that I loved about your mom—and remember like they were yesterday—are the everyday things that we did *outside* the bedroom. The things she did with you and Doris when you were kids, the way she would actually listen to my stories about the kids in class, how she would always dress up for Halloween and go trick or treating along with you; I loved the way her face sort of glowed in the evening sun. I miss your mom so very much, sweetheart, not because of the sex. I miss *her*. She was the most wonderful thing to ever happen to me.

"Sam was going to be your husband. You had a beautiful relationship that neither of you would have ended if you hadn't seen the one thing that doomed your future. I think that deep inside, you want what you had with Sam. But Gary is a different person, with his own virtues and vices. He's a good man who shows respect to everyone and that is hard to find nowadays. But the one thing that makes me think that he's the man you've been looking for, is the way I see him look at you; like you're the prize of a lifetime." He brought his hand up and lightly stroked her cheek. "And you are. I wouldn't be so sure about him if I hadn't seen that look in his eyes."

"He may not have that look anymore, after what I said."

"He's hurt," he shrugged. "Go to him and tell him that you're sorry. Tell him how you feel. It'll get you two talking."

"I suppose."

"That's what you want, isn't it? Real conversation? Well, here's your chance. Just be sure to apologize *without making excuses*."

"You mean, now? It's eight o'clock at night."

"Now," Harold said firmly. "Don't let him go to sleep feeling like a heel."

"What if he says he doesn't want to see me again?"

"Then go back again tomorrow. Then the next day, then the next until he listens to you. This is about *his* feelings, not yours."

"You're right," she said. "I deserve to be chewed out."

"I doubt he'll do that," Harold smiled. "But remember one thing: Make-up sex is for *after* you're married."

"Oh, Daddy."

"Don't 'Oh, Daddy' me. You two don't have the best track record for restraint. Just keep your heart open and your legs closed."

Pam stared, open-mouthed at her father who simply took her by the arm and guided her out the front door.

***

Tara was awakened by a bright light shining in her face, so intense she felt it as well as sensed its brightness through her eyelids. She opened her eyes and squinted. It was the sun, reflecting off of something on her dresser. She rolled over and was assaulted by the light shining through the bedroom window. *What's going on?* She thought as her mind began to clear. *I don't have a window on this side of the...*

She opened her eyes and saw that she was not in her own bed. Nor was she in her own home. She sat up, anxiety taking hold of her as she tried to orient herself to her surroundings. The walls of the room were a bright yellow, unlike the light blue in all the bedrooms in her place. On the walls were family portraits of complete strangers. On the dresser from which came the bright light was a silver-framed wedding picture at least forty years old from the looks of the hairstyles and clothes. The subjects of the portrait looked familiar. She slid out of bed and went to the dresser to get a closer look. *The Nielsens? Oh God! How did I get here?* She looked up at her reflection in the mirror and screamed at the sight. Her clothes, arms and neck were covered in dried blood.

***

Ray Brandt was not at all comfortable with this kind of call. He'd responded to many like it when he was a Maricopa County Deputy and no two were alike; but each and every one had the potential to be deadly. The caller said she was a neighbor of the Nielsens and she heard some kind of argument going on in the house, then she heard someone scream. She wouldn't give her name for fear the Nielsens might find out, but all calls to the Marshal's Office were automatically traced, so it took only a few seconds for Ray to see that it was Beatrice Cort, who lived next to the Nielsens. He parked the patrol car two houses down so he could watch the windows and outer parts of the house until Cindy arrived to back him up. He only had to wait three minutes for her patrol car to pull up behind his.

"This is an unusual call," she remarked.

"Yeah, it is," Ray nodded.

They walked around the house to the back fence and looked over it—no one. Ray walked to the front door while Cindy stepped back to keep a full view of the front, her hand on her weapon. Ray looked into the living room through the window as he passed. There were two figures on the floor but it was too dim inside to make out who they were or what their condition was. At his signal Cindy went to the wall next to the window and drew her handgun. Ray radioed

Sheriff's Office dispatch and advised them of his status and that he was knocking on the front door now. He started softly but when no one opened up he knocked harder, calling out to Ted and Deanne, but still no answer came. He radioed S.O. dispatch again.

"I see blood on their clothes, Ray," Cindy said as she shone her flashlight through the window.

"There are people on the floor in there and there's no answer. We're going in."

"Ten-four, Paul One."

Cindy went to the opposite side of the door from Ray and brought her gun up as Ray stepped back and drove his heel into the door just above the knob, sending it swinging open as the lock broke free of the door frame with a loud cracking sound. As Cindy stepped through the door and began scanning the room Ray walked over to the two on the floor, his weapon drawn, and began to check for vital signs on the people, but straightened up and cursed when he saw who they were.

"*Dammit!* Just what I was afraid of," he spat. "It's the homeowners," he advised dispatch. "They've been worked over; butchered."

They headed carefully down the hallway and checked each of the four rooms starting with the bathroom. There the sink and vanity were stained with the orange-pink traces of washed-off blood. Cindy noticed a few medium lengths of hair in the drain. She pulled back the shower curtain and saw evidence that someone had showered blood off of their body.

The kitchen and dining room were cleared in a moment. Ray moved to the first bedroom. No sign of anyone; no readily noticeable signs of struggle. A check of the master bath had the same result. He repeated the process for the second room and came up empty. The third and final room in the house brought a macabre surprise. The bed linens, strewn on the floor, were stained with bits of blood and a trail of bloody clothes stretched across the floor, ending at the closet. He stepped back into the hall and using the wall as cover he looked through the doorway into the room. Cindy moved to a backup position behind him.

"Whoever is in the closet," he called, "come out, showing me your empty hands first."

"Do you hear me?" he said after a long silence. He walked over to the door, stood at the doorframe and lean over to open the door. He counted off mentally with his weapon at the ready as Cindy kept her gun trained on the closet door; three...two...one—he yanked the folding door open and discovered, to his shock, Tara Stone in her underwear, balled up with her knees against her chest, her eyes wide with terror and staring through him. She was trembling and her skin was white as paper.

"Dispatch, we have a live 101 in the back bedroom," Ray said into his radio. "She appears to be in shock. I need an ambulance right away."

The sight of Tara sent a chill through his body.

This can't be happening.

***

As Jason Hadley awoke from a restful sleep, he lay in his bed looking up at the beams in the ceiling and allowed his mind to drift. This really was a beautiful town. Not the best-planned one—the main part of it was in the middle of a meadow surrounded by ridges and small hills so the spring run-off was likely a problem—but the setting was perfect; especially where his place sat. The beautiful view of Graham's Alpaca Ranch, with its dense stand of quaking aspens bordering it on the west and the stream running through the center of the meadow, was well worth the price he paid for the house, let alone the seemingly endless, rolling hills covered in tall Ponderosa pine forest. He got up out of bed, took his robe from the closet and put it on. Today, he decided, was going to be a relaxing one, sitting on the porch and watching the clouds float by while he went over the files on the three computers he'd taken from Brent Carval. He needed a day of inactivity considering the busy week he'd had. He wasn't young anymore and even taking on amateurs like Brent and his friends wore him out now. Then again, he was going to be seventy years old in a few months. The body can only do so much at his age.

Gadgets, he thought. Nowadays, if you don't have some proficiency with gadgets you're in trouble. Fortunately, there was a wide array of them that didn't take much training to use. *Poor Brent,* he thought. *He really believed he had everything covered and that no one could break through his firewalls or decipher his codes. He really needed some real-world experience before going into business for himself.*

Tomorrow he needed to follow up on any leads he found in these files, and hopefully he'd find and remove whoever had paid Brent and his crew to do the café shooting. Fortunately, it was generally believed to be racially motivated, so that kept Ray out of his hair.

Ken is a very good man, he thought. *I hate to see him and Min going through this, thinking they're not safe here. I'll have to find some way of putting their minds at ease when this is all over.* This was his town now. God had placed him here to live out his final years and he was going to make sure that when He took him to his reward, Summertown would be even better than when he arrived.

It's the perfect place, he thought to himself. *I can fulfill my promise to Herb, build my hotel and still be available for anything I'm called to do. Yes, God really does give us exactly what we need if we remain patient and obedient...even when obedience is hard.*

The vision of Tara, laying in in the middle of the Nielsens' living room, flashed across his mind's eye. He squeezed his eyes shut and shook his head and said aloud, "Stop!"

It was God's will, no doubt about it. And feeling remorse for doing His will is tantamount to blasphemy. So, stop feeling sorry for people that were meant to be removed from this world, and get on with your work. There's too much to be done for you to be dwelling on things that should be forgotten.

Chapter Twenty-four

Reno drove up the I-17 in the black of night. There were no street lights and he felt almost insulated from the world; encapsulated within this car that he had stolen from the parking lot of a grocery store in the central part of Phoenix. He didn't know what kind of contacts Hadley had in Arizona, so he took pains not to leave a paper trail like rental documents or credit card transactions to give him any warning of his arrival. He drove along at the posted speed limit, watching rather detachedly for police. He estimated a two hour drive to Flagstaff, then straight to Summertown. He looked in his rearview mirror and saw that the same pickup truck was following him that had gotten on the highway thirty minutes ago. It might have been a coincidence, as this was an interstate highway with thousands of cars traveling on it daily. But he couldn't afford to take a chance. He pulled off at the nearest exit and headed west on Pioneer Road. He passed the entrance to the Pioneer Living History Museum with the pickup following in the distance. He picked up speed, looking for the next gathering of buildings or houses, knowing that whoever was following him wouldn't make any foolish moves until he was out on the open road and away from any witnesses. He eventually reached Anthem Way where he managed to get back onto the highway and head north again. The truck was, of course, right behind him so he decided to make the first move. He braked hard and yanked the wheel to the left, sending the sedan into a sideways skid that became a wide, arcing turn when he punched the gas again and drove across a turnabout intended for police vehicles. He hit the brakes then punched the gas once more as he turned onto the highway going the opposite direction. The pickup kept going northbound without even slowing down. He kept driving until he came to the next exit a few miles down the road, then he waited until the very last second before he suddenly veered off down the ramp. He blew past a stop sign and once more took two hair-raising left turns that took him right back onto the highway going northbound. A highway patrol vehicle turned on its light bar and blew its siren and after a moment's consideration, he decided to pull to the side. As the trooper walked slowly up to his passenger-side window, hand on weapon, flashlight shining through the back window, Reno saw that it was a young female and she was very nervous. *She probably called for backup,* he thought. *She should have waited for them before approaching me.* Just as this thought was occurring to him the pickup that had been tailing him sped up to them and stopped just short of the patrol car. It was too dark to see anything past the glare of the headlights until the bright flash of multiple gunshots lit up the spot just to the right of the vehicle. The officer arched her back and screamed then fell forward onto the road and lay motionless. Reno wasted no time in slamming the car into reverse, turning the wheel toward the road and flooring the accelerator as bullets gutted the right side of his car. The shooters were already in motion and didn't have time to avoid his car before he shifted into drive and t-boned them, catching the driver's-side door and ramming the wheel man into the gunner of the team. Reno could see the driver's head whip out the window and hang there as the effects of whiplash kept him from recovering. Reno shifted into drive, revving the car to keep it from stalling, then he slammed the shifter into reverse and rammed the truck once more, this time keeping his foot on the gas when he saw that he had broken the vehicle's inertia and was pushing them over onto the shoulder, sending the attackers' pickup rolling sideways down the berm. When it finally came to rest it was upside down and the weight of the fall had crushed the roof. Reno jumped out of his car, ran down the steep slope where the truck lay and searched as fast as he could for a weapon. After sweeping the ground about halfway around the car, his foot struck something hard. The weapon the killer used; an AK-47 from the feel of it, and the magazine was still attached. He left it where he found it so that law enforcement wouldn't tie him to the killing of the trooper. Then he went about the grisly business of searching the mangled bodies for anything he could use.

Three minutes later he took a side trail away from the road, now equipped with a Glock .45 automatic, a Smith & Wesson .357 revolver, a small, high-intensity flashlight and the ID from the gunner, whose photo was just blurry enough to allow him to use it as his own if necessary. It was a slow trek, walking on as much rock as possible to avoid leaving too many footprints for the police to follow; and they would certainly follow, with one of their own down. He was only two miles across the desert when he heard the sirens in the distance. He decided that he couldn't afford to be careful anymore, so he broke out in a steady run until he found a ranch about four miles to the northwest. There he stole an old pickup truck and drove up the interstate a few more miles, stole a different car at Rock Springs and hauled it down the nearest side road until he found an on-ramp to the I-17. By the time the story hit the news he was in Camp Verde where he spent thirty three minutes hiding his vehicle then finding and stealing another car. He didn't have time to be evasive anymore. They knew where he was and where he was headed. So he drove straight toward Summertown, constantly checking his mirrors and cradling the revolver in his lap.

***

Gina and I sat on the couch together, quietly watching television but neither of us were paying much attention to the show. Gina was laying back with her legs in my lap and taking glances in my direction when she finally spoke.

"How are you feeling?" Gina asked.

"Guilty still...of course," I said. "I know it isn't my fault, but that doesn't keep me from feeling responsible for how things turned out."

"Jimmy, you know that you had nothing to do with Tara doing what she did," Gina insisted. She sat up then and reached over and started rubbing my neck. "It's one thing to go get drunk after you find your ex with somebody else, but to do what she did to Orin and Deanna?" she shivered at the thought. "They haven't told anybody exactly what she did to them, so you know it must have been horrible."

"I still can't believe she did it."

The very idea that Tara was capable of killing would never have entered my mind. But there was no doubt that she had done it.

"Why don't you come over to my place? Maybe stay the night?" Gina asked sweetly. "You could use a change of scenery and I'd love to wake up next to you in the morning."

"Well…"

"Just to sleep, Jimmy," she said. "It'd be nice to sleep next to you."

"OK. I really don't want to be alone."

"Don't worry," she said, patting my leg comfortingly. "I'll sing you to sleep and you'll have sweet dreams, and forget all about that icky stuff out there."

"Promise?" I asked, only half-joking.

She reached over and ran her fingers softly through my hair.

"I promise," she smiled and looked at me with—how do I describe it—devotion? Or something like it. At that moment I knew we had somehow passed from "friends with benefits" to something deeper. It felt good, and yet I still felt that it was short-lived. I didn't even know if I was really cut out for a quiet, domestic life anymore. God knows I wasn't any good at it.

***

Reno had made it to Flagstaff as the sun was coming up. He had taken the time to pull off the road, into the brush outside Munds Park and take a three-hour nap because he knew if he didn't rest he would be useless if he ran into any more of TiZo's thugs. Or were they Jason's? He wasn't sure at this point who was after him but he knew he didn't stand a chance without sleep. Now, very much in need of a big cup of coffee and some breakfast, he stopped at the Denny's at the south end of town. As he pulled into the parking lot, he made note of a black, four wheel drive Dodge Ram with Arizona plates that had been driving behind him since it got on the highway about ten miles back. It was the kind of car used by many people in Flagstaff with its heavy snows in winter and rugged terrain in summer. It was so obviously a non-descript vehicle that his inner radar immediately alerted him. *I'll just have to keep going,* he decided. *I'll go straight to that café I read was there and ask for him. He's bound to be known around such a small place.*

He pulled out onto Milton and headed to the next traffic light and prepared to make a U-turn, go down to Lake Mary Road and head to Summertown as fast as he could without drawing attention from state patrolmen. He looked in his rearview mirror and saw the black Ram pull up to his bumper; or trunk to be more precise. Their motor was loud and intimidating and the driver revved it up over and again.

When he turned, he turned as tight as the old Impala would go but that pickup was obviously modified for off-road and it stayed with him. *Easy,* he told himself. *Keep calm and don't do anything until you get down the road a bit. Your chance will come.*

He drove on until he saw the sign for Marshall Lake, a marshy grassland that only filled with water in very rainy seasons. He recalled looking at a map of the area and seeing that the road to this lake had a sharp, hairpin turn. He turned left onto the road, then followed it to the right. He saw the switchback coming and started to slow for it. *Don't stop, old girl,* he said to the car, patting the dashboard. *We're almost there. A few more minutes and I'll give you a little rest.* He spoke too soon. The black Dodge Ram suddenly appeared behind him and before he could take evasive action it rear-ended the Impala with such force that Reno was thrust hard into his seat and his head struck the headrest and bounced. He was stunned briefly and by the time he could clear his head the Ram was right beside him, driving its front right bumper into the front left quarter panel on Reno's car, forcing him off the road. He had only a split second to cross his arms over his face and brace himself against the steering wheel before he struck one of the roadside posts, which brought the car to a dead stop. His head throbbing painfully and his wrists strained from cushioning the impact, he reach down and fumbled for the .45 automatic that had fallen. He looked in the side mirror. The truck stopped at an angle behind him and two tall figures got out carrying what looked like shotguns. As one of the men walked up the driver's side of the car the other began to round the rear corner to go up the passenger side, pinning him in the car where they could blast away until he was nothing but a big lump of raw meat. Reno lunged to the right, threw the passenger door open and fired his pistol at the first thing that appeared. The bullet struck the side of the shotgun's barrel and ricocheted into the air; the force of the impact knocked the weapon out of line long enough for Reno to throw himself out the door, roll over then fire two more rounds. The first missed by a mile but the other hit his assailant in the center of his chest, dropping him instantly. Before he could get on his feet, the second attacker fired through the driver's side window, sending pellets and glass everywhere; some striking Reno in his right side and back. As excruciating as the wound was, Reno knew he had to move now or be killed. He dropped to the ground alongside the car and laid as flat as he could, then he took aim at the ankles of the gunman who was now rushing to head him off at the back of the vehicle. A shot into each leg brought a yelp of pain and caused the man to tumble forward onto the ground on the other side of the car. The killer tried to bring his shotgun to bear on his enemy but Reno's gun was already firing. The gunman thought hiding behind the rear wheel would at least protect his vital organs, but every bullet Reno fired sliced through the sidewalls and found their marks. Before the tire flattened, his enemy had been hit three times.

He got up, walked carefully around the front of the car and slowly headed toward the killer. The vacant, open eyes of the man and the pool of bright-red arterial blood, some of which had sprayed heavily onto the side of the car, told him all he needed to know but he advanced with weapon ready anyway. A check of the man's pulse confirmed that he was dead.

No good wasting a good truck, he told himself. He took only enough time to wipe all surfaces he had come in contact with inside the car, then he jumped into the truck and headed back onto the highway and on to Summertown. As he passed the south shore of Upper Lake Mary a police cruiser with lights flashing sped around the bend and rocketed past him. He had almost no time left, he knew. They were probably responding to a call from someone about shots fired in the area. Fortunately the place was obscured by a thick stand of trees on one side and the topside of a mesa on the other. In the unlikely case that there were witnesses, they would be too far away to offer a physical description. But the tire tracks would tell them that it was a pickup truck, and they'd probably think back on the one that passed them on Lake Mary Road. He had to get rid of this truck as soon as possible.

Reno drove as far as he dared, then pulled off the road and followed a narrow forest path as far east as it took him. When it ended he found himself facing a natural embankment of dirt and granite among a dense stand of pine and aspen trees. If he was lucky this spot would prevent anyone from seeing the truck until he was well away from here and headed toward Summertown.

He parked as close to the embankment as possible, making sure that he was directly under the trees to keep from being easily spot by aerial search crews. Then he wiped every surface he could find. The one thing he couldn't clean was the deep-red stains on the upper part of the driver's seat where he had bled. But that couldn't be helped. By now, they had certainly found the car and the bodies and probably figured out that he was wounded. He had to get out of here and find Jimmy Stone as fast as he could without being seen, even if he had to trek through these hills on foot—which it looked like he was going to have to do.

***

After spending most of the day looking, Jason found the file he was searching for, complete and only minimally encrypted. After having broken Brent's password protection Jason was able to find the encryption key and read the contents. It was a very short spreadsheet file, intended to grow much larger with time, which listed the name and contact information of each client as well as the target's name and all pertinent information needed for the completion of each job. There was only one job listed and as he had suspected, he was the target. The client was anonymous, of course—what kind of fool would give their real name when hiring an assassin—but there was a chat room address listed in the contacts field, as well as a drop location for picking up cash payment. The date for pickup was only a few days ago which, to Jason, meant that the client lived a distance away, probably overseas; it takes time to send cash from a long distance, especially if you're doing it surreptitiously. He found the cash in the antique safe that stood in the corner of what served as an office. The door of the safe was still slightly ajar, which said something about the lazy-mindedness of the owner. Ten stacks of $20 bills, twenty bills in each stack, were neatly arranged along the bottom shelf. An array of jump drives hung from key hooks on the inside door of the safe, each with a small label.

Brent, for all his inexperience and overconfidence, had taken the clever precaution of hiring David Corbett to kill Ken Shirazi, equipping him with the exact model of gun that his friend had used to do the actual job. Brent even supplied the ammo Corbett used...or more accurately, *tried* to use. The cartridges were loaded with wax-core, copper jacketed bullets. This made it look like the real thing and allowed the cartridge to eject after firing, but the wax melted before it even left the barrel while the thin jacket probably made it as far and the road before falling to the ground. This was why there was no evidence to refute the belief that Corbett was the shooter. There were no instructions given as far as escape routes, so it was simply Corbett's stupidity that caused him to run across an open field where he was spotted and ultimately killed.

It was an open and shut case as far as the police were concerned, which made it that much easier for Jason to conduct his search for the person who had paid for the hit. If he hadn't spent that little bit extra on the services of a top hacker, he wouldn't have been able to get to Corbett's place before the Sheriff's detectives, and he wouldn't have gotten the notepad that held all of the contact instructions that Carval had given him. *It just goes to show,* he thought, *that if you want the best chance of success, you pay for the best help.*

As he read the next line in Brent's notes Jason spotted something that rang a bell. The ID that his client gave on the Tor network was HRooster92. The first thing he needed to do was get some help tracking down the owner of this ID because the Tor system was way out of his league.

It was time to listen to the recording he made of his interview of Brent Carval. He had been avoiding it; it was an aspect of his profession that he detested. He hated making another person suffer. He had no qualms about killing as long as it was justified but torture, though a necessary evil in some situations, made him ill. The muffled screams, the blubbering, moaning, and muttering through the agony was often unintelligible at the time, so he learned to record the sessions and listen to them later, after he'd gotten everything he could from his prospect. And in this case, although it took very little time to get Carval to talk, what he said was so hard to understand that he knew he would have to play the recording several times to get everything.

Chapter Twenty-five

I awoke to the sound of Foreigner's "Hot Blooded" at a volume too high for human safety. Before they got to "Check it and see", a slender white arm shot out and slapped the snooze button on the alarm clock, bringing blessed silence back to the room. I reached over and touched the face of the lovely young woman lying next to me, cupping her cheek in my palm and feeling the softness of her skin. The squareness of her jawline and the cleft in her chin complimented the shape of her small, almost pixyish nose and when she opened her clear blue eyes she seemed to look right into my heart. I was falling. I wasn't just the victim of a lustful crush, I was actually falling for this girl and it made me giddy with joy and scared to death at the same time.

"Good morning," she whispered. She grinned warmly and reached her arm around my chest, then laid her head on my shoulder. "Did you sleep OK?"

"Oh, yes," I smiled. "The best I've slept in a long time."

"See? We don't have to have sex to have a good time together."

That made me laugh.

269

"What's so funny about that?" she demanded.

"I've always had a great time with you. Long before we ever started sleeping together I enjoyed just…being with you."

"I know," she said. "But things are different now."

"Yeah," I agreed. "Sex does change things. No matter how hard you try, you can't stop that from happening."

"Does that mean you regret it? Do you want things the way they were before?"

I looked into her eyes again as she stared up at me, nervously waiting for my answer. This was yet another opportunity to stop doing what I knew was wrong. Even if it hurt her, I knew that ending our affair was best for both of us in the long run.

But when I finally spoke I said, "Of course not. Are you kidding me? I'm crazy about you."

It was true, but I knew it was the wrong thing to say. I should have told her that as much as it hurt us both, I needed to stop this. I should have reminded her that I was still legally married and had no right to be in another relationship until my divorce was final. But I didn't have the guts. The very idea of hurting Gina in any way was unthinkable. Her warmth, her loving affection filled me with a joy I'd forgotten existed. I couldn't be without her. She'd become too much a part of me.

"I love you," I said before I could stop myself.

Her eyes opened wide, her mouth opened but no sound came out. She sat up in bed and stared at me as if I'd just said I was from another planet. She stayed that way for what seemed a long time, then she leaned over me and looked me squarely in the face.

"Say that again," she commanded. "And look me in the eyes when you say it."

"I'm in love with you, Gina," I said matching her gaze. "It doesn't matter how you feel about me, I love you. I just had to say it. It's the truth."

I had barely finished the sentence before she kissed me so hard my mouth started to go numb. She held me there, lying under her, our lips practically welded together. She finally released me, but only long enough to wrap her arms, legs and neck around me as much as she physically could, then she started laughing.

"I love you so much, Jimmy Stone. I fell in love with you a long time ago, I just didn't want to admit it to myself. I didn't want to get hurt again."

My heart swelled inside my chest. In my mind there was music playing, more beautiful than I ever imagined. I was ecstatic. Then the alarm clock went off again, this time playing some Weird Al Yankovic song. Gina reached over, grabbed the offending instrument and yanked it off the nightstand, disconnecting the plug at the same time. Then she chucked it across the room until it smashed to pieces against the far wall. She turned to me, smiling sweetly as if the sudden, violent act never happened.

"I have to get ready for work," she said. "You can stay here and sleep if you want, and be waiting for me when I come home."

"Like a 'kept man'?" I gasped.

"Like a *sex slave*," she said in that awful Russian accent.

"Like a slave of love," I corrected in the same dialect.

"Mm. Your accent turns me on," she purred. "Where'd you learn to do that?"

"My mom."

"OK, that killed the mood."

"No, really," I laughed. "She was Ukrainian. I am too, actually. I was born there."

"You never mentioned that before."

"Well, I really don't remember much of it. She brought me to the States when I was seven."

"Was your dad Ukrainian or American?"

"American."

"Are they still alive?"

"My mom passed away about ten years ago, in an assisted-living place in Sun City. I have no idea whether my father is still alive or not. I haven't seen him since they divorced."

"He never tried to keep in touch?"

"Nope," I said as unaffected as I could. "The last memory I have of him, he walked right past me as he was leaving the courtroom. He didn't even look at me."

"Wow," she said. "That's cold."

"Yeah, well, I'm over it," I said. "My mother was more than enough for me and I don't have any complaints."

"C'mon, babe," she smiled sympathetically. "Anybody who goes through that is likely to feel abandoned. It's not like your dad died. He left you." Then she added, "Mine didn't even acknowledge me as his daughter until I forced it on him."

"Forced it? What, did you tie him up in your basement until he signed your birth certificate?"

"Almost."

I hesitated a bit before asking, "What do you mean, 'almost'?"

"My mom was sixteen when she met him. She cleaned offices in the building where he was vice president of some marketing company. I don't know how they met, I just know he seduced her and when she told him she was pregnant he threatened to kill her if she ever told anybody."

"Married?"

"With two sons."

"Scumbag."

"Asshole."

"So how did you force him to acknowledge you?" I asked.

"I looked him up. He lived on the lake in a fancy house. When I told him who I was, he threatened me just like he did my mom. Thing is," she grinned wryly, "I'm not like my mom."

"What did you do?"

"Well, first, I tried to get my mom to charge him with statutory rape, but she wouldn't. Then, I found out that there was a statute of limitations for that and it had already run out. But I looked around and found a lawyer who took the case on contingency when I told her my story. To make a long story short, we won. He had to pay back child support equal to what he'd spent on his boys, and since they were adults by then he had to pay big."

"Wow."

"Yeah. His wife left him about halfway through the trial and filed for divorce."

"That probably ruined him."

"I hope so," she said gaily. "After we got that fat check, we moved to Champaign where I got my teaching degree. I never went back."

"You're a tough little thing, aren't you?" I said.

"You got that right," she smiled. "So are you, Jimmy. You lived your whole life knowing your dad didn't want you, yet you don't seem bitter."

"I was, growing up," I admitted. "I got in a lot of fights at school, especially with groups like the Junior ROTC guys and the Boy Scouts."

"You?" she laughed. "Baby, you *are* a Boy Scout!"

"I wasn't then," I said. "I didn't join any gangs or do drugs or anything like that, but I just couldn't stand the Scouts. Back then I called them Hitler Youth."

"Now, that is *wrong*," she scolded, which would have been more effective if she weren't giggling at the same time.

"I know. They bugged me because most of them had dads who went on the outings and did the projects with them. Then everybody would get together for special dinners where they handed out little feathers and badges when the kids did crap like learning to sharpen a knife. Hell, I learned to use a knife when I was eight."

"Eight!?"

"Long story."

She waited for me to say more. When I didn't, she said, "You were jealous."

I just shrugged and nodded my head. "I didn't appreciate my mom, or realize that I really didn't need my father, until I got to high school," I said.

"What happened there? Were you visited by an angel or something?"

"You joke, but angels are real," I replied. The skeptical look on her face told me we had a lot to talk about as far as our beliefs were concerned. "But no, he wasn't an angel. He was leader of the Newman Club at Sunnyslope High. I was a freshman. He was a lay minister at St. Jerome Parish."

"He was a father figure?"

"Actually, no. He never let me get attached that way. He was maybe thirty-five, I think, and he always acted like everybody's big brother."

"So how did he help you get over your anger with your dad?"

"By being a big brother," I said simply. "By reminding me that God had provided me with a parent who loved me and who had been taking good care of me. And that was enough."

"No lightning bolts, no voices from the sky…"

"Nothing but a guy who I respected showing me *I* was worthy of respect, and that it was my mother who deserved the credit for that. He listened to me when I needed someone to talk to."

Gina laughed and shook her head. "Your teen years sound like a Hallmark Movie."

"Not quite," I said.

"I'm sorry," she said contritely. "I don't mean to make fun."

"No?" I bristled.

"No, really. It's just that I lived in hell for the first half of my life and had to fight for everything I ever got. My mom was always afraid to stand up to anybody because she didn't want me to get hurt. It sounds like your mom was a hard-ass. You never needed to protect yourself, your mom took care of you."

"I was just a wimpy little kid who ran to my mommy whenever I had a problem, is that it?"

"I didn't say you're a wimp, Jimmy," she laughed. "I wouldn't be with you if I thought that. I know it was hard growing up without a father. And I'm glad you learned to let it go. I just grew up in a tougher world."

"Maybe," I conceded. "Anyway, that's all in the past."

"I don't think so," she said warily. "I struck a nerve, didn't I?"

"Don't worry about it."

"Don't be like that," she said, laying her head against my neck and stroking my back. "Tell me what it was like growing up with your mom."

"This isn't a counseling session, Gina," I said coldly. "You wouldn't believe me if I told you what I had to do when I was a kid. But that has nothing to do with who I am now."

"Don't close off from me, please," she begged.

I hesitated. This was something I never told anyone before. But she wanted to hear it, and if she couldn't handle the truth, then…

"OK," I said. "I'll tell you why I never talk about my childhood. My mother took me here to the States after she divorced my father in Ukraine. He was some kind of CIA guy who couldn't keep his pants on. As far back as I can remember, she was always afraid he would try to kidnap me and take me back to wherever he was working, just to spite her. So, she signed me up for karate lessons, boxing lessons, judo lessons, she had me go out for track at school so I could out-run whoever might try to snatch me. At one point, she had me spend my after-school time with some old Russian man she'd found who taught me how to spot when somebody was following me. And then I got *more* self-defense lessons from him—*Systema*, he called it. I spent most of my childhood learning to avoid being kidnapped, or learning how to escape from a kidnapper. But I never— *never*—went camping, never got to stay overnight at a friend's house, never learned what it was like to just hang out with my friends. And do you know why?"

Gina was wide-eyed. She shook her head expectantly.

"Because my mother was afraid my father, who never showed any sign that he gave a *damn* about me, was going to steal me away. That's why."

I was angry now. I always got angry when I thought of how much I missed out on growing up. I wasn't angry at my mother, she was trying to protect me the best she could. No, I was angry with my father. He'd gotten inside mom's head and she lived the rest of her life worrying about me. I never saw her talk to anyone that didn't have something directly connected to my education. I never saw her with friends—I never knew whether she even *had* friends. Herbert Stone stole my mother's happiness and I could never forgive him for it.

"Baby," Gina whispered as she touched my cheek. Her hand instantly calmed the tension I felt all the way through, even the muscles of my face. "That's in the past. You grew up to be a good man, and that's what your mom wanted, I'm sure. So, she got what she wanted most in life." She moved closer to me and spoke tenderly. "You have a beautiful daughter, lots of friends, a grandbaby on the way and now you have me. Your life turned out great."

"That's true," I replied, embarrassed now that I had allowed her to see the screwed-up side of me. "I took the long road to get here, but you're right. Even with all that's happened, I still have a good life. I only wish…"

"Stop," she said, putting her fingers to my lips. "Stop wishing things were better for Tara, or for your mom, or whoever else's life you want to fix. They made their choices and you made yours. You're only responsible for you, Jimmy. You have it good because you do the right thing. And even when you do something wrong, you own up to it. That's why God, or The Universe, or whoever you want to give credit for the good things in your life, has taken care of you."

"I am so lucky to have you," I said smiling. "If I didn't, I'd be so busy kicking myself that I wouldn't have time for anything else."

"It goes both ways, Babe. I think that's why we were meant to be together." She snuggled closer to me and began running her hand down my chest.

"Aren't you going to be late to work?"

She looked over at where her alarm clock used to be, then reached over and picked up her watch next to the lamp. She let out a laugh and said, "I'm already late. What's another few minutes going to hurt?"

About an hour later Gina and I walked out the front door of her little house, hand in hand and kissed each other goodbye before she got into her car and drove the five blocks to Summertown School. I had made the transition from close friend, to friend with benefits, to boyfriend and I was finding it increasingly easier to forget the fact that I was still married to Tara.

Chapter Twenty-six

It was very cold in the forest this time of year, and for a man who spent most of his life in the Caribbean it was unbearably cold. Reno tried to stay warm by running through the rocky terrain, staying under the canopy of Ponderosa pines as much as he could. But his body was increasingly unable to retain its warmth. He began to shiver uncontrollably until exhaustion set in. He couldn't be more than ten miles away from Summertown, he was sure. But if he didn't find some kind of shelter he was going to freeze to death.

He half-jogged, half-walked for about half an hour until he spotted a large pick-up truck with a fifth-wheel trailer attached, the leveling bars set and the roll-out awning on the side of the trailer locked open. Since there was no furniture set up they were either just now arriving or, more likely given the time of day, getting ready to leave. There were probably very few campers around here at this time of year, so he decided that this was about the only chance he had of getting warm. He hid behind one of the larger granite boulders nearby and watched for signs of life. He only had to wait a few minutes before a man in a thick winter coat opened the door to the trailer, stepped down and went to the generator on the side, where he began pulling the draw-cord to start it.

While the man was occupied with the generator Reno quietly worked his way closer, moving from tree to tree until he was within about fifteen meters. When the generator sputtered to life, he used the noise of the motor to cover his movements and ran quickly to the stranger and striking him three times on his shoulder, just at the base of his neck. When the stunned man's knees buckled Reno pushed him forward into a face-down position then, grabbing the collar of the man's jacket he pulled it over his head to keep from being seen by him. Then he took the man's neck in the crook of his arm and squeezed until he passed out. It happened so quickly that the unlucky camper didn't have time to resist.

"Bobby?" came a female voice from inside the trailer. "Are you OK?" The sound of footsteps thumping toward the door prompted Reno to quickly climb over the hitch and circle the trailer from the other side. As the woman, apparently around her middle 50s or so, stepped out of the trailer she saw her companion on the ground, motionless. Before she could scream, Reno's arms were around her neck, applying the same technique that had subdued Bobby. He opened the trailer door and quickly surveyed the interior to confirm that they were the sole occupants, then he dragged each of them up the short steps and onto the floor of the living room. Keeping their jackets covering their eyes, he found some belts and electrical cords and bound them together then tied them to the legs of the table, making sure that it was firmly anchored to the floor.

He searched the man and found the keys to the truck, looked through the tiny closet in the bedroom and took a few sweaters and a black ball cap, then he opened the refrigerator and took a few things to eat. He wasn't sure when he was going to eat again, so he drank most of a carton of milk and ate two packages of lunch meat, then took a few apples and a bottle of water before he headed for the door. It hadn't occurred to him that he should check his wounds. He had gotten used to the hot ache that radiated from them and he was too occupied with getting the truck unhitched so he could get out of there. He was almost to the driver's door when he realized that if he didn't start the heater his victims could freeze to death. He spent a few precious minutes looking for it and turning it on. The couple was stirring when he stepped down again from the trailer and walked over, got into the truck and took off. He knew that he should have taken off as soon as he got the keys and some food, but he couldn't leave two innocents to freeze.

That was what separated him from Jason. He cared about what happened to people.

The clouds were forming and it looked like it was going to snow. Reno pushed the gas pedal a little harder as he forced the truck up a steep, off-trail grade. He knew that the ridge he was on would eventually offer a view of Summertown to the west, but he didn't know exactly when. He just had to keep hugging the ridge and hoped that he made enough progress to make the trip a lot shorter before he ditched the pickup. He also hoped fervently that the snow would cover any tracks he left and buy him time to find Jason and kill him before the police found him.

***

"Cindy, we have a call from DPS," Ray Brandt said. He had called call her at home, by phone instead of radioing her. That meant he didn't want the locals listening in on their scanners.

"What's up?"

"I need you to post yourself at Babbitt and Lake Mary. There was a shooting outside Marshall Lake. Two Hispanic males were found dead next to an older model sedan. DPS says the tracks around the scene look like a mid-to-full sized truck or SUV was their but is now gone. The responding officer said he passed a black Dodge Ram on the way there. The pickup was headed our way."

"A black Dodge Ram," she repeated back. "Anything else?"

"That's all," Ray replied. "The officer couldn't make out the driver."

"Understood. If I spot them, do I detain them or do you want me to wait?"

"Call it in and wait for Gary or me to back you up. If they run, follow and call it in. Our main concern is keeping them out of our town."

"Got it," she said. "On my way." As Cindy got up from her couch, the game show she'd been watching was interrupted by a news flash about the shooting near Marshall Lake, with a live aerial shot of the sedan with its doors open. Two body-sized sheets lay near the back end of the car on each side. *Either the shooter has some training, or he's really lucky,* she thought. *I hope to God Gary doesn't spot him and go cowboy on us. He could get himself killed engaging somebody like that on his own.*

***

Ken was standing at one of the tables in the corner as I entered the café, talking to a middle-aged man with thinning blonde hair and a husky build, who had a big sheet of paper covering the table. It looked like they were making plans. Seeing me, Ken waved me over. I was glad to see him smiling for a change.

"Jimmy, this is Chris Miller. He's the contractor who'll be remodeling the restaurant for us. Chris, this is Jimmy Stone, my accountant. Well, actually," he chuckled, "he's pretty much everybody's accountant around here."

After exchanging greetings with Chris, I listened as Ken explained that he was going to rearrange how the café was set up.

"I'm having all of the front windows taken out," he said. It's all going to be one big wall. The entrance will be on the side…"

"You're taking away one of the best parts of this place," I said, pointing to the snow floating gently on the wind outside. "The view you get from those windows…"

"Those windows are the reason I almost got killed," Ken interrupted. "Who knows who else might have gotten hurt as well if that idiot wasn't such a bad shot."

"But changing the way you do things…"

"Is just common sense," he insisted. "Keeping things as they are after what happened would be stupid. I'll admit, I was scared for a while after. I almost put the place up for sale."

"Really?"

"I was talking to brokers about it last week," he nodded. "But the other day I was praying for answers and it came to me: Selling out would be running away from something that will always be with me. I can't change what I am, and I can't change the fact that there are bigots out there willing to kill me out of blind hatred. No matter where I went, that would follow me just as it always has. But I don't have to make it easy for the next guy, either. That's why I'm rearranging the place so that won't happen again. At least not as easily as it did."

"I see," I replied. "I understand now."

I looked at the planned layout and discussed the projected costs with Chris.

"This is not going to be a cheap job," I said. "I'm not sure it would be wise to open that pizza delivery place while this is going on."

"Oh, that's off," Ken grinned. "Ever since the shooting Min's barely let me out of her sight. She says she regrets even bringing it up."

"She realized she can't live without you," I said. "At least something good came out of it."

"God does that, Jimmy," he smiled.

"Yeah," I nodded. "I have to be reminded of that sometimes."

The bell over the front door rang and a man walked into the restaurant. He looked eerily familiar but I couldn't quite place him. He was tall, close to my height and had tightly curled, short, black hair, similar to Ken's. He wore a dark jacket and black cargo pants and walked with a pronounced limp, favoring his left side. His complexion was ashen and I wondered if he might be ill.

He sat at a stool and leaned on the counter, looking all around the room. His expression was hard to read. Chad greeted him with a cup of coffee and a smile and the man instantly became someone different from the one I'd just observed. He sat up, grinned and seemed to start engaging Chad in a friendly line of banter as if they had been friends for years. It unnerved me somehow. He was only there for a few minutes, during which he apparently asked directions judging by the pointing and waving that Chad was doing. Then he stood up, put some cash on the counter and headed for the exit.

"Thanks," the stranger smiled and waved as he walked to the door. Then he turned around just before going out the door, his eyes suddenly on me for a long moment. Then he sighed and shrugged, waved again and walked out the door.

"Hey, Chad," I said as I walked to the counter. "Who was that?"

"A friend of Mr. Hadley's," he replied. "He said he used to work with him at the mission in Haiti and now he lives in Tucson."

"Hm. He knows Jason but he doesn't know where he lives?"

"He said he lost the address, but knew he lives in Summertown."

"He could have called him if they were friends."

"He said he wanted to surprise him," Chad smiled, finding my apparent suspicion amusing.

The thought that I should know this guy nagged at me. He seemed to know me somehow. Where on earth did I meet him? He was tall, slim...*Miragoane!* I had no idea what caused me to think of it, but the memory of him escorting me to the airport and standing guard until I got on the plane was vivid. No question, he was that guy. What was he really doing here, and how did Jason know him?

***

Reno left the parking lot by way of the back exit so that they wouldn't see what his vehicle looked like. He took a circuitous route, looking around to make sure no one had been waiting for him; he was sure they knew where he was going, so it was simply logical to expect a welcoming party.

He didn't think that whoever was chasing him would stop with just two guys in a pickup truck, judging by the kind of firepower they carried and the fact that they had twice been waiting for him. And the police would surely find him once those two in the woods untied themselves and called for help. There was no way of telling how long he had but no matter what happened, he was going to kill Jay Hadley.

Two minutes later he turned onto the short, winding street that led to Hadley's house. Now he would find Jay, tie him up and kill him slowly, let him know what hell will be like for him. He'd dreamt of this day the whole time he'd been laying in the hospital. No matter what kind of past they had, all that mattered now was that Jason deserved to die.

Chapter Twenty-seven

Jason Hadley had been watching the roads, listening to police radio traffic and knew the time had come. Reno's cover had been blown and he'd barely gotten out alive. Now he was coming to him here, of all places. The fact that he'd gotten out of the country was a miracle by itself. *Lord, help me hide Reno,* he thought. *Give me the wisdom to do the right things to protect him.*

He watched as a large, white pickup truck with a fifth-wheel hitch in the bed climbed the street to the house. Two icy hairpins were easily negotiated and now there was just the straight run to the front of the house. When he saw Reno's face through the windshield of the truck, his heart sank. His godson's face was a mask of death. Reno pulled into the garage, barely missing the far wall. The moment the truck was far enough in, Jason closed the garage door and ran to the driver's door. As he opened it Reno greeted him with a pistol pointed at his chest, held low and close to his waist so that Jason couldn't take it away.

"Get back," Reno barked. When Jason didn't obey immediately, a fist shot out and struck him in the solar plexus, doubling him over and knocking the wind out of him. Reno dragged himself from the car then shoved him back hard. As Hadley lay on his back, gasping for air, Chatelaine kick him in the face then jumped on his chest, landing with both knees digging into him. Then he straddled his chest and hit him hard in the temple, knocking him out.

***

It was dark inside the house and the only sound Jason Hadley heard was a metal-on-metal scraping. He was awake now, after a short forced nap and he was beginning to familiarize himself with his situation. The cord around his neck pulled tightly at his jaw and lifted his head at an uncomfortable angle while the weight of his body kept it just tight enough to cause excruciating pain but not enough to choke him out. His wrists and forearms were bound together behind his back somehow, stretching his chest back, allowing no leeway at all for him to squirm out of the ropes. He was seated on a chair, probably since is legs were bound to it and his chest was strapped to the back. He was very effectively immobilized.

"Reno, why?" was all he could say.

"Don't pretend anymore," Chatelaine said contemptuously. "I know you were behind my assignment to Boudreaux's staff and I know why. He told me, just before I *killed him.*"

"What happened?" Jason begged. "Please, tell me. I don't understand. Why are you doing this…?"

"This is just the beginning, you bastard!" Reno spat. He punctuated his words by punching the older man squarely in the face, fracturing his nose. Blood sprayed out and down Jason's mouth and chin and he choked against the cord around his neck. "*You murdered my family! You killed them the same as if you were there!* Boudreaux told me! You set me up! He told me you were partners!" He grabbed Hadley by the hair and pulled down hard so that the loose around his neck bit into his throat. "I spent two years sending *bullshit* to MINUSTAH while you and that son of a bitch bought and sold young girls and drugs and guns and anything else you wanted without any fear of being caught!" He slapped Jason hard across the face. "Then, when he decided he didn't need me anymore, he sent his little brother to my sister's house." He struck again, with his bare knuckles. "You let them rape and torture Mireille and Soraya! Soraya was just a little girl!" He grabbed Jason's broken nose and twisted, eliciting a grunt of pain from his victim. "*You took away everything that made my life worth living, and I'm going to make you regret the day you were born!*"

Jason Hadley's mind was a cloud of agony both physical and mental. Mireille and Soraya dead? *Oh, my God, please help me. How?* He looked up at Reno and despite his foggy vision, he could see that Reno was rapidly running out of strength. He had lost a lot of blood and he had expended a lot of energy just to get here. His once-handsome face now had the look of death. "Reno..." he croaked out through his constricted throat.

"Shut up!" Reno slapped him again. He picked up a knife that he found in one of the kitchen drawers. It was a long, narrow blade and it was dull.

Reno's lips curled up in a feral snarl as he said, "You're going to die now, like a slaughtered pig, and my hand will be on the knife that kills you."

***

I walked up the steep drive to Jason's house, almost slipping a number of times on the ice that had accumulated along the edge of the road. I knew that I would be interrupting something, but I'd gone too long without answers and I wasn't going to wait anymore. When I arrived at the front I could hear shouting coming from somewhere inside. Whatever was happening, it wasn't a joyful reunion. I rang the doorbell, and the shouting stopped. I waited several minutes then I turned to go, but then the door opened. Standing in the entry was the guy from the cafe, his face even more blanched than it was at the café and sweat beaded on his forehead.

"Hi, Jimmy," he tried to smile. "Jason and I were just talking about you. I'm glad you stopped by."

He gestured for me to enter and as I did, I saw Jason sitting in the middle of the dining room, a wire noose of some sort tied to his neck and anchored to a hanging lamp. I felt that old, familiar sensation of being struck in the head by a big bell and saw a burst of stars, then blackness.

***

"Any news on the suspect yet, Chief?" Gary asked over the patrol car radio.

"None," Ray replied.

"Should we take a look around the east end of the hill? If he's trying to get away, he'll probably come our way."

"Maybe, but there are a couple of other spots along the way where he could have picked up another car and we'd never spot him without a physical description."

"True..."

"But go ahead and take a look around in that area just in case," Ray said. "Cindy, you copy?"

"10-4, Chief," Deputy Noe's voice shot back. *She must be as bored as I am,* Gary thought.

When he got to the corner of Babbitt and 7th street he waited the two minutes for Cindy to arrive, then they stepped out of their cars and made a careful search for signs of a vehicle entering from the forest nearby.

"There's nothing visible," Cindy reported via radio. "The snow has already covered every square inch of ground. Even under the trees."

"It's been three hours," Ray said. "If he was coming our way he would have been here by now. Let's go ahead and stand down, but keep your ears to your radios just in case."

***

I didn't have any idea how long I was out, but when I awoke I had a bad headache that occupied my entire skull. I squinted my eyes and gradually opened them, the throbbing only slightly worse from the light entering my head. I was sitting on the couch, facing the arched doorway that opened to the dining room where Jason was still trussed up. My arms were crossed over my chest and taped fast by a quite a lot of duct tape. I looked down at my legs and saw that they were strapped together the same way, at the knees and also at the ankles.

"I'm sorry for the rough treatment, Jim," Reno said. He was leaning against the wall next to Jason and was no longer hiding his condition. "Your arrival was a surprise and I no longer have the strength to be gentle."

"What…"

"I'm about to kill this man," Reno replied matter-of-factly. "He played me for a fool, then he had his friends kill my family."

"What…"

"Is that all you can say, 'What'?" he chuckled weirdly. "Did I hit you too hard?"

"Reno, you should sit down," Jason managed to say through gritted teeth. "You've lost a lot of blood…"

"Not as much as you're about to lose!" Reno snapped. He swung a backhand slap across Jason's face but he lost his balance and fell forward, landing hard on his hands and knees.

I held my breath as I stared at him. Chatelaine fumbled for the knife then struggled back to his feet, leaning on the dining table next to him for support.

"Alright, Jason," he mumbled as he slid his way along the wall. "I'm not going to last any longer so…" He picked up a long kitchen knife and with considerable effort lifted it until it was just above his shoulder, the pointing toward Jason's chest. "I'm…taking you with me."

"No!" I screamed.

I threw myself forward and jumped, with all my strength, toward Reno but I only made it a few feet before I dropped to the floor. Looking up frantically I could see I should have saved my strength. Reno had begun to crumple to the floor, hitting his head on the table on the way down.

"Jimmy, help me out of this!" Jason ordered urgently, wiggling his now-purple fingers. "We have to get him to a bed and stop his bleeding or he's going to die."

"What the hell is going on?" I demanded as I worked the fingers of one of my hands free enough to begin tearing away at the edges of the tape on my torso.

"I'll tell you as soon as we get him stable. Now help me out. He doesn't have much time."

"I'm working on it," I grunted. "It's going to take a little time to get this tape off."

The thumb and index finger on my left hand were sore from clawing at the tape, tearing a fiber or two at a time. But once I had a little more wiggle room I was able to use my whole hand, then my wrist, then things went much more quickly. It probably took quite a while to get free, but with all the effort and concentration involved, it seemed much shorter. As soon as my arms were clear enough for me to reach my legs, I was tearing myself free, then I was on my feet and helping Jason out of his noose.

As I worked on the electrical cords that were tied around his wrists and arms, I said, "We need to call…"

"No one!" he snapped. "We call *no one*. He can't afford to be taken to a hospital. If there are any more of those men who did this to him he'll be a sitting duck. We have to take care of him here."

"What's this 'we' crap?"

"You'll help," he said assuredly. "You're not the kind of man who runs."

"How do you know…?" I didn't bother finishing the sentence. I knew he was right. I was going to help, no matter how stupid the idea was, because Jason said so.

Jason promised answers to all my questions, "and a few answers to questions you didn't know you had," if I didn't call 911, but instead allowed him to take care of Chatelaine here at his house. Of all the harebrained things I'd done, this was probably the dumbest. I had no reason to trust him, yet I did. Somehow, I was sure that he was a victim in this mess and if I'd only let him practice medicine without a license, I'd get what I wanted. Stupid. But he assured me that he knew what he was doing.

As soon as he was free, Jason got up from the chair and stumbled to his pantry. From the top shelf he took down a big, red toolbox. He carried it, limping all the way, over to where Reno lay, still unconscious on the floor. Once he had massage some circulation back into his hands, he opened the toolbox and revealed a virtual portable emergency room.

"Come sit down over here, Jimmy," he commanded. "I'm going to take a little blood from you and give it to him."

I sat obediently, not speaking. I watched as he prepared what looked like an IV needle, somewhat thicker than I had expected it to be. He smiled at my dubious expression.

"I've done this more times than I like to remember," he said. "From the jungle, to safe houses, to the mission, I've mended all kinds of cuts and broken bones, helped with sick patients at the clinic in Miragoane... Here, this is going sting a little. Ready?"

He slid the needle into my arm and attached the IV tube. "Sting a little" was an understatement. As large a gauge as that needle was, it felt like he was shoving a drain pipe into my arm. I watched as my blood made its way down the into an IV bag hanging on the chair next to me.

"How do you know my blood is compatible?" I asked. "Won't it do more harm than good if I'm not a good match?"

"In his condition," Jason said gravely, "the need for blood trumps any worries about blood type. But I know you're compatible."

"How?"

"He's your brother."

There are so many ways to be introduced to long-lost family members. You can get a letter or email from them, be a guest on an Oprah special, go on Jerry Springer...

"What!" I started to stand up but Jason just put a hand on my shoulder and gently guided me back into the chair.

"Half-brother, actually," he said.

"What!"

"I guess he did hit you pretty hard," he smiled.

"How?"

"Well, Jimmy," he said patronizingly, "your dad had children with a young woman after he moved to Haiti."

"He was in *Haiti*?"

"Yes," he said. "But that's a long story."

"I'm not going anywhere."

He shrugged, turned to Reno whose ragged breathing could be heard in the background. He removed the man's jacket and shirt, surveyed the wounds on his back and sides. They looked small but if they were bullet holes, the damage was going to be worse inside, where I couldn't see.

"Are you going to dig those bullets out?" I asked uncertainly. Hadley may have had some field medicine training of some kind or another, but I was pretty sure that he wasn't a surgeon.

He reached into the box and pulled out a metal cylinder about an inch thick and the same in diameter. He touched it to the wound that looked to be the shallowest, judging by the lump where the bullet appeared to have stopped.

"A couple of them are close enough to the skin," he nodded. "As for the rest, I think he'll heal better if I just leave them in."

"But won't he get lead poisoning?"

"These are shotgun wounds," he said as he began washing the areas with a washcloth and bowl of hot water that he'd brought from the kitchen. "And they struck at an oblique angle—see the long streak this one on his side made? That means they probably didn't go in far enough to damage any organs."

"But pellets are made of lead."

"Not these," he replied and held up the metal cylinder. "That's what this is magnet is for. Lead isn't magnetic, but these pellets are. Reno got lucky—well, as lucky as a fellow can get when he's hit with double-ought buck. This is steel shot." Seeing my confusion he explained, "A while back, a law was passed requiring steel shot to be used around waterways. Lead was contaminating them. As long as I give him some antibiotics, I'm pretty confident he'll get better."

"How do you know all this?" I asked, growing frustrated with the ease with which Jason was handling the whole experience. This was clearly a stranger sitting before me, who had been playing a part the whole time I'd known him. "And why do you have all these medical supplies? What do you really do? Nobody comes out this far looking to kill a missionary, so don't bother trying to get me to believe that one."

"Very good, Jimmy," he replied. "You worked that out so fast."

"Cut the crap and tell me the truth!" I demanded. "You know things about my life that I don't, and I want you to tell me. Now!"

"All right," he said. "You have a right to know. It won't be pleasant, but I'll tell you the truth."

"So what, are you a spy? The whole time I thought you worked for the missions, were you working for the CIA?"

"A spy?" he chuckled derisively. "That's a very romantic word for what I did. I supervised intelligence gathering in the south provinces of Haiti; mostly a clerical job. I reported to your father."

"Why does Reno think you killed his family?"

"Because he's so grief-stricken and full of rage that he has to blame someone, even if what he was told is a lie," he said sadly. "The man who told him that I sold him out was evil. He enjoyed torture, both physical and mental. If he said what Reno says he did, it was a final insult. A last wound to inflict before he killed him."

He took the bag from the chair and after disconnecting it from my tube, he prepared Reno's arm for his transfusion. Chatelaine's face was white, his lips gray. If I hadn't heard him breathing I would have thought he was dead.

"Do you think he'll make it?" I asked. "Without getting medical attention, I mean."

Jason nodded. "I'm confident that all he really needs is this blood, me sewing up the holes in his side, and enough rest to allow his body to recuperate."

"Who shot him?"

"That is a very good question," he replied gravely. "And I have the answer. But he won't believe me until I can show him the evidence."

"How will you get that if you have to take care of him here?"

"I have it here. But that can wait," he said calmly. "Reno comes first. We'll need to get rid of that truck in my garage. We need to drop it in the woods somewhere south of here so no one…"

"What's this 'we' stuff again?"

"Jimmy," he pleaded. "I need to protect him. If he gets arrested, it will take no time at all for the people hunting him to locate him and finish the job. As long as no one knows he's here, he'll be safe."

"I don't want to get involved…"

"You already are," he replied patiently. "He's your family. And you're *his* family…the only one he has left now."

"It's easy to say, 'He's family. You have to watch out for him now', but he's really just a stranger. The fact that the same man conceived us doesn't make him family."

"I know you better than that," he said. "There isn't anything you won't do for friends or family, and now that you know the truth…"

"But I *don't* know the truth!" I insisted. "I'm only hearing your version of things. How do I know it's really true?"

"What do you want me to do?" he asked.

"I don't know," I muttered. After thinking about it for a moment I just shrugged and said, "Tell me what you know about my father. Tell me why he left me. Tell me how I have a family somewhere I never knew about until now. Just start talking, I guess."

"Alright, Jimmy," he began. "Herb Stone was a good man and a patriot. But the day he met your mother—the one who gave birth to you—was the beginning of the most difficult chapter in his life."

"What do you mean?"

"Olga Pivtorakozhukha," he explained, "was your mother in the most important way: she raised you and loved you as her own. But she was really your aunt, your birth-mother's older sister."

I stared blankly at him, unsure of whether or not this was the truth. If it was, I decided that I should be shocked, but I was still waiting to be convinced.

"Your father was a very handsome guy," he went on. "He had a magnetic personality and a knack for recruiting lonely women, sometimes secretaries, sometimes women in even higher positions; our nickname for them was 'Agatha'. They were common targets among espionage organizations. Herb had a talent for romancing these ladies and making them feel like they'd found their knight in shining armor. He left a trail of broken hearts all over Eastern Europe when he left."

"Mom," I said to myself, trying to get my mind around the idea.

"Yes, your mom," he nodded. "She was a…"

"A clerk at the Ukrainian Embassy. I know."

"She was a sergeant in the Soviet Army," he said, shaking his head. "She decoded field intelligence reports for the GRU, Soviet Military Intelligence."

"She…she was a spy?"

"She was a cryptologist," he corrected me. "And she had unimpeded access to classified material that we wanted."

"My mother was an 'Agatha'," I said, as if saying it aloud would help me understand it.

"Olga Pivtorakozhukha was a lonely young woman," he said. "And, like many of your father's other recruits, she fell in love with him because he was the first man to ever treat her like a lady."

That had a ring of truth. Mom was not an attractive woman. Of the few photographs that she owned of her family they all showed a group of square-jawed, flat-browed Slavic men and women who would have made perfect extras in a film about Russian peasants. She often talked about growing up with her seven brothers and two sisters, but the only pictures she had were of her parents and a few of her brothers.

"Which of my mom's sisters gave birth to me?" I asked.

"Vira," he replied. "Olga was twenty-seven and Vira was nineteen when Olga brought Herb to Makariv, her hometown to meet her family."

"So…my father seduced Vira?"

He kept his eyes on what he was doing as he removed a needle, some thread—sterile thread, I supposed—and began wiping one of the clotted-over wounds on Reno's back. It started bleeding again, so he put a folded gauze over the hole and pressed hard.

"Do me a favor and open one of those bottles of alcohol," he said. He was perfectly relaxed, no sign of nerves about sewing up a bleeding bullet hole in his friend's body. I did as he asked, then I helped roll the patient over onto his side so he could breathe. Jason took the gauze off of the wound, opened the hole with two fingers then poured the alcohol straight into it. I winced, knowing how much it must hurt, but Reno showed no sign of awareness. When he finished with that, he began to stitch up the wound.

"Jimmy," Jason said in a low and earnest voice, "there is nothing about this whole affair that I haven't deeply regretted until this day."

"How do you know all this you're telling me?"

"I was stationed at the U.S. Embassy in Kiev, as part of the Marine security detail, after my first tour in Vietnam. I let it be known that I was interested in clandestine work and Herb took me under his wing, groomed me for the job. He had me doing a lot of leg work."

"Like what?"

"Nothing glamorous," he said. "I did pick-ups and dead-drops, shadowed people; simple things but stuff he needed someone he could trust to do. That's why he chose me. I was a marine, I could take care of myself and whatever happened, he knew I wouldn't talk."

"And you know everything about my family because you worked for my father? Was he in the habit of sharing his personal life with employees?"

"I wasn't just an employee, Jimmy," he replied. "Herb and I were the closest of friends. We had to rely on each other during some scary times, always afraid we'd be caught and thrown into a Soviet prison, or maybe even killed. That kind of pressure either brings people closer or tears them apart."

He finished tying off the stitch work then moved to the next hole, located on Reno's side, under his left arm. There was swelling around the edges.

"It looks like it's getting infected," I said. "I hope it doesn't get worse."

"I have some antibiotics in the box over there," he said nodding toward the big, multiple-drawered tool box that contained his medical supplies. "It'll take most of what I have to keep it down, but I'm pretty sure he'll be OK. He's Haitian. A Haitian's blood is usually full of antibodies because they're exposed to a lot of disease and germs most of their life. What would have you bedridden for a week would probably cause him to lose no more than a day or two of work." He checked Reno's face and neck and added, "He doesn't have a fever yet, that's a good sign."

"So, why did you come here?" I asked. "You obviously have a reason other than retirement, and don't feed me that crap about closing your eyes and pointing at a map. Tell me the truth. Why are you here?"

"To keep a promise I made to your father," he said. "The last year of his life he knew he didn't have much longer to go. He'd had two heart attacks within, I think, a five or six month period of time and the doctors had told him that if he didn't have major bypass surgery he had no chance. He refused, he was afraid he wouldn't live through it. So, he called me and I visited him at the hotel where he was staying. He gave me a copy of his will, then he made me promise him that I would watch over you when he was gone."

"If he really cared that much, why didn't he come see me himself? My mother has been gone for almost ten years now. He could have given any story he wanted."

"He never would have lied to you, Jimmy," Jason said. "Open another bottle of alcohol, will you?" He had finished sewing up a third wound and was moving up to the place just under Reno's arm where there looked to be a long, nasty gash.

He spent extra time on this one, working a long, narrow pair of forceps carefully into the wound and digging every-so-gently until he managed to grab the pellet and slowly pull it out. I was sure that a surgeon would have had a better technique, but he got the job done. After spending even more time packing the hole with gauze and taping it closed, he stepped back and inclined his head. I took that to mean the conversation could continue.

"If I was so important to him, why didn't he try to keep me from leaving with mom?" I asked. "The last thing I remember about my father was the look on his face when the judge told me to leave with my mother. He just stared at me. He didn't smile, he didn't touch me, he didn't cry…"

"I was there, Jimmy."

"Where? I don't remember anybody but my mom and my dad. Nobody else was there but the three of us and a judge."

"The courtroom was full," he said shaking his head. "Your parents' divorce was just one of a dozen other cases that had to be heard that day. I was in the back, watching. Your father didn't touch you because if he did, he wouldn't have been able to let you go. And Soviet courts weren't friendly to Americans."

"I remember differently," I said.

"Of course you do," Jason said paternally. He finished off the wound and turned to look at me. "You were a little boy. Your whole world was being turned upside down. As far as you were concerned at that moment, there was only you, your mom and your dad." He smiled faintly and added, "I even remember what you were wearing; a navy blue suit that your father had made for you. You looked so grown up in that courtroom, standing there like a little soldier standing at attention; your little lips quivering, but you weren't going to let anyone see you cry."

"Stop."

"You were staring at your dad the whole time, probably hoping he'd put his arms around you and tell you everything would be fine."

"I said stop."

"If only you could have seen into his heart, you would have seen it breaking into a thousand pieces."

"Shut up!" I said, choking back a sob. "I don't want to hear it!"

"You're going to hear it whether you like it or not!" he snapped. "Herb Stone was my best friend. He was like a brother to me. Watching him fall to pieces as we left that courtroom broke my heart. And knowing that you spent your life believing that he didn't love you makes me so angry I can't stand it."

"If he loved me so much, then why did he let my mom take me away?" I demanded. "My mother told me his attempt to get custody was just a show so he wouldn't look bad. You just bought into his lie."

"Your *mother* lied, Jimmy," he said. "She hated your father for what he did to her sister and for cheating on her. She loved you very much and wanted to make sure you didn't grow up to be like the man she despised. So, she blackmailed your dad to arrange passage from Kiev to New York. She said if he didn't guarantee political asylum for the two of you she would turn herself in to the KGB and tell them everything."

"Yeah, about that," I said. "How was it that she wasn't arrested or killed when she married my father? I know they wouldn't just let her keep handing over secret documents to the enemy."

"That's very true. Actually, she had reported your dad's contact with her at the beginning. From the very start, she gave us false information, supplied by the KGB."

"Disinformation," I said. It was a word I'd heard my mom use when she told me stories about the KGB and how they controlled things.

"That's right, disinformation," he said with a touch of surprise. "That's what the Soviets called it. Your mother kept passing us false information so good, it was corroborated enough by other sources that we accepted it as reliable. It was long after she had taken you to the states and had settled in Phoenix that we learned that everything she gave us had been fabricated."

A groan emanated from the patient on the bed. Until that point I had forgotten he was there. We watched silently to see if Reno was waking up, but his stirring subsided. After waiting another minute or so, I spoke again.

"Did she spy for the KGB here?" I asked, half-jokingly.

"No," he replied. "As soon as she got passage to the States, she left the trade. Everything she did from then on was for your benefit. I'm sure of that because when we found out she'd burned us we checked her out from every angle possible."

"And the KGB just let her quit? That isn't how mom described them to me. They never tried to kidnap her or shut her up?"

"Oh yes, sure they did," he said as if that was a silly question. "Olga was very handy bait. The FBI kept you and your mom under surveillance for a long time and as soon as they spotted Soviet agents sniffing around you, they swooped in and quietly arrested them. It made their counterintelligence division look really good."

"How do you know all this?" I asked yet again. "I thought espionage was a need-to-know kind of thing."

"It generally is," he nodded. "But that was a long time ago. Most of that stuff has been declassified. The *entire* story wasn't documented, but after spending a little time in the archives, I was able to figure it out, based on my memory of events and my knowledge of how things are done in my business. Plus, I have a few friends in the FBI."

"OK," I said, relenting for now. "So, tell me about my—biological mother. Why did she give me up?"

"She didn't," Jason said sadly. "She died in childbirth."

"Me?"

He nodded. "She was very small and slender. Very different from Olga. I don't know exactly what caused it, but she lost too much blood."

I didn't know how to react to that. It was sad, I knew. I could only imagine how it must have hurt mom—Aunt Olga? No. The woman who gave birth to me deserved better than to die on the table of a hospital, but she was really just how I came into the world. The one who made me who I am, she was my mother. And as much as I tried to feel like I'd lost a part of me, I just couldn't. As shocked as I was at this new revelation it didn't change anything. It all happened a long time ago and had nothing to do with me other than how I got my deep-set eyes and square chin. Everything else, my mom said, I got from my father. This stranger who gave birth to me meant nothing, and I couldn't manufacture grief for her if I wanted to.

"And I was just given to my mother—Olga, I mean?"

"Pretty much as simple as that," he shrugged. "Your father married Olga and claimed you as his son so that you wouldn't grow up a bastard. In fact, he spent the first six years of your life trying to get you away from your mother."

"You say that, but I do remember some things. I remember sitting up at night, staring out the window wondering if he would come home. He never did." Finally getting myself together, I added, "And it no longer really matters now. Sure, it may be part of what made me the person I am, but it was over 40 years ago. If I spent my whole life moaning about how my dad didn't love me, I'd be a basket case. My mom, whether she was my biological mother or not, she raised me and made sure I knew that she cared about me. I never felt abandoned and never felt alone. So, let's just drop the subject."

"Whatever you say," he said. He went back to work again.

It only took a little while to finish sewing Reno up. Then he pulled out another IV bag that looked like saline solution and hooked his patient up to it.

"It's getting late," I said. "Gina's probably wondering where I am."

"You'll come back later to help get that truck out of here?" he asked more like he was confirming a prearranged meeting than asking for help.

"I'll be here," I sighed. "When?"

"Two. And watch to make sure the cops aren't out. Coming up this street, you can be spotted just about anywhere in town."

"I'll walk up," I said. "It'll give me more time to cuss myself out for being so stupid."

"It's important that Reno doesn't get caught, Jimmy."

"I'm not talking about that," I said. "I'm talking about believing what you've told me. My head tells me it's a load of crap, but my heart says it's the truth."

"That's why people love you, Jimmy," he smiled. "You lead with your heart."

Chapter Twenty-eight

Tara Stone sat on the bunk of her jail cell, staring at the wall and wondering what would be coming next. She'd spent the last few days with three different psychiatrists but she was still unable to remember one bit of what she'd done that night. The knowledge that she had done such a vicious thing had weighed on her mind so heavily that she could think of nothing else. *I should have seen it coming*, she told herself. *I knew I was capable of it, but just didn't want to believe it. Now Orin and Deanna are dead and I'm...* Three days of sitting here, thinking about her demon-self had eaten away all the false layers of her personality. She could see herself as she really was, now that she was left alone to face it down.

She'd spent so much of her life denying the hate she harbored, without justification, against anyone she thought had a better life than she did. The envy she felt whenever she saw someone happier than her just wouldn't go away, no matter how much she prayed, no matter how often she went to mass. She was so ashamed of it that she dared not talk about it for fear that she would lose friends, or worse—ruin the image they had of her.

She knew she was starting to unravel over the course of this past year when she was stuck dealing with the consequences of coming back to Jimmy. It was a year spent as a servant to her husband, something she swore she'd never do again after what she had endured in her first marriage. And the idea that Jimmy wasn't able to give her the affection she wanted was so much harder than she expected. She had needs, after all. Everything changed so quickly, she couldn't keep up. One day she's changing Jimmy's bandages, another day she's watching Gina strut around Jimmy's apartment after getting from Jimmy what he should have been giving *her* all those months...then she's waking up to find out that she's capable of the most horrendous acts...

She knew she was going to be either in prison or in a mental hospital for a long, long time. They didn't let people like her out. The icy grip of fear enveloped her heart and squeezed until she was sure it would kill her.

Do it, she thought, her teeth clenched against the psychic agony. *Get it over with. I can't take it. I don't want to live the rest of my life like this. Just kill me and get it over with.*

Left alone to her thoughts, she spent each day in this torture. She had to get out there. She had to get to Jimmy and tell him she was sorry. She had to convince him that it wasn't her that killed Orin and Deanna. It was something inside her. She never would have hurt them, no matter how much she hated them. She would never hurt anybody.

But she knew that was a lie. It *was* her. She killed them. She cut them up then went to sleep in their bed. If only she could remember, she could face it. But she couldn't think very clearly right now.

The drugs that she had been given kept her stable, but she felt as if she were moving through water; she could barely feel anything, it was like she was wearing invisible gloves. Was this how she was going to have to live the rest of her life? Was this the only way she was going to be able to keep from hurting someone else?

"My God," she moaned. "Please, just take it all away. Just kill me now. I can't bear it. I don't want to live like this!"

Seemingly in the blink of an eye three detention officers appeared in the doorway to her room, two of them holding leather restraints.

"Hey," the short, stocky man with sergeant stripes on his sleeves said not unkindly. "How are you feeling? We heard you shouting. Do you need to talk to someone?"

"Don't pretend you want to listen to me!" she sneered. "If you were just going to listen to me talk, why did you bring two others with you with straps in their hands? You're going to tie me up again!"

"We don't want to do that if we can avoid it…"

"Don't lie to me!" she screamed. She angrily slapped the mattress as the three officers spread out, taking positions on each side of the room. "I didn't do anything! Keep your hands off me!"

Tara slid back and braced her back against the wall, then pulled her knees up to her chest and wrapped her arms around her legs in hopes of defending herself against what she knew was coming.

"Look," the sergeant said. His voice was gentle but firm. "We don't have to do this…"

But it was too late. Tara's emotions had escalated beyond the point that words could do anything to calm her. She snatched the pillow next to her and threw it at him, screaming obscenities loud enough to be heard throughout the unit. Two minutes later, she was being carried down the hallway to an isolation room. She was wrapped in a full-torso restraint blanket that prevented her from moving her arms. Despite the fact that her legs were hobbled she twisted about, trying to kick the officers as they labored to get her to the room and restrained.

Don't let it take control of your mind, she told herself. *Don't let it change you…*

***

Gina was sitting on the couch when I walked in my front door. I hadn't realized just how late it was until I looked at the TV and saw that the news was on.

"Where have you been, young man?" she said, trying to mask her concern. "I tried to surprise you by coming early and cooking supper for you, but you surprised me instead."

I'm sorry," I said. "Something really important happened and…"

"What happened to you?" she asked, getting up from the couch and walking to me. "There's a huge knot on your head. What happened?"

I went to the bathroom and looked in the mirror. Sure enough, the spot where Reno had clobbered me was swollen like a golf ball and it stood out from the side of my head.

I thought fast and said, "Man! I didn't think I fell that hard. I slipped walking down the drive to Jay Hadley's place. He wanted to talk to me about his retirement plan and what deductions he can make on his taxes."

"And that was the 'really important' something that kept you tied up for hours?" she asked skeptically.

"Well, it's the end of the year," I shrugged, trying to remain casual yet apologetic. "He just wanted to know if he was getting everything he could out of his current accounts without getting punished by the IRS."

"Hm." She obviously didn't buy it, but she wasn't going to press me on it. "Anyway," she said, tossing her head to signal the beginning of a new subject, "I cooked your supper and it *was* great. But now, it's cold and needs heating up." She got up and headed for the kitchen, acting like an unappreciated housewife. It was the cutest thing I'd seen in a long time.

"Everything you cook is perfect, sweetheart," I said in that syrupy, 1950's, husband-in-trouble tone that I knew she'd catch.

"Don't give me that crap," she snapped. "You come home late with a knot on your head, your shirt looks like you slept in it and there are sweat stains all over it. Tell me right now what happened!"

"I just told you," I insisted.

"James…whatever-your-middle-name-is…Stone…"

"Pivtorakozhukha."

"What?! *Whatever!* You're lying to me about something and I want to know why!"

"Gina, please. Just trust me," I pleaded. "I can't talk about it. I promised."

"You just got your ass kicked by somebody and you want me to drop the subject?"

"I didn't say anything about getting my butt kicked…"

"It's obvious. And I won't have it."

"What was that?" I said, her tone beginning to get under my skin.

"I said I won't allow you to go getting beat up again. You're not made of steel, you know."

"So I've been told." I took a deep breath in and let it out slowly. "I promise I'm not doing anything dangerous. Not now, at least."

"Not now?!"

"Don't worry…"

And 'round and 'round we went until I finally gave in and promised her I wouldn't go back. We made up the old fashioned way, with hugs and kisses, enjoying a quiet evening of a cold supper and late-night TV. Afterward, I drove her home and got back to my place just in time for a very brief nap. Then I walked back to Jason's house, avoiding the few street lamps in town and taking advantage of the natural cover of the trees and hedges that lined the main roads. I stopped in the shadows behind a pine tree and took a look around to make sure I wasn't being observed. From where I stood, I could see a Marshal's Office SUV parked on the corner of Babbitt, facing Lake Mary Road. It was probably Cindy. She liked stationing herself at the highway at night and waiting for the rare speeder. I stayed behind the trees and remained aware of where I walked in relation to the lights and shadows, no problem making it to Jay's place unnoticed.

Jason opened the front door before I had a chance to knock. He ushered me into his living room which had been cleaned up since I was last there. When I asked what he was going to do, he shook his head.

"I don't want you to know more about this than you need to," he said. "I won't expose you to more risk than necessary."

He showed me everything I needed to take care of the patient for the time he was going to be gone and said, "Do *not* untie him, under *any* circumstances, do you understand?"

"You get no argument from me," I replied. "I still have a headache from the knot he put on my head."

After giving me final instructions about drugs and dressings he went to the garage, opened it manually, opened the driver's door of the truck and shifting it into neutral he gave it a hard backward shove then hopped in and backed it out of the driveway, continuing down the street in the dark, never starting the motor until he was at the turn onto Tubman Lane. He kept the headlights off until he got to

Lake Mary Road, then he headed south and disappeared from view. I was impressed, not only by his ability to drive backwards down a street with multiple turns in the middle of the night, but doing it with no power steering in a big pickup like that was quite a stunt.

It was at least an hour and a half before I heard the back door open and saw Jason walk through the doorway into the living room. He was sweating heavily despite the snow that covered his head and shoulders.

"I'm getting too old for this clandestine stuff," he chuckled. He walked to the wood-burning stove and took off his jacket and scarf. "I'm glad it started snowing again. No trail to follow."

"You walked all the way back here?" I asked. "You must not have parked very far away."

"Don't worry about where I parked the truck," he said. "If, in fact, I did. For all you know, somebody stole it and drove it out of state."

"So it's headed out of state?"

"Who knows?" he shrugged.

"Gotcha," I said, obviously a bit slow on the uptake.

"How's the patient doing?" he asked.

"He's been asleep the whole time," I said. Then, without segue I asked, "So, why didn't my father ever try to see me?"

Jay didn't bat an eye. He obviously expected questions. "Your dad was a very proud man," he replied. "He didn't want you to see him the way he was in Haiti. He had been a pretty big deal in Ukraine, but in Port-au-Prince? He felt like a failure."

"What do you mean?"

"Well, that whole affair with Vira destroyed his career. It hurt mine quite a bit, too," he added with a toss of the head that made it seem inconsequential. "I was demoted to Lance Corporal and sent back on combat duty when my CO found out that I'd been working with the CIA without authorization."

"They sent you into combat?"

"Three tours."

"After the first one you'd already done?"

"Yes," he said. "Four tours in all. I think they were hoping I'd be killed in action, but God had other plans."

"And my father was sent to Haiti as punishment as well?"

"Pretty much," he nodded. "They wanted him out of Eastern Europe. It was too vital a place to risk anymore embarrassment. They put him in Haiti, watching Papa Doc and his VSN goons ruin their own country."

"Why didn't he just quit if he didn't want to go?"

"Your father was a Company man. He hoped to redeem himself somehow. But after he spent a year or so in Port-au-Prince during Papa Doc's regime, he realized that there was very little that his expertise would be called on to do. He started living the life of a bourgeois white while doing his job as required. That was how Reno here, and his sister, Mireille came into the world."

"What, did he sleep with another source's sister there, too?"

"A hooker."

"A *what?*"

"A Carrefour prostitute," he said, grinning at my surprise. "It wasn't the crowded, dirty mess back then, that you recall driving through. There were places where a man could take his pick of the girl by race, height, age, whatever he wanted. And when he was finished, the girl would bathe him and dress him."

"So, he fell in love with a hooker? My God, he had to have hit bottom."

"He had at that point," he nodded. "But ironically, that was what brought him back. When the girl told him she was pregnant with his child, he took her out of the whorehouse and set her up in a place in Delmas. He stopped drinking, stopped womanizing, and started actually doing his job."

"He believed a *hooker* when she told him she was pregnant with his baby?" I asked skeptically.

"Not at first," he replied. "At least not with *his* baby. After all, what are the chances that a woman who has sex with men for a living is sure which of them got her pregnant?"

"Exactly."

"But he did believe that she was pregnant," he said. "And for whatever reason, he was in love with her." He smiled and added, "And it turned out that the babies were his after all. The older they got, the more they looked like him." He glanced at me and said, almost tentatively, "You look like him, too. You definitely have your father's looks."

I mentally thanked God for that, since the alternative was to look like…Oh, yeah. Mom didn't give birth to me. And since I had no idea what Vira looked like I was going to have to take Jay's word for it.

"When did you go to Haiti?" I asked, looking to change the subject.

"Right about when your dad was at his lowest. He'd requested I be hired as a contractor using the cover of a missionary. I've always been a believer, so that worked out well. They protested a little because of my history with your dad, but they didn't gripe too much. They probably figured, 'What's this guy going to screw up down there? It's just

Haiti'. That's still the opinion in Washington to some degree, 'It's just Haiti'."

"So, you worked with the missions and wrote secret intelligence reports while he got drunk and screwed around with whores."

"Yes," he grimaced and I wasn't sure if it was at the memory or at my bluntness. "But, as I said, meeting Seline changed things."

"I just can't understand how a man with his knowledge and worldliness would fall for someone he was paying for sex. It just doesn't make any sense."

"Well, Seline was an incredibly beautiful young woman," he said. "And I recall a certain special—*warmth* about her that wasn't at all common among women in that trade."

"But she was a hooker."

"A hooker who was being kept in a house of prostitution," he nodded. "Do I need to tell you what it's like there?"

"I can guess."

"Like just about any other man would, I suppose, Herb saw a vulnerable young woman who needed rescuing. The more he visited that place, the more attached he became."

"Attached to a hooker."

"That is just how things happen when we place them at God's feet, Jimmy. I prayed for that man day and night. I didn't want to lose him to the demons he was carrying around."

"You're still talking about a prostitute, Jay. I don't see God making these changes."

"Seline left prostitution because of it, Jimmy," he explained. "Your father quit drinking and went back to being the man he once was because he had children to support. They had given him something to live for. Trust me, God's hand was in it. His ways are mysterious."

"They sure are," I replied and shook my head. "Seeing as you never mentioned them getting married."

"They didn't marry because she didn't love him."

"You mean, he moved her into an apartment, paid for everything even though he knew she didn't want him?"

"I told you he loved her, Jimmy. That's what real love does. What does the Scripture tell us? Love never asks anything in return. He never did. He provided a home for his children and their mother, yet received nothing in return—sure, Seline was very grateful. But Herb never slept with her again, because he didn't want her prostituting herself, even for him."

"Wow," was all I could think to say.

I wondered if I was capable of that level of selflessness toward a woman. If what Jason was telling me was true, Herb Stone really had become a better man, living out his life in virtual exile from the position of respect that he had held in Ukraine. It sounded like he had gone from being respected by everyone else, to learning to respect himself. It gave me food for thought.

"I'd better head home," I said, trying unsuccessfully to suppress a yawn. "It's been a late night and I still have work in the morning."

Jason went to the front window and looked out. "Yes, now is a good time," he nodded. "It's still snowing, so your footprints will be gone by the time you get home."

After slipping twice on the slope down to Tubman Lane and bruising my left knee the second time, it was an easy walk through the quiet streets to my place. Snow was falling gently, the big, puffy flakes floating on a light breeze until they landed softly on the ground. The light from the few street lamps in town reflected off the pure white covering, giving everything a strange, peaceful glow.

I looked at my watch and was surprised to see that it was only 4:30 in the morning. In the brief span of ten hours my self-identity had been changed completely. I realized why my mother pressed me into fighting sports like boxing and karate, never asking me if I liked it or not; why she taught me always to be aware of my surroundings. My entire childhood from the time we came to the States until my senior year of high school was spent, one way or another, learning to avoid being kidnapped.

Cloak and dagger. You hear about the world of espionage and it seems so far removed from the real one that it may as well be just a bunch of fairy tales. Then one day you're introduced to a couple of its practitioners, listen to them talk and see that these are real people, the cloak and dagger stuff really happens and it has impacted your life in the profoundest of ways.

I slid into bed and was out like a light. In my dreams, my father was arguing with my mother as a strange lady in the shadows screamed at him in Ukrainian. I didn't really speak the language anymore, but I could tell that she was very, very angry.

***

Jason touched his thumb to Reno's eyelid and gently slid it open. "You can open your eyes now, 'ti Frere," he said genially. "I know you're awake."

Reno's eyes opened and remained so without blinking or squinting.

"It's time to talk about everything that's happened today," Jason said. Reno looked at him placidly, not making a sound. Jason sat in a chair next to the bed. "So, you didn't think of the possibility that someone else betrayed you?" he asked, half-accusingly. "After all we'd been through together—after all I've done for you and Mireille—you actually thought that I would do such a thing?"

Reno didn't answer. He looked away, stared at the ceiling and shook his head. After what seemed an interminable silence which Jason didn't break, Reno finally spoke.

"Boudreaux said it was you," he said at last. "Why would he lie if he was about to kill me? There was no reason for him to make up such a thing."

"Except to hurt you just one more time before you died," Jason replied. "He loved torturing and exerting power over his victims, you know that better than I do. Sending you to your death thinking you were betrayed by your closest friend is exactly what he would do."

Chatelaine's eyes began to move around the room while looking at nothing in particular, seeming to imagine scenarios, or maybe recalling things in the past. "But who else knew I was working Boudreaux?" he asked, less certain than before. "Just you and my field officer."

"You didn't mention it to Pastor Jacques?"

"I'm not stupid, Jay," Reno retorted. "I know to keep my assignments secret."

"Then, why did Philippe call me to say you had been blown and were coming to me for help?"

"You're lying," Reno snapped.

"Think about it, Reno," Jason said. "Why would I open my garage door, unarmed, and let you drive in and pull a gun on me?" Jason asked. "If I was in on the killing of Mireille and Soraya, I'd have never let you near my home. You would have been dead long before you got on a plane."

"And these holes in my body came from out of the blue?" Reno sneered.

"You know how I work, Reno," Jason replied quietly. "Do you think I'd ever use men who couldn't guarantee that you'd disappear without a trace?"

"Everybody makes a mistake sometime," the younger man said, but the mask of hatred had cracked a bit. He was considering Jason's words.

"And while you were on the way here," Hadley added, "someone tried to assassinate me." When he didn't get a response, he went to the kitchen table and picked up the file he'd built on Carval then brought it to Reno. "Lucky for me they were amateurs. As it was, they almost killed an innocent. This is evidence I found in the shooter's home."

Reno said nothing, but his expression softened ever-so-slightly. He scanned the material in the file as Jason silently turned pages, looking away occasionally as if refusing to accept what was there on the page. But with each new page, accompanied by screenshots of email instructions given by the client, realization dawned on him. He gasped in a deep, shuddering sob.

"Oh Jezi!" he choked out. "Oh *God,* I almost killed you!" He tried to lift his hands to his face but was stopped by the restraints. He rolled his head from side to side and moaned, cursing himself in Kreyol.

"Reno, stop," Jay said, firmly but kindly. "You'll tear your stiches. Take it easy."

"I tried to kill you," Chatelaine said, self-loathing dripping from his tongue. "How could I..."

"In our trade, we learn to *distrust* easier than to trust," the older man replied, putting his hand on Reno's forehead and stroking it like a father comforting a sick child. "You were blinded by your grief, looking for someone to blame. Anyone would have lost their sense of reason."

"But you said I should have known better," Reno replied in a child's voice. "And I did know better, but I still believed the bastard that killed Mireille and Soraya rather than you."

"There will be time later to grieve our losses and regret our mistakes," Jay said. "Right now, we have to be focused. You need to heal up enough to leave town. Then, when you're ready, we'll avenge the girls together."

He began untying the ropes holding Reno down.

"I was so sure it was you," Reno whispered almost to himself. "How could I?"

Jason pulled a knife from his pocket and cut the rope from Reno's arms, legs and torso then he went to the side table and picked up a syringe filled with clear liquid. He injected the contents into Reno's I.V.

"You need to sleep," he said. "And you've got too much on your mind to fall asleep on your own."

"I'll be fine," Reno said.

"You will now," Jason grinned wanly. "You have some of your brother's blood in you now, and with what I just gave you you're going to sleep the day away." He patted his godson's face paternally. "And I'm not going anywhere until you're ready to travel. We're going to mete out justice to those who deserve it, and we're going to do it together. God is on our side."

Reno nodded lazily, the sedative having taken effect. "Jimmy gave me his blood?" he asked absently.

"That's what families do, *'ti Frere*. They help each other."

But Reno was already asleep. Jason arranged the pillows around his patient then walked to the living room couch where he stretched out and kicked off his shoes.

Father, he prayed, *give us strength to overcome those who have harmed Your children, over whom You gave me charge. I ask that You will strengthen me and use me as the instrument of Your retribution. As You have always done since the day that I accepted Your call to be Your servant of justice, I pray that You will empower me and give me the wisdom to know who should die, and to deliver death according to their deeds. Show me also to whom I am to show mercy, if that is Your will.*

Being the scalpel of God was a heavy responsibility, especially when one must bear it alone. Reno knew that he killed, but he had no idea that it was by command of the Most High, not for money. The money he took from those he removed from the earth was used to fund his operations. Seeing the cash, when there was cash to see, allowed Reno to believe that his 'Ton Djé was a professional.

Jason was at peace with his calling. God doesn't give any man more than he can handle as long as he places his hope in Christ. It was by meditating on the Word that he was able to fight off the feelings of guilt as he killed the Nielsens in their own home according to the Most High's command. And it was keeping his thoughts on the Father that helped him through the task of moving Tara to their living room that terrible night and preparing the scene for discovery the next morning. *No one knows the mind of God*, he reminded himself. *You heard the Voice and you obeyed, just as you always have. Obedience and faithfulness are all that He requires.* And the reward for faithfulness would be great when he reached the end of his days on earth.

Hadley smiled a bit at the thought as he drifted to sleep.

Chapter Twenty-nine

Gary smelled the enticing aromas of pancakes, bacon and coffee. He opened his eyes and sat up in bed, looking around for Pam who had stayed the night with him, but she was already up. *Well, of course, idiot.* He shook his head and wiped the sleep from his eyes. *She's cooking breakfast while you lay here like a lazy bum in your own home.*

He pulled himself out of bed and put a pair of shorts on, and then made the short walk to the kitchen where he saw his new girlfriend standing with her back to him at the stove, wearing one of his uniform shirts and apparently nothing else.

"Good morning, officer," he said. "Aren't you a little underdressed to be out on patrol?"

"That depends," she replied, turning and winking at him. "Maybe after breakfast you can teach me to use your handcuffs."

"Oh, you are a bad girl, aren't you?" he walked over and wrapped his arms around her then began caressing her from behind.

"Whoa there, mister," she laughed. "I'd like to do something besides *that* with you sometimes, you know."

"Well, if you don't want to do...*that*," he said undeterred, "then you shouldn't be walking around wearing nothing but my shirt. It turns me on."

"Oh. So if I want to avoid getting dragged into bed with you, I have to wear overalls and a turtleneck?" She knew where this was going, and she was debating whether or not to resist the temptation.

"No, you'd probably turn me on in that, too." He began kissing her at the base of her neck, where he learned she was particularly sensitive.

"Oh, God," she purred. "You don't really want me to finish cooking your breakfast, do you?"

"I'm having my breakfast right now," he said lustily. He swept her up then and carried her to the bedroom.

Later, as Gary showered, Pam lay in bed and stared at the ceiling. *This is wrong,* she thought. This wasn't a relationship; it was a sex partnership. It left her feeling cheap and dirty. She was a Christian; at least that's what she had professed all of her life. Now she wasn't sure what she was, because a Christian woman shouldn't just jump into bed with a guy if she isn't married to him. Here they were, acting like newlyweds, and they hadn't talked at all about where their relationship was going...if anywhere.

I can't keep doing this, she thought.

She got out of bed and dressed, then she went to the living room and sat down on the sofa. When Gary got out of the bathroom, she was going to let him know where she stood. If he couldn't respect her feelings, then he wasn't the right guy for her.

***

The dim glow of pre-dawn shone through the café's front windows. Steam rose from Marshal Brandt's and Deputy Noe's coffee cups, as they pondered the same mystery that had puzzled them for weeks.

"It's like this guy dropped off the face of the earth," Cindy said. "We couldn't track him past the campsite where he stole that couple's truck. A big four-wheeler with a fifth-wheel trailer hitch is hard to lose, but that's just what we did. We lost him."

"Well, Gary had the right idea, at least," Ray replied. "The guy did head into the woods. And, he made it quite a distance, considering the amount of blood he was losing along the way." He shook his head in bewilderment, "But, as large as this area is, a DPS helicopter, a Sheriff's Department helicopter and two squads of police officers should have been able to find some evidence of where he went."

"That snow helped him a lot," Cindy said.

"Yeah, it saved him. He had to have either been able to stop the bleeding somehow, or he has friends somewhere near here, because we haven't heard so much as a whisper from any of the hospitals. And, what really gets me is that we don't have any leads on the truck!"

"Yeah," Cindy nodded. "Like I said, it's hard to hide that big of a vehicle, especially one with a great, big fifth-wheel hitch mounted in the middle of the bed. And, there aren't any reports of abandoned vehicles that match that description. So, unless he managed to get it to a chop shop, he's bound to be long gone."

"Need a refill, guys?" Min asked as she poured more coffee into their cups without waiting for a reply. "Where's Gary? I ain't seen him in a couple days."

"Gary has the next two weeks off," Ray smiled. "He needs a little time to relax after the month he's had."

"He's on suspension, you mean," Min winked. "I know about it."

"You do?"

"Yeah, Gary was moanin' about it for a couple of weeks. He was wondering when you were going to make him take the time off."

"Yeah, well, I couldn't spare him 'til now," Ray replied. "I just hope he remembers why he's getting it. Waiting two months to enforce a suspension kind of weakens the punishment. But, the Council insisted that I do it. So, there you are."

"It'll work out, 'Dad'," Cindy teased. "He's a good boy, and you raised him right."

"He's already got a father, Cindy," Ray bristled, "who did raise him right. And, I'm sure he'll make good choices. Now, let's order breakfast before Min kicks us out of here."

Min smiled at Cindy and took down the usual order of eggs and sausage for both officers, then headed back to the counter. When she got there, she whispered in her husband's ear then went through the double doors to the back room. Ken, an impish grin lighting up his face, walked to Ray and Cindy's booth and whispered, "I smell a new pool in the works."

"No more pools!" Ray demanded.

"Ray," Ken raised his hands in surrender. "I'm just calling it as I see it."

"Pools are bad news around here."

The Marshal's cellphone rang. Ray saw that it was from the Coconino County Sheriff's Office.

"Summertown Marshal's Office, Brandt speaking," he answered.

Cindy Noe watched as her boss's countenance faded to white, and his eyes closed, apparently in anguish. The conversation was short, Ray told them he would call them back soon.

"What's up?" Cindy asked.

"Bad, bad news," the marshal sighed, closing his eyes and bowing his head.

***

It took me awhile to figure out what had just interrupted my deep and restful sleep, and when I did, I looked at the alarm clock next to my bed and was filled with apprehension. I got out of bed and put on my robe, then stumbled to answer the front door where someone was ringing the bell every few seconds. Ray stood in the entrance when I opened it, his face somber.

"Jimmy…"

"When did it happen?" I asked. Somehow, I knew Tara was gone. I knew it the moment I heard the doorbell, and seeing Ray standing with that somber look on his face confirmed it.

"Sometime late last night," he said sadly, not bothering to ask how I knew. "I'm so sorry, Jimmy. I wish…"

"I know," I said, waving away the kindness. "I had a feeling something would happen. I couldn't be sure what, but I just knew *something*…" I couldn't finish. I just stood there with my clouded vision and hazy mind, numbed by the news. "How did she die?" I asked flatly.

"It was reported that she…" he sighed, shook his head and went on, "She hung herself."

"How? She was supposed to be monitored. They weren't supposed to let her get hold of anything…"

"She took her shirt off and twisted it up, used it as a rope," he said sadly. "She did it after lights-out, between bed-checks."

"Oh, my God," I moaned. The idea of her watching and waiting to do herself in, planning for it, made me nauseous.

"Jimmy, let me call Jessie for you."

"No. No, thanks, Ray," I said hastily. "I don't want to upset her."

"Then, let me call Gina. Anybody. I don't want you to be alone."

"That makes two of us," I said humorlessly. "But, that's what I am. And, that's how I'll handle this. Alone."

"Jimmy…"

"Ray," I reached out and put my hand on his shoulder. "I appreciate you coming here and telling me in person. I really do. And thanks for trying to help. But, there's no way of fixing this. My wife is dead. No matter what happened between us, she *was my wife."* Then I remembered what that meant, and I sighed resignedly, "And now, I need to call her brother and break the news."

"If you want, I can do that," Ray offered delicately.

"No," I shook my head. "It should come from me. He deserves to hear it from family."

"Well, if there's anything I can do…"

"I know," I said. "Thanks again."

"Call me if…"

"I will. I promise."

The last of my self-control deserted me the moment I closed the door. As soon as I heard the click of the latch, I sank to my knees and wept bitterly.

Chapter Thirty

The days passed slowly as I made arrangements for Tara's funeral. The worst part, by far, was telling her brother, Ed. I had never heard him cry before and prayed I would never hear it again. I could feel his anguish through the phone, as his moans mixed with desperate pleas to God that it not be true. And asking why, over and over again. As painful as it was for me, my sadness was nothing compared with this man's. Though Tara was a few years older than him, he had taken on the role of big brother, watching out for his sister ever since their father, who raised them after the death of their mother from ovarian cancer, passed away when Ed was in his junior year of high school.

He had helped her get out of an abusive marriage, had helped her pay for college and was always there for her as she battled with the depression and mental illness. He didn't marry until she moved to Summertown and had clearly begun a happy new life. She had been the single most important person in his life, and now, suddenly, she was gone. I offered to have her body sent back to Indiana to be buried with her family, but he turned me down.

"She was miserable here, Jimmy," he said. "The only time she ever let herself be really happy—even though it was only for a little while—was her time in Arizona. She should be buried there."

I almost offered them the use of the house, but thought better of it. That was where Tara and I had lived together. It was the last place she had lived, and there were too many bad memories associated with it to be a good place for her family to stay. Instead, I told him I would get one of the many rental homes in town made ready for them.

He thanked me for telling him, then he began to weep and moan all over again. Then, through his sobs he said, "Goodbye", and hung up. I was still holding the phone to my ear with the dial tone humming long after the conversation ended, lost in my thoughts and praying that God would somehow ease the pain of this poor, tender-hearted guy.

I was incredibly busy this time of year as it was and making funeral arrangements, as necessary as they were, just added to the stress of the season. But, the hectic schedule did help keep me from getting morose for too long, which Jessie had warned me about a couple of days ago.

"Papi," she said, "you are always kicking yourself for past mistakes. You need to stop it. You can't change the past. Just move on and count your blessings. Whenever you get down in the dumps, think about what you'll do when your grandson is born." Then she grabbed my hand and put it on her belly so I could feel him move.

That short bit of contact with the tiny life that was growing in my little girl's tummy sent a rush of warmth through me that put everything in perspective. Jessie was right. It was what Gina had told me before, and yet. I turned around and let the hard times get to me all over again. God had given me all of these wonderful blessings and no matter what else had taken place around me, He was still watching over me, just as He always had. Despite all of my myriad shortcomings, He never left me.

***

The day of the funeral was clear and lovely, the kind of day Tara loved to spend down at Tubman Park near the pond, watching the ducks and geese swim over the areas of the water that weren't frozen over. Despite the friendships that she had lost in the past year, most of the town turned out to show their respects, many coming to offer their condolences to Ed and me.

I felt foolish sitting in the section reserved for bereaved family members. I had filed for divorce weeks before she died, and I was in a committed relationship with Gina now.

But, Ed practically begged me to sit with him and Gloria. He was holding up very well, I thought. But then, Father Duplesy began the mass and the poor man just fell apart. He buried his face in his small wife's shoulder and wailed and wept for the rest of the service. I had feared that, because Tara had committed suicide, the Funeral Mass would not be given for her. But, the father said she was absolved of the sin of self-murder, as she was clearly not in her right mind at the time.

It was a short service, and I was only half-listening to the priest. Most of my thoughts were taken up with trying to remember Tara the way she was when we were deeply in love. Those brief few years of married joy were so very sweet that, as long as I allowed them to stay at the forefront of my memories of her, the pain and the guilt that I carried were made less painful.

After the somber graveside committal service where only about half of the original congregation attended, we met at the house Tara and I had lived, for a small reception. Ken and Min insisted on taking care of everything, and Chad did all of the setup of the tables and chairs. I don't know what I would have done without them. Gina looked terribly sad, sitting in the chair where Tara would read and stare out the window in springtime. She spent much of the time looking at Ed and Gloria. I couldn't quite work out what was on her mind, but I could see that this whole day was deeply affecting her.

Jessie and Tom sat together on the sofa, saying nothing. After all, what could be said? We had lost Tara long before she took her own life. Today was merely a formality. Unlike most funeral receptions I had been to, even my mother's, no one had a happy or humorous story to share about the deceased. It was as if no one could remember anything about her. Ed was still too heartbroken to get through a sentence without crying. So, I felt that it was my duty share something.

"You know," I began spontaneously, my voice cracking a bit. I stood up from the chair I was occupying and continued. "You know, Tara had an impish sense of humor." I cleared my throat and went on, working hard to grin as I spoke. "But one thing she was very serious about was her job. She loved teaching." People nodded in agreement. "Every night, she would talk about how each of her students was doing. They were like her own children. She worry about them like a mother would; if they were eating right, if they were fitting in with the rest of the class, you name it, she worried about it. She was warm, she was caring and she was a good woman. That's what I want us all to remember her for. Not this...*evil sickness* that took her away from us, but the real, kindhearted, loving Tara we'll all miss." When Ed began to sob, I knew I'd said enough. I sat down and put my arm on his shoulder. I wished there was some way to alleviate some of the agony he was going through, but I knew that was impossible.

I hoped that others would share, but that didn't happen. Even Harold Chapman, the most jovial guy I knew, was silent, his eyes glued to the floor. After a while the few that were there filtered out of the house and soon we were left alone to clean things up.

Gina had stayed through it all, never saying a word. She didn't sit next to me. The only time she had any contact with me was to offer me a cup of coffee, then she went and sat back down. I couldn't guess what she was thinking of the whole time. Then, after Ed and Gloria left, she got up from her chair and walked over to me. She wrapped her arms around my waist, rested her head on my chest and squeezed me tight, holding me like that for a long, long time. It was then that it finally occurred to me why she had remained in the corner, out of the way. It was out of respect for Ed, whose grief was great enough not seeing that his brother-in-law had moved on with his life. She didn't want to cause him any more distress than he was already going through. At that moment, I decided that I was going to marry this woman…but not yet. I wasn't going to make that kind of mistake again. I was going to take this one slowly and carefully.

Chapter Thirty-one

It was another pleasant day in Clearwater, Florida. The view of the Gulf of Mexico this time of year was beautiful and the air was just warming up to a brisk coolness that made a walk along the beach something that Ted Linelli looked forward to. He stood on the deck of his home and breathed in the soothing breeze, looked down at the beach only twenty yards away and saw no one. He'd worked a long time and taken a lot of chances to be where he was today, and it was all worth it. Smiling, he went back inside and headed for the stairs.

"Labadee," he called to his personal assistant. The house was silent. "Labadee!" he shouted. Still there was no reply.

Linelli stomped from room to room, calling and searching for some sign of the man whose contract required him to be immediately available twenty-fours a day. Not one to take his authority being flouted lightly, he got angrier the longer he spent searching.

"I should never have hired you, you stupid, lazy-ass Haitian," he said aloud. "If Francois wasn't your cousin I'd have kicked your ass out my house the first day!"

When he arrived in the lounge at the back of the house he had lost all control of his temper. He was about to leave the room and continue his search when he spotted Labadee's head behind the bar, like he was crouched down close to the edge of the counter.

"What the hell are you doing hiding from me?!" he shouted. "Are you drunk? I told you about drinking during the day…"

Something was wrong. Labadee wasn't moving.

"Labadee…?"

Linelli walked nervously toward the bar but stopped abruptly when he saw one of the burly Haitian's legs sprawled toward the Arcadia door that led to the terrace. The door was open, allowing the soft Gulf breeze to waft through the place, and on that breeze there was another scent that Ted knew well. It was the scent of death.

"I feel badly about your man," someone behind him said. "He was in the wrong place at the wrong time."

Startled, Ted turned quickly to confront a man he hadn't seen in many years, and certainly hadn't expected to see alive. Jay Hadley had hardly changed. He still looked to be about sixty years old, with that same thinning gray hair.

His features were somewhat square and his eyes were a cold grey-green. The expression on his face was hard to read.

"But these things happen, don't they?" Jay went on. "You know that as well as anyone, don't you, Ted?"

"What the hell are you doing here?" Linelli demanded while trying to will his legs from shaking.

"That's the businessman's way, isn't it?" the intruder smiled coldly. "Straight to the point." He pulled a Glock pistol from his waistband and held it in his open palm. "Since when does a mild-mannered Christian man, owner of a respectable building supply business, need his personal assistant to carry one of these?"

When he didn't receive an answer, Jason began walking slowly towards Linelli who stood motionless, strangely fascinated by him. He removed the magazine from the gun and racked the slide, ejecting the unfired cartridge. The loud 'pop' it made as it hit the parquet flooring echoed off the bare walls of the room and made Ted flinch. Hadley pressed his thumb on the side of the gun and the slide closed with a solid, metal-on-metal 'clack'. Then he tossed the weapon away to his left, like one would discard a worthless piece of trash.

"You know, you should never hire people who haven't been referred to you by reputable sources." Seeing Linelli's puzzled look, he explained, "Going on the Tor network to hire a killer nowadays is like pinning an ad up on a laundry room bulletin board. You never know who you're going to get, or if they can do the job." He stopped only a few inches from Linelli and smiled. "The men you hired to kill Reno Chatelaine failed. He's a trained professional, they were just a bunch of gang-bangers who thought the job was an easy way to a quick buck. Reno's doing well, by the way, but—it's probably stating the obvious—he's *very* unhappy with you." Jason stopped and opened his arms, and added, "And, as you can see, the guys you hired to kill *me* failed. They failed miserably…but they did keep excellent records."

Linelli didn't see, but definitely felt Hadley's hand shoot forward and grab his groin, squeezing his testicles like a vise then quickly pulling out, away from him until he felt them tear. He screamed, doubling over in agony. A hand on the back of his head shoved it down hard until his face met an upward-swinging knee. His own knees buckled and he crumpled to the ground, unable to feel anything from his nose to his chin, his hands cradling his ruined manhood.

"You'll be answering some questions, Ted," Jason said casually. "And if I don't think you're being truthful with me, I'm going to hurt you again, very badly." He knelt down and pinned one of Linelli's arms behind his back and threw him onto his stomach, then added, "I know that you came to the Lespri Bondye Mission looking for a source of young girls and that you managed to lead Jacques Philippe—a man of God—down the path of evil. He was weak and you knew it, so it was probably easy to easy to talk him into it. Philippe must answer for his sins, but you will be held accountable for, not only yours, but every other soul you led down the road to hell. You can plan for a very, very painful death, Ted. Or, I can end your life quickly if I think you've been especially helpful." He grabbed his victim's face and twisted his head so that he could look into his eyes again as he said, "Either way, I've been appointed to send you to your judgment, for the sins you've committed against God's children. So, prepare your soul."

***

Philippe Jacques smiled broadly as he invited his friend, Reno Chatelaine into his home. He raised his hands to the sky and began to shout praises to God for protecting his friend, breaking into song and embracing him. But when the embrace wasn't returned he stepped back and looked closely at the young man's face. All sense of affection or friendship had disappeared. His friend knew the truth about him now, he could tell. Philippe looked behind his guest to see if there was anyone else with him, then he shrugged and casually waved Reno into his home.

"I have nothing to say to you," Jacques said as he closed the door behind them. He walked to the sofa then sat down, then picked up the remote control for the television and turned it on, acting as if Chatelaine's presence was something merely to be ignored. Reno felt the change in this man whom he'd loved and trusted for most of his life. He now saw under the mask that Philippe had been wearing for so long and it sickened him to his core.

"'Nothing to say'?" he said incredulously. "You have been selling the children you took in to your orphanage, and you have nothing to say? You killed your own wife when she found out about it—no, you didn't even have the courage to do it yourself, you had someone else do it for you. You conned us into moving you here, where you've been living like a king through the misery of defenseless children…and you have 'nothing to say'?" He stood directly in front of Jacques, blocking his view of the television. "You sold a child that Jimmy brought to you for protection and you took his money every month for the past twenty years, money that was supposed to pay for *her needs*. And to pretend to be a man of God all of this years…" his voice choked off as he tried to contain his rage.

"I make no apologies for what I've done," Philippe replied flatly. "It was business. No life is more important than another. Their lives were no more important than mine.

Simply because I took advantage of the opportunities given to me doesn't make me a monster. We all end up in the same place in the end."

"No," Reno said emphatically. "The innocent children you sold to the Boudreaux brothers are in heaven right now. But you are going to hell."

The look in Philippe's eyes signaled surprise. Reno could see that Jacques hadn't realized how much he knew.

"So, you know about my business with Francois Boudreaux," the older man shrugging derisively. "So what? Francois is dead and so is Michel."

"Why should I believe you?"

"I don't care if you believe me or not," Philippe said. He was trying his best to act unaffected, but the twitch in his right eye gave him away. "He was the one who shot you at Mireille's house. You shot back and killed him. And when you did that, you took away my suppliers. Now I have to look for a new connection among Francois' aides. Do you know how long that is going to take?"

"You really think that I'm going to let you live after what you've done," Reno said, incredulous. "How can you honestly believe such a thing? You tried to kill me. You tried to kill Jason…"

"That was my partner," Jacques said, confidently. "He is the enforcer in this operation, and that is why I know you won't dare kill me."

"You had the nerve to sell those children to the worst kind of human garbage, yet you didn't have the courage to kill me yourself?"

"'Those children' were dumped at my doorstep by their parents because they were a burden to them," Philippe countered. "They couldn't feed them, so they expected me to do their job for them. Well, I am no less important than any of those little *freluké*. I spent years helping them, pretending to love them, caring for them while I watched my wife get old and fat and ugly. My 'reward' for loyal service to a 'loving God' was to work myself to death caring for someone else's children and to live the rest of my life with a woman I could barely look at? I admit it to you now: the mission was a business. I started it so that I could make a living, and that is all.

"At first, I thought, 'Look at all of these poor children. I can share whatever I get from the rich people I meet and we can all survive together.'" He laughed, "How naïve I was. It took only a little while to realize that the rich will throw you only a few crumbs from their table and expect you to survive. And the children just kept coming, each of them with their mouths open like little birds. Their mothers would

363

bring them to me and say that they couldn't take care of them anymore. I tried to say no, but Denise would always take them in anyway."

Reno watched Philippe's face become harder and colder as he spoke. *How could we have been conned by such a man?* he thought. *How could we have been so blind? Did any of us even bother to look into this man's eyes to see the monster inside?* Looking at him now, it seemed impossible that they could have missed such pure evil.

"I watched while TiZo and his gang enjoyed themselves, dancing, gambling and driving new cars, spending their nights with women I would have killed for," Jacques said. "And then I would look at my sweet wife Denise, with her warm smile and motherly face…and her *fat* arms and *big, flabby* stomach, her nose that got bigger as she got older, and I grew to hate her—yes, *hate her*, even though I knew she did nothing to deserve it. Because the same 'God' who let men like TiZo live in luxury, never worrying about where to find their next meal. He allowed them to simply *take* whatever they wanted without fear of punishment, but He made a man like me live in squalor, getting his pleasures where he could get them. Then, Francois came to me and made a business proposition." He sneered and said, "At first, I refused, like the good Christian 'shepherd' that I was supposed to be. I thought he might be trying to test if I was legitimate. But when he sent TiZo, who threatened to burn down the mission and just take the girls he wanted, I knew that I was in business."

"You didn't give any thought to the children you were selling."

"Of course I did," Jacques replied indignantly. "I am not a monster, despite what you may think. I was fond of many of those girls. But it was either they stay and we starve together, or they go where they would be fed and clothed and I would be paid for my services. For years, I had to think about how I was going to feed fifty people on the tiny donations we received from people in the U.S. who thought they were so *holy*, so *generous* for sending a few dollars a month out of their *thousands...!*" Jacques stopped himself in mid-tirade. He sighed, shrugged and said, "I took what I wanted—only a little bit of what I *could* have taken. If God judges the affairs of men, then He'll surely take a look at what I've done for Him and be merciful. After all, if your wonderful *Tonton Djé* can go around killing people in the name God, why can't I send a few children to places where they'll be clothed and fed regularly, and all they need to do in return is show a little affection to their benefactors?"

"Whoever you are," Reno said, staring at Philippe as if facing the devil himself, "you've destroyed enough lives. Today, you are going to die."

"If I die, so will Jimmy and his family," Philippe replied with a malicious grin. "Do you really think I'm in this alone? My partner will kill you and everyone in your family. He…"

"Are you referring to Ted Linelli?" He shook his head slowly, emphatically. "Jason killed Ted Linelli three hours ago."

Philippe Jacques' eyes widened and the wicked grin on his face disappeared.

"Before he died," Reno went on, "he told Jay everything about your filthy little 'business'. He admitted that he was the one who told TiZo to kill Denise because you didn't have the balls to do it yourself. Actually," he smiled coldly, "he admitted it because he was getting his ears torn off with a pair of pliers." He took out a pair of leather gloves and began putting them on as Jacques watched in terrified anticipation. "He also admitted to hiring the men who tried to kill me in Arizona…*and* the amateurs that tried to kill Jay." Reno moved his fingers around and clenched his fists in the gloves to get a good fit. "And when Jason wouldn't put him out of his misery, he told him that you were the one who gave Boudreaux information about my family." He grabbed the old man by the collar of his shirt and yanked him forward. *"You're the reason my family is dead,"* he snarled. "And I'm going to kill you for it."

Jacques pulled away, shrank back into the sofa and screamed, *"Jean Baptiste…!"*

A hard backhand from Reno shut him up.

"You're alone, *'Pastor',*" Reno said with ice-cold menace. "Jason and I killed your two stupid apes while you were having your afternoon nap. Maybe you should have spent a little more money on *real* protection instead of a couple of fat, lazy *macoutes.*" He slapped Philippe across the face again and said, "What luxury, to be waited on hand and foot, spending your afternoons in bed…" he struck him again, "while the ones you've made your money from are raped and beaten, starved, forced into drugs, or just killed to make room for another poor, defenseless victim. You know perfectly well that those boys and girls you have been selling are treated like animals. They aren't 'fed regularly and clothed', you piece of *shit!* They're *raped!* They're *beaten!* They're *mutilated and killed,* their bodies are thrown away like garbage. You've known this all along, and you've pretended to be a *servant of God* for all of these years. You will be judged for your sins and you will burn in *hell* for them."

He pounced on top of the old man and watched him shrink into the sofa, his hands up to defend himself from another slap, terror now visible on his face.

"I'm going to kill you now, *salop!*" he said through clenched teeth. "And I am going to do it slowly."

"Reno, don't," Jason said. He had entered the room a moment ago, but Reno had been so intent on exacting revenge that he hadn't noticed. "We gain nothing by torturing him. We already have all the information we need. Revenge won't make the pain go away."

"I know," Reno growled. "But that doesn't mean I have to make his death quick."

"Reno, please!" Jacques begged. "*Please…!*"

Chatelaine's hands were already around the man's throat and squeezing. Philippe gripped Reno's wrists and tried frantically to pull them away, kicking at the air, trying to wriggle out of Reno's grasp. He threw flailing strikes at his killer's face, tried to gouge at his eyes but Chatelaine simply head-butted him in the face without even loosening his grip. The younger man was just too strong.

Strangulation is a horrible way to die, as Jacques Philippe was discovering. His eyes bulged and his face turned a deep purplish red as his brain began to use up its remaining oxygen supply. His mouth opened and his tongue protruded from it like some creature desperately trying to escape from the dying organism that it had called home until now. His lungs burned from the desperate need for the air that they would never again hold. After a long, agonizing struggle Philippe Jacques collapsed and his hands fell away from his killer's arm. Reno continued to squeeze Philippe's throat until the man's vacant eyes stared, half-closed, into space, a mix of terror and anguish frozen on his face.

"It's over," Jason whispered. He had waited until his godson's rage ebbed, never leaving his place nor trying to stop him. "We need to leave. We need to put all of this behind us now."

With difficulty, Reno pulled his hands from his victim's neck, the muscles in his palms now aching from the strain. He stood up and allowed Jason to check Jacques's pulse while he caught his breath. He hadn't realized how much energy it had taken from him. Then, without another word, they went about removing all evidence of their presence. When they had finished they left the house, Jason dropping a large manila envelope on the dining room table on the way out. As they exited through the back door, they stepped over the body of a large man, lying face-down in a puddle of his own blood.

Chapter Thirty-two

"Ray, why don't you just grab her by the hand, drag her to the church and *make* her marry you?" I asked.

"What do you mean, *make* her? Did you ever *make* Corinda do anything?"

We were sitting at the counter of the café while Ken filled our cups and listened as Ray vented his frustrations. After months of trying to talk Corinda into marrying him, he was no closer to a wedding than he'd been when she put him off the first time.

"Well, of course not," I shrugged. "But that's because I'm a wimp. You're not. And," I tapped the badge on his shirt, "you're a 'man in uniform'. She'll do whatever you tell her, if you just turn on that commanding presence of yours."

"You're not a wimp, Jimmy, and you know it," he replied. "As far as my 'commanding presence' goes, I tried that. It got me nowhere."

"Just give her some time, Ray," Ken said. "She'll change her mind."

"I doubt that, Ken," Ray replied. "It's been almost four months."

"Are you still seeing each other?"

"Well, yes, of course."

"Then she still wants you. Just give her time and she'll come around. Trust me."

Ray shook his head. "I'm getting to where I almost don't care."

"You're not breaking up with her, are you?" I asked, alarmed.

"Well," Ray lowered his voice and looked around the room. "I'm giving it serious thought. I don't need any more stress in my life right now."

"I can understand that," I replied. I looked over my shoulder to make sure we were the only ones within earshot before I went on. "But let me share something with you that you had better never, ever tell Corinda I said....*promise*?"

They both shrugged and nodded, which I took as assent.

"If I had it to do all over again—despite everything I've said about her—I'd never have let Corinda go. She was a good wife. She's a loyal, warm, caring woman. A great cook. Even when she gained weight, she was always beautiful. You won't find another woman like her, Ray. I'm lucky getting another chance at love with Gina. But I wouldn't have needed it if I'd been wise enough to see what

I had. If I had done what I should have, and worked to save my marriage to Corinda, she'd still be mine. But the fact is, she's not. She's yours. She's in love with you. Don't throw that away. Be the man she always wanted but never got when she was married to me."

Ray let that sink in. I knew it was a lot to absorb. After all those years of bad-mouthing Corinda, here I was saying that I wished I'd never lost her.

"All right, Jimmy," he said at last, his voice a little hoarse. "I'll give it another try. You're right. I shouldn't throw away a chance to keep Corinda in my life." He got up, put an arm around my shoulder and gave me a warm man-hug. "And thanks for sharing that. I know it had to be hard."

I nodded, unable to speak. He had changed his mind entirely because of what I just told him and I didn't want him realizing that it was the biggest load of manure I'd ever shoveled up in my life.

"Yo, Bubba!" Cindy Noe shouted from the front door of the restaurant. "Harold just called! He's coming down here to talk to you! He says it's urgent!"

"Well, it can't be that urgent if he wants to meet at the café instead of meeting me at the office," Ray replied.

"Well, he sure sounded agitated."

"Oh, alright," he sighed.

Two minutes later, Harold arrived with his daughter, Pam and Gary Callan in tow. Harold was clearly not a happy camper, but Pam was smiling brightly. She stopped at the door and raised her left hand to display a big, gold wedding band with a little, square-cut diamond.

"Guess who just got married!" she squealed as Gary stood bashfully behind her, hoping that no one would notice him.

"I told you I would have won that pool!" Ken crowed.

"What!" Ray shouted before he could stop himself. He gulped twice, breathed in deep and tried again, keeping his voice as even as he could. "Wow. Well, congratulations, you two. That's great."

"Cut the crap, Ray," Harold barked. "You're as shocked as I was." He turned to his daughter, who was not at all bothered by his reaction. "Do you have any idea just how *stupid* what you've done is? You hardly know each other!"

"Well, they do in the Biblical sense," quipped Ken. This got him a hard smack on the back of the head from his wife.

"You're not helping," growled Harold.

"I'm just saying that the marriage has been pre-consummated…"

"Ken!"

"It's done, Daddy," Pam said firmly. "So, you can be happy for us or you can sit and stew over it. But we're married and that's that." She took her new husband by the hand and pulled him toward the front door. Gary remained silent, following his wife like an obedient Labrador retriever.

They were almost out the door when Harold threw his arms up and said, "OK, you win!" He waved them back into the room and walked over them, his arms open. "You're both adults and you can make your own decisions." He hugged his daughter. "I just want you to be happy, sweetheart. If this is what you really want, then," he held out his hand to Gary who took it nervously, "welcome to the family, son." Then he put his hand on the young man's shoulder and added, "If you hurt her, I'll kill you."

"Daddy, don't be such a goofball."

"I'm dead serious, boy."

"No he isn't," Pam assured her husband.

"Oh, yes, I am!"

"Daddy, you wouldn't try to kill the father of your grandbaby."

Harold looked stricken. "The father…"

"I didn't get a chance to tell you at first," she said, barely containing her glee. "I'm pregnant!"

No one spoke. Harold's eyes were wide with shock and his mouth hung open. Pam's smile disappeared as she suddenly realized that her dad may be having a heart attack. She and Gary took him by the arms and anxiously led him over to a chair and sat him down as Ken ran to the fountain and got him a glass of water. I got out my phone and began to dial 9-1-1.

"Daddy?" Pam said, hoping that her father wasn't too far gone to hear her. "Daddy, can you hear me?" She took his face in her hands and in panic she wailed, "Please, Daddy. Daddy please stay with us. Daddy, please don't die!"

Ray and Gary were at Harold's side in an instant. Ray put his finger to his friend's neck to check his pulse, Gary reached for his father-in-law's shirt collar and began to loosen his ever-present necktie. But the instant that the men made contact with him, Harold bolted up from his chair, causing Pam to jump back and scream while Ray and Gary grabbed his arms to control him.

"That's what you almost did to me, you little brat!" he shouted. "Were you trying to kill your father? Is that what you were trying to do? Well, that's what it would have been like if you had!"

Cindy Noe burst out laughing. Ray sighed and sat down on the floor where he'd been kneeling. Ken groaned in relief and Min caught herself snorting with laughter.

I told the dispatcher it was a mistake and there was no emergency, but she said paramedics were on the way and she couldn't cancel a 911 emergency call.

Pam was still trying to catch her breath from receiving the fright of her life when her father took her in her arms and said, "Congratulations, sweetheart. It isn't under the circumstances that I'd have liked for you, but the man responsible," he scowled at Gary who was still in defense posture and just now realizing there was no threat, "did the honorable thing, and I'm glad."

Pam had recovered and now she was livid. She pushed her father away and pointed an accusing finger at him.

"You're *a—jerk!*" she shouted, barely stopping herself from using another word. "What if you made me go into labor? I would have lost the baby!"

"How far along are you?" Harold asked, worried.

"Five weeks."

"Oh," he laughed. "I doubt you were at risk, sweetheart…"

"How do you know?!"

"I just do!"

"Oh, you know *everything, don't you?*" She grabbed Gary by the hand and pulled him behind her as she headed for the door. "Well, I suppose if 'Doctor Chapman' says there's nothing to worry about, then we can get back to our honeymoon, can't we Gary?"

"Uh...yeah, sure," he replied, embarrassed that she had brought up their intimate activities in public.

"I mean, the marriage may be 'pre-consummated,'" Pam said, throwing a look toward Ken as she spoke, "but we're going home right now and just *keep on consummatin' it!*" She dragged her husband a few more feet then stopped again, turned around and shouted at the top of her lungs, "We're going to consummate the *hell* out of it!" she opened the door then stopped again and shouted, "*We're gonna frickin' consummate it 'til neither of us can walk straight!*" Then she opened the door and yanked her meek and obedient husband, his face now a deep red, outside with her.

Cindy was beaming. "*God,* I love it here."

***

It was finally beginning to warm up a bit in the afternoon. I had been visiting Jason at his house pretty regularly since he came back from driving Reno to Miami in February, and we had become pretty close. When I told him about Tara's suicide he was so deeply affected that I could have sworn he almost cried. I hadn't realized until then just how much we all meant to him.

Today we were enjoying the bright, breezy, mid-March day, sitting on the front deck of Jason's home and drinking the only real coffee I could get my hands on that I didn't brew myself. I made terrible coffee, so I was grateful that Jason served the good stuff without lecturing me about the dangers it held to my digestive tract.

"Refill?" Jay asked, filling my mug without waiting for a response.

"One more cup and that'll be it," I said. "I have to fall asleep sometime tonight."

I leaned back in my chair and surveyed the layout of the town. I never knew just how great a view this place had. Everybody said it was just a shack but whatever Jay did with it, it certainly wasn't a shack anymore. The walls were painted, the beams in the ceiling were stained and varnished. The kitchen was completely redone with granite countertops, walnut cabinets and stainless steel appliances. He'd had a big picture window installed next to the door leading out to the deck and from the living room, on a clear, pre-spring day like today, you could see for miles.

"How's Reno doing out there in Miami?" I asked. "Has he found work yet?"

"No," Jay replied. "He doesn't really need to work at this point. He's put in for medical retirement from the State Department and that should go into effect in about another month. I offered to help him out until he starts getting regular checks, but he says he has plenty of money saved."

"How did the trip back home go for him?"

"Hard, of course," he grimaced. "Robert's parents wanted him to stay with them. But he told them he couldn't live there anymore. The memories are just too fresh."

"I can only imagine."

"Yes," he agreed. "They offered to buy the house from him—Robert and Mireille named him in their will after Soraya. He took them up on it."

"Did they have life insurance?"

"A big policy," he nodded. "When that passes through probate, Reno told me, he's going to donate it to UNICEF."

I almost asked why he didn't donate it to Philippe Jacques's ministry, but I caught myself. The news report of Philippe being killed in his home by a rival sex trafficking syndicate had rocked me to my very foundation. Ted Linelli, the man who had ridden with us in search of a doctor for the pastor's dying wife, was also implicated. Jason said that the last he had heard from a friend at the Haitian Consulate in Miami, they were still making arrests in connection with the slave ring. Jason and I spent many hours talking about it over the last several weeks and it boiled down to one simple and obvious fact: men are capable of all kinds of good and all kinds of evil.

"Ted and Philippe—especially Philippe—they fooled us all, Jimmy," Jason had said. "They weren't the first men to lead double lives, leaving heartbreak and pain in their wake, and they won't be the last. Things won't improve until Jesus comes back."

"True."

"The one thing news like this does, is it reminds me that none of us are immune to sin. And remember, God doesn't differentiate one sin from another. Sin is sin, period. As Jesus said to the Pharisees when they brought the adulteress to him, 'Let him who is without sin cast the first stone.' I try very hard not to cast stones at anyone, because I know very well what I'm capable of."

"Yeah, I can relate," I replied.

"Which brings me to ask the question: When will you be making an honest woman of Gina? I know you two have been getting very serious lately."

"It's a little early," I replied. "Tara's funeral was…"

"You've got a grandbaby coming in a few months," he interrupted, "He'll need all the good examples of healthy relationships possible. You should marry the woman you've been sleeping with all these months."

"You know, you're awfully quick with relationship advice. How is it you never got married? You never even talk about having dated. Why is that?"

Jason smiled wistfully as he looked at me, his head tilted a bit like he was considering my words.

"I never had a chance to have but one."

"What do you mean, 'never had a chance'?" I asked. "Did you take some sort of vow of celibacy or something? How is it, as old as you are…?"

"I did have a brief relationship with someone during my second tour in Vietnam," he said. "She was a sweet young girl of about eighteen, I was about twenty-three, I think. We liked each other lot." He smiled and nodded at the memory. "But then I got injured in the field. We were on patrol in an area we heard was crawling with VC. A buddy of mine was walking ahead of me. He stepped on a mine and was killed almost instantly. Shrapnel sprayed everywhere. It hit me and one other guy in my squad. He got just a few deep cuts around his legs, I think. But I was rendered…" he sighed and shrugged, "impotent. One piece of flying scrap metal went into my groin and took away my ability to have children, and another sliced through my thigh, next to the femoral artery. I would have bled to death if it had struck just a couple of millimeters over."

He held my gaze and said with conviction, "Jimmy, I know it doesn't seem like it would be, but I can tell you with absolute certainty that the single best thing to happen to me—the event that set me on the path that I have followed for the last forty-five years—was losing the very things that had led to the downfall of not only your father, but many, many other men. God placed me at that spot, in that jungle. He guided the path of that shrapnel. Everything that happens to us is ordained by Him. He had singled me out for His work and He guaranteed that I wouldn't be distracted by lustful desire, by removing that part of me from the equation."

What do you say to that? A man tells you that he thanks God for castrating him; that it was the best thing that ever happened to him and you say… What?

Jason smiled in that fatherly way that set me at ease. He could tell I was searching for words that would suit such a revelation.

"Enough about me now," he said, taking me off the hook. "When are you going to ask Gina to marry you?"

"But…"

"But you're older than she is. But she deserves a younger man. But, but, but. Bull!" he slapped the table and made the mugs jump a little. "You wouldn't have had me tell her everything if you didn't plan to marry her."

"Stop thinking about the past," he said. "Think with your eyes on the future. You had joined herself to another and broke her vows long before the divorce was filed. You need to do what is best for you and your family."

"That's what I'm doing," I insisted. "Yesterday, I got my summons for court."

"I thought you were already given a trial date."

"I was," I said. "This is a summons for a civil trial. Jarrett is suing me."

"Oh, no."

"Exactly."

"Why didn't you tell me about this yesterday?"

"What could you do?" I asked. "I'm a big boy, and I can take responsibility for my own actions."

"But your inheritance…"

"I don't want it."

"You don't want *2.4 million dollars*?"

He waited for my response but I couldn't seem to make my mouth work.

"Jimmy?" He waved his hand in front of my face and repeated, "Jimmy? Are you OK?"

"Did I hear you right?"

"Two million, four hundred thousand, three hundred forty dollars," he nodded.

"How…?"

"Very canny investing during his career," he smiled. "And it's all in cash."

"Cash! Where?"

"That you don't need to know," he grinned. "The less you know, the better. So, don't worry about lawsuits. Or anything else, for that matter. You're father has you taken care of."

I closed my eyes and tried to take it all in. After spending my life hating him, then learning that the reasons for his absence from my life weren't entirely his doing, it was very hard to handle. The guilt I was feeling was irrational, but I felt it nonetheless.

"Jimmy," Jason said. "Just take the money and take care of your legal troubles. Your dad left it for you to use as you need it."

"What about taxes? Probate? How do I know this money was made legally?"

"You don't, and you won't," Jason replied flatly. "It is safe, it was earned by your father because it was all he could give you. I can give it to you in annual increments, or I can give it to you all at once. I prefer all at once. You can buy a safe and keep it…"

"That would be illegal!"

"So is aiding and abetting a criminal," he said. "But you helped me get Reno out of the country."

"That was different."

"Was it? You were taking care of family. Your father was taking care of you, his family, when he worked for this money. You'll be taking care of your family when you take this money and use it for their needs."

"I can take care of my…"

He looked at me skeptically. How could I take care of my family when I was almost guaranteed to have to pay a settlement of untold magnitude, which would leave me flat broke, with only enough to pay my bills.

"Let me think about it," I said curtly.

"Take all the time you need," he replied. "You have a lot on your plate right now. The most pressing of which is asking Gina to marry you."

Jason…"

"Jimmy, you know it's what you want to do, and you know it's the right thing to do."

I did respond right away. Instead, I sat and stewed over being told what to do with my life, as if I was some kid fresh out of high school. But after the initial indignation subsided, I came to accept the obvious wisdom of Jay's words.

"You're right," I said finally. "I'll just have to ask her. I don't know what I'll do if she says no."

"You know she'll say yes," Jason chuckled. "There are few times that I've seen two people better suited for each other. Gina has a tough shell, but inside, she's soft and gentle. And she is in love with you. Don't make her wait around, Jimmy. Make her your wife."

I thought about that as I walked home, the sun's rays stretching across the little clearing from the west, smoke rising from the chimneys of a few of the homes in town. I'd been putting off asking Gina to marry me because of what I thought others would think. I thought that the "Poison Tongue Club" would spread rumors, like Gina and I had been having an affair while I was married. Or that I was lonely and needed a wife. But it really didn't matter what they thought. They were going to say what they wanted to say, no matter what I did. I needed to ask Gina to marry me because I loved her and couldn't imagine my life without her.

I changed direction and headed to Gina's house. I decided that I'd better ask her now while I had my courage up. I knocked on her door and waited for several minutes, but she wasn't home. I headed to the school, but it was already closed for the day and everyone had gone home. I went to the café where Ken told me Gina had been there for a little while but left. He said she looked preoccupied. Her car was still in the Little Creek parking lot, so I kept walking down the front strip of town. After checking the General Store and Corinda's hair salon I went into Smokie's where I found her sitting on a barstool, talking to Margie.

"Do you know how many places I've gone to, looking for you?" I asked.

"You found me, didn't you?" she replied brusquely.

"What the heck's wrong with you?" I volleyed back.

"I should ask you the same damn question," she snapped back, a slight slur in her diction. "I was just having a quiet drink and talking to Margie here, and you come barging…"

"Gina's pregnant, Jimmy," Margie said, cutting Gina off in mid-rant. "She didn't know how to tell you, so she came in here and had a few glasses of wine." She addressed the lady in question and said, "And that's all you're getting tonight, young lady. You're carrying a life around now, and I won't be responsible…"

"You're what!" I shouted. The bar wasn't full, but I had gotten the attention of those who were there.

"You knocked me up!" Gina shouted. "So what? It's not like I haven't been through it before."

"Marry me!" I shouted at the most ridiculous time I possibly could have.

"Bite me!" she replied. "I don't need your Catholic guilt. If you really wanted to marry me, you would have asked me before this." She stepped down from her stool and began fishing through her purse. "I don't need a man to raise a baby. I'll get by just fine."

"Like you did last time?" I demanded. "Do you remember who went through that with you?"

"Don't talk about that," she said. "We're talking about now."

"It's the same thing, Gina," I said as I walked closer to her so we could talk without the rest of the room hearing. "I went through it with you then, and I want to be there with you now."

"I'm not a charity case, Mr. Stone!" she shouted, her voice breaking. "I don't want you marrying me just because you think you have to."

"Well, that's just tough," I said. "Because I really do have to." I took her shoulders in both hands and faced her as I said, "I have to ask you to marry me right now because if I don't I'll have to wait until tomorrow. And I've waited way too long as it is. I can't stand the idea of life without you, baby or no baby. I want to share every single part of my life with you. I need you and regardless of what you claim, I think you need me, too. I love you, Gina, and I want you for my wife." Feeling like an idiot, I got down on one knee and asked, "Gina will you marry me?"

"No," she said as she paid her tab and began to leave.

"Yes, dammit!" I demanded. "I love you! You love me! We belong together, and you know it!"

"*I* know it," she replied. "But do you *really* know it, or do you just want to marry me so your baby will have your name?"

"Gina, I came here looking for you because I couldn't go another minute thinking about you, without having you with me. I went to your house, I went to the school, I went to the café and if I didn't find you here I would have gone out looking all the way to Payson if I had to. I want you to marry me. I love you."

Without saying another word, she turned and left. I followed her out to the front where she stopped outside the door and leaned against the wall, as if posing for a photograph.

"Now," she said, straightening her hair. "Ask me again."

"Gina, will you marry me?"

"No."

"What?"

"You didn't call me by my full name," she said, as if everybody knows that.

"OK," I replied contritely. "Gina Albright, will you marry me?"

"No."

"What now!"

"You didn't get down on your knee."

I closed my eyes, took a breath and let it out. Then I knelt on the sidewalk and looked up at her lovely face and asked, "Gina Albright, will you marry me?"

"Actually, my middle name is…"

"Are you going to marry me or not!"

"Of course, stupid! If I didn't want to marry you, I would have left the moment you walked into the bar."

"Holy crap. Is this what I have to look forward to for the rest of my life?"

"What do you think?"

"I think I'm screwed."

"Smart boy."

I stood up then and took her in my arms and kissed her. A little voice in my head was scolding me, reminding me that only a couple of months ago, I was burying Tara. I ignored it. I couldn't change the past, no matter how recent. I could only do my best now to make a good future for myself and those I loved.

***

A big part of what made the wedding great, for me at least, was that I didn't have to do a thing. The moment we announced our engagement, Gina was swept up into the capable arms of Jessica, Pam and Min. Pam was especially enthusiastic because she had missed having the chance to plan her own wedding. I watched as Gina began to show ever-so-slightly and her face took on that beautiful glow that every expectant mother I've ever seen has.

When the day of the wedding finally came, everything was in its proper place…and God help the man who even set foot in the bride's house. Corinda had generously volunteered her services, making an unprecedented house call to give Gina the makeover she'd never admit to always wanting. I later discovered that Corinda even threw in a brief Spanish lesson. *Pendejo* is the word Gina likes the most, apparently. Neither she nor Jessie will tell me what it means, but I have a pretty good idea.

I spent half of the day drinking the watered-down coffee they served me at the café as Ken kept asking me if I knew what I was doing. Each time I said yes, he'd then ask, "Are you sure?" He kept at it until Min came and pulled him away by his ear.

Father Duplesy officiated, Ken was my best man, Gina's stepfather, Carl, gave her away and Jason gave a beautiful toast at the reception. The highlight of it all though, was when Jessie went into labor on the dance floor.

On the tenth of June at 7:03pm, I received the most wonderful wedding present a man ever got. Andrew Kenneth James Shirazi came into the world, weighing 8 pounds and 3 ounces, and measuring 20 inches exactly. He came fully equipped with all the standard features, along with the added bonus of a head full of pitch-black hair.

"That's one for the books," Ken laughed as we all got into our cars to follow the ambulance into Flagstaff. "Just married, already pregnant, and Gina ends up a grandma before she's a momma."

You should have seen the look on the triage nurse's face when Gina went to the window in her wedding dress and identified herself as "Grandma Stone", her own baby bump on full display. Then in came Corinda, with Ray in tow, flamboyantly identifying herself as Grandma Stone, as well. I couldn't help but wonder what was going through the nurse's mind.

I took just enough time to go and kiss my little girl and her little boy, then hug my son-in-law. Then I took my wife, who was sitting in the corner trying not to show her disappointment at being upstaged on her wedding day, and let it be known to those who would listen that we would be back in a week. Gina and I needed to savor every moment alone together that we could, because in just a few more months there was going to be three of us. And I wasn't as young as I was when Jessie was born.

"Do you realize that when our baby graduates from high school I'll be pushing seventy?" I said as we drove down the interstate to get on a plane for our trip to Hawaii.

"You've said that before, about a dozen times," she chuckled. She patted my knee and said, "Don't worry, Babe. We can have a couple more kids. That way, you'll always have someone to push your wheelchair around."

More kids? I thought. *What, is she trying to kill me? I wonder how much a vasectomy costs.*